SHADOWS OF THE UNLEASHED

Jon Rowlison

Part I - Demon Sword

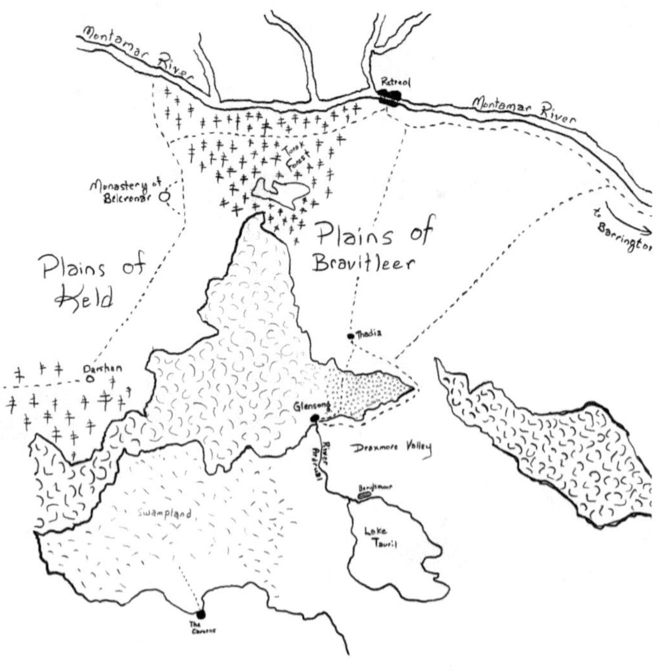

Montamar River
Montamar River
Retreol
Torak Forest
Monastery of Belcronar
Plains of Bravitleer
Plains of Keld
to Barrington
Thadia
Darshen
Glensong
Deaxmore Valley
River Reinall
Berghtmoor
Lake Tauril
Swampland
The Caverns

Prologue

Jairin hid behind the pedestal, heart pounding. His mother was going to be furious. The large tapestry had been a family heirloom for generations and he gathered that it was worth quite a lot by how much she fussed over it. The six-year-old prince wondered if they would make him pay for it. Maybe there was a market where parents would sell children who couldn't pay for things they had ruined. He only meant to look at it, lying out on the large table in the receiving room. It was the lantern; that stupid lantern. He didn't drop it. He had no idea how it fell from his grasp. Why did the bad things always have to happen to him? He ran his hands through his messed-up, tangled hair. Just an hour ago, he'd been worried that he was going to get in trouble for getting dirty before their meeting with the emissary of something-or-other. That seemed irrelevant now.

Boom!

The immense blast came from the far end of the hallway, rumbling through the whole second level of the castle. Jairin turned his head, eyes wide, down the hall to the side entrance of the throne room.

Aftershocks ripped through the hallway past the prince, the unmistakable sound and feel of stone smashing against stone. He was ordered by his father never to enter the throne room unless invited, but this had to be an exception. Jairin rose and then ran down the hallway to the great door that separated the throne room from the corridor. The guards were absent from their post at the entrance. Screams and shouts rang from the other side.

Jairin reached up slowly to pull the door handle. His hand, shaking, was close when he stopped and pulled it back. He took a deep breath, swallowing with some difficulty through the lump in his throat, and then reached up again. This was a bad idea. With a trembling hand, he pulled the handle and opened the door just enough to poke his head inside.

Through a thick cloud of dust and debris, he spotted an overturned table nearby. Jairin ran in and hid behind it for better view. Very little could be seen through the swirling dust. What was the smell in the air? It was a marriage of dirt and iron that he hadn't smelled before.

It took a few moments for his eyes to adjust. Something was moving through the cloud. The beast was immense, nearly the full height of the room, shaped more-or-less like a large man.

The ceiling crumbled as the massive creature made its way through the room. Jairin struggled to hold back an incredible scream and fell back, landing on his rear-end. One of his father's gold-robed priests was holding a staff up to the creature. It moved surprisingly fast for something so large. It turned its head and Jairin saw it look in his direction. Had it seen him?

Tears streamed down the prince's cheek. He was too young to die. He'd done nothing to anger anyone or anything; nothing that someone would be killed for, anyway. He tried to stand up, but found himself paralyzed. At last, he saw his father approaching the creature with his sword drawn.

The priest recited an incantation. The creature rose up and seemed to grow even taller. It unfolded massive wings, laughing. It reached out an arm toward the priest, releasing a red mist from its hands, like a shower of sparks. The priest screamed briefly and then his robes fell shapeless to the floor.

Something inside Jairin snapped. He had never seen anyone killed before. His grandmother had died several years before, but she had been very old. It was normal for people to die when they were old. He knew people were killed in battle for a noble cause as well, but this wasn't a battlefield. This was his home. People don't get killed in their own home, and there's just no reason to kill a priest. How could there be anything out there in the world that would kill a good man without reason? Jairin's mind ran in circles trying to figure out what the priest had done to make this creature so mad. And if it was mad, why was it smiling and laughing?

The prince backed up, at first keeping his eyes on the beast at the far end of the room while keeping his head lower than the table top as best he could. He needed to escape. As he neared the door, he turned to run.

"Boy!" a loud voice boomed. There was a loud crunch as the beast crushed the table with another heavy step.

Jairin turned quickly to see the creature holding his father aloft in one hand. The king struggled to break free of the massive hand to no avail. The creature bled from the opposite arm, seemingly it's only wound.

"Get away!" the king yelled to his son. The expression on his father's face made him look surprised, but also greatly disappointed. Was he angry with me for disobeying his rule about coming in here? Maybe he knew about the tapestry too.

"Find the—" His father would never finish that sentence. Jairin tried to bravely wipe the tears streaming down his cheeks with his silken sleeve only to have new ones take their place.

The immense creature stood full before the young prince, out-stretched wings breaking away more of the ceiling. It looked down at Jairin and said in a commanding voice, "Go forth, child. Tell everyone that the demon Gestron will sweep across the land like a glorious plague. Anyone who resists me will be destroyed."

Jairin cowered on the ground, trying to cover his eyes. The demon released his grip on Jairin's father, dropping him. There was a sickening sound as the body hit the floor, like a bag of dry firewood and rotten vegetables being thrown into the refuse. The king's eyes were rolled back in his head, his body misshapen and crushed.

The demon turned and flew from the ruined throne room. Crashing and screaming continued throughout the castle, but Jairin sat frozen.

It felt like an eternity before anyone came to the throne room. The king and over a dozen castle guards lay dead and dismembered. The smell was sickening; iron, seared meat and hair, freshly-split wood… death. The priest's body had been incinerated to the bone. Jairin lost nearly everyone he loved that day. They found his mother's body in the afternoon, headless, on the floor of the nursery. The kingdom was gone. When the immediate threat passed, Jairin let out his imprisoned screams.

He released the sound from his gut and something else escaped with it. Jairin looked around the room through teary eyes. His faith and wonder had suffered a grievous blow. A new sensation pushed his fear to the side. He had learned how to hate.

01 The First Morning

The scream came from the chamber next door.

Jairin awoke with a start. Another night terror? He sat up in his bed, swiveled around, and set his feet on the cold stone floor of the monastery. Hurrying to Zael's room, he knocked twice and then entered. He found her rocking back and forth slowly on her bed. The attacks were less frequent now as Zael stumbled her way through her mid-teen years, but it was still a struggle. Sweat dripped from her brow as she blinked in the dim lantern light coming from the hallway. Her eyes darted around the room. "Where am I?"

"We're in the monastery, remember?" He sat on her bed and wiped her brow with the sleeve of his night shirt. She leaned against his arm. "I'm here, Zael. You're going to be okay. It was just a dream." She brushed the stray lock of light brown hair from her eyes, then took his hand and managed a tremulous smile.

His parenting skills weren't as refined as he'd like, but he was much better now than when he'd first found her near the monastery five years ago. She had clung to him that day, and he had been acting as her guardian ever since. He could probably pass for her father, though at thirty-five, he would only have been twenty at her birth.

Zael made signs to Jairin that she was hungry for breakfast.

"All right, get dressed and meet me at my room." Jairin returned to his chamber to change out of his sleeping clothes.

A few minutes later, she knocked on his door and together they made their way downstairs to the dining hall.

Zael picked up the cornbread and took a bite. Chewing, she set the rest of it down to grab her pencil. "Talsmede Dragons?" she wrote on the paper in front of her with a shrug, turning it so Jairin could read.

He contemplated whether the fiery red flowers would work with the yellow and blue spring blooms she'd already selected. He nodded. "I think they'd work quite well. Perfectly, maybe."

She knew Jairin didn't love flowers and other growing things the way she did, but she loved that he had tried to be part of her gardening plans. Zael wondered why her own father couldn't have been more like Jairin. She pushed the thought of her birth father quickly from her mind as it made her stomach turn. Jairin was always patient and gentle, and the monks were kind to her too. They had often told her how impressed they were with her eye for designing spectacular arrangements in the west garden.

Their flower garden planning was briefly interrupted by the distant deep ringing of the bell at the front entrance. Several relatively quiet minutes passed. She looked to Jairin, who seemed equally puzzled. She continued drawing in a few more sections of her flower garden plot, looking up periodically to see if anyone had entered the room.

One of the monks popped his head around the corner into the dining hall. "Gathering! There's a gathering in the great hall immediately. Everyone must attend."

The few monks still eating breakfast got up and filed into

the hallway. Zael and Jairin set their plates and utensils in the dish pit and left the dining area.

The great hall was nearly filled with monks—some in black, some in brown, a few in green or red. Zael looked around. It must be something important to call everyone here. She'd never seen a meeting in the great hall—at least not one to which she had seemingly been invited.

Benedict, the head monk, stood at the front of the hall with a tired-looking, scared stranger. The leader of the order had a gray beard and gray monks' robes. Wrinkles across Benedict's forehead and in the corners of his eyes gave him a wizened look. Zael had heard he was over 160 years old. He was the oldest man she'd ever met, though it wasn't impossible for someone to live to their bicentennial birthday.

The stranger, by contrast, was dressed in a plain shirt and trousers, caked with dirt.

Benedict raised his arms, and the side conversations trailed off to a hush. "Attention. I need everyone's attention, please. We have a visitor, and I need you all to hear him out." He turned to the stranger, standing to his side. "Go ahead."

The man cleared his throat and started hesitantly. "They were horrifying—shadows and—people dying and sick and —unnatural—"

"Please, friend." Benedict said as he handed him a cup of tea. "Take a few breaths, focus. We need you to tell your tale from the beginning, like you just told me."

The stranger took a few moments to collect himself and shakily raised the cup to take a sip. The gathered monks began to talk amongst themselves and Benedict again motioned for them to stop.

"I am Arik," the stranger said almost as though he was asking. He looked younger than Jairin, but more worn. He cleared his throat and made brief eye contact with a few monks before continuing, "I'm a... I was a rancher and horseman outside the city of Darshen, to the south. A month ago, everyone in my village began to get sick. A plague was raging through our lands. It looked like influenza, but it kept getting worse. Most people became paralyzed and died a few days later."

Worried monks looked around at each other, murmuring, "Why did he come here? He'll give us all a deadly sickness." Several got up to leave, but Benedict broke the discussions again. "There's nothing to worry about here. Please, sit. Let Arik finish his tale. Time has passed, and Arik doesn't have the plague. I can promise you that we are safe here."

A monk in brown stood up. "How do you know that?"

"We are protected here. Let him finish, Brother Ayrle." Benedict motioned to Arik to continue.

"The sickness killed off not only the people in my village, but most of our stock of steer and horses. The few that lived were deformed and lame. They had to be destroyed. The plague also brought with it unnatural shadows."

Jairin perked up and looked at Arik with a new interest. He believed he knew what was happening. These sounded like the shadows from the catacombs. They had festered there, emerging to ravage the south lands. After so many years, they might finally be moving west beyond the mountains. He waited to see if the details matched up.

Benedict straightened his robe and gave it a tug at the waist where it had ridden up just a bit. He squinted an eye and nodded, looking briefly to Jairin and then back to Arik, who was continuing with his story.

"We saw shadows in broad daylight running from house to house, like they were looking for something. They weren't regular shadows, like something in front of a light would cast. They moved around on their own, just like you or me."

Voices erupted again. Benedict let them talk amongst themselves this time for a few moments.

"Okay, please quiet down," Benedict said. "Arik, how did

you not get sick?"

"I don't know. Maybe fate had other plans for me. Most of the people of Darshen died. My village became a ghost town. There were so many dead lying in the streets and in their homes that even if we didn't fear catching the plague or mind the nauseating stench, we didn't have enough people left to bury them all. I took my last able horse and rode toward Retreol to escape. I saw this monastery on the road as I came north. Please, save me." He looked around, watching the faces of the crowd as they processed what he was saying. "This cloud of shadow is getting bigger, spreading… I came as much to warn you as I did to save myself."

Jairin glanced at Zael, who looked fearful and pale. He'd heard enough.

Jairin stood and waved his hand. Benedict called on him to speak. Jairin raised his voice to be heard above the din. "I think I know what is ravaging the south lands. Shadows destroyed my own kingdom many years ago."

The gathered monks looked around in surprise. They'd known since his arrival that Jairin wasn't like them. Many of them suspected he'd bring trouble one day; leaving for weeks at a time on unknown errands, coming back at all hours of the night, and refusing to wear a monk's attire. He was here to meditate and certainly liked his privacy, but he wasn't on the path of enlightenment that they were seeking. …And the young girl he'd adopted as his daughter? What possessed the child that made her faint in the middle of a sentence and wake up screaming so many times? This man they had taken in when he had been no older than Zael threatened the quiet halls of their monastery. Would this plague be coming for them next, after all?

Jairin continued, "If these shadows are what I think they are, they'll be coming north soon, right to our door. They are harbingers of something far darker and far more powerful.

They serve a demon, the same one that destroyed my kingdom. They have been destroying towns and villages in an ever-growing area, killing those they come across."

Benedict's eyes widened. "How do we defend ourselves against such a rising storm?"

"We can't. This is something I have to stop at its source. There is something that I have been keeping from you, my brothers." After fifteen years of silence about his past, Jairin shared his story with the monks.

"I am the son of King Marax."

02 Disclosure and Departure

All eyes were fixed on Jairin. The borders of the Kingdom of Tarquin had extended even beyond the borders of the monastery. They were familiar, for some only as tales from their childhood, with what had happened at the castle some twenty-five odd years ago. Violence, death, and the shattering of the kingdom had plunged everyone into lawless times.

One of the brown-robed monks addressed Jairin. "You would have us believe that the tales of demons in Castle Glensong were true, Brother Jairin?"

"Yes."

"You were there? You witnessed this? How did you escape when so many were killed?"

Jairin nodded. "I was a young boy. I was spared as a warning, to spread the word to anyone who would stand against him."

The monks squinted and shifted their positions as they looked at their brother who claimed to be a prince. One spoke up, "You didn't warn us. You haven't said a word about this in the fifteen years you've lived among us?"

"I was scared. I still am. The seers said that a warrior would arise to reclaim the kingdom after an age of chaos.

That warrior would be the king's son. I am his only son."

Zael pulled out a small board and began writing on it in chalk as Jairin spoke.

The chatter in the room was still low. Benedict ran his fingers through his beard as if straightening it. He liked Jairin. Despite the gossip, he had never really caused any trouble. He also knew where Jairin had come from and had always suspected that he might have been more than he seemed. We all had to be something before we came to the monastery, he thought. He had made promises many years ago that Jairin would be kept safe and watched after. Benedict had always known the young man wasn't destined to be a monk. "How do you intend to stop this demon?"

"I've researched this tirelessly for years. I have a plan, but..." Jairin looked directly at Benedict. "I can't tell you. Anyone who knows what I'm doing puts my plan in more danger. More importantly, it puts them in danger as well."

"Are you saying we should just sit here until the shadows come to knock at our door?"

"No," Jairin replied. "I'm not telling you what you should or shouldn't do, but I won't put the order in danger, and I won't let you do it either. I can't tie my own fate into someone else's. This weight was put on me a long time ago."

"We are sworn to protect each other here." Benedict wasn't giving up on his question. "There's no need for this secrecy, Brother Jairin."

"I'm sorry if you feel like I'm leaving you in the dark. If what Arik says is true, it's time for me to leave. I need to try and put an end to this. You can defend yourselves however you need to. I think you are better protected here than you would ever admit to me, my friend." Jairin smiled. There were things Benedict and the other leaders didn't share with him. They were preparing for new constructing in the monastery. Why were they building up space in the library when they already had so many empty shelves? Why did the animal tracks he found always veer wildly away from the grounds? Something was going on here that nobody would talk to Jairin about.

Benedict seemed to know more. Not many of them did, but a few of them were keeping secrets. Here, in this place, they had some protection. There was magic at work here that nobody would acknowledge or discuss with outsiders or with Jairin.

As the discussion continued for several more minutes, it was clear that Jairin and Benedict were both steadfast in guarding the rest of their secrets.

Jairin excused himself to gather his belongings. He turned to Zael to see if she was going to follow him from the hall. She held up her chalkboard for him to read: *You aren't a 'chosen one.' The seer was just a crazy old woman.* She signed to her father: "I am scared. I knew this day was coming. I'm coming with you."

"We'll go to Retreol first and see how you're doing," Jairin said. "We'll figure the rest out once we all meet up."

Zael nodded.

Jairin put several sets of clothing into the pack lying on his bed and then lifted up the small down mattress he'd slept on these many years. This was going to be dangerous. He wondered if he should sneak out quietly and leave Zael here in the protection of the monks. There was no guarantee that Retreol would still be safe in a few days or in a month, but the magic here in this monastery seemed strong enough to keep everything away.

He pulled something out from under his mattress; long and slender, wrapped in a plain brown rag. Jairin set it down on the bed and removed the tattered covering, revealing the bright, ancient sword. The fine lines cut into the steel formed intricate patterns and words whose meanings had been lost through the ages as the language evolved. The lantern light in the room danced on the polished surface of the masterfully crafted blade.

Someone spoke behind Jairin. "Why would a monk need that kind of weapon?"

Jairin turned to see the stranger, Arik, the survivor from Darshen, looking into his room from the hallway. He must have followed them at a distance on their way back to the rooms.

Jairin looked at him. "You've regained your composure, I see. Wouldn't it be smart to have a sword with which to protect yourself?"

"Of course. But that kind of weapon looks like it was made to do much more than that. Why would a monk need such a fancy sword?"

Jairin sighed. "I'm not a monk."

"But you live in a monastery."

"Not anymore—"

"You isolate yourself from the outside world."

"Yes, but—"

"You sit here amongst monks, in solitude."

Jairin's body tightened. Who did this young man think he was, that he should come here and argue with the Prince of Tarquin? "I came here to do research in their library. When I was little, I heard this monastery was a sanctuary, a place where the shadows wouldn't be able to find me."

"Safe for you, or safe for them?"

"Both." What kind of question was that? Jairin wondered what he needed to do to make this horse rancher go away. "I won't put these monks in jeopardy. I'm trying to pack. We're leaving for Retreol soon."

"I'm going with you," Arik said.

"You're what? I don't remember inviting you."

Arik crossed his arms. "I was headed to Retreol, too. Let me come with you. I can fight, and there's safety in numbers." His tone had grown bolder.

"You have no idea what you're asking," Jairin said. "You have your whole life ahead of you. Why would you put it in danger to follow me?" Personal feelings aside, Jairin didn't have any objection to having the young man come with him as far as the city. There was safety in numbers out in the wild lands, but why did it have to be this guy?

Arik shook his head. "I don't have a life. I had one, but the shadows took it from me. I think we have something in common. I want to kill this demon just as much as you do."

"I can't let you throw your life away on this."

"I'm a survivor. I don't plan on dying. I'm doing the best I can to accept that I've lost everything. I figure we can get a little further by combining our efforts."

Jairin sized the horseman up; fit and with the hands of a worker. He looked like he could hold his own in a fight. If this horse rancher had a lust for revenge, he would be a great asset. If he could use a sword, Jairin could use the help —even if it would be harder to sneak into the caverns. "You've signed yourself up."

Arik smiled. "Are you always so secretive?"

"Yes," Jairin said. "Are you always so pushy?"

"Absolutely."

The two men stared each other down for a few moments and then grasped wrists, joining forces with a shake of forearms.

Jairin put the sword into a plain scabbard. "I promised Zael that I would bring her as far as Retreol. Once we get there, we'll see how excited you are about going after the shadows."

Arik asked, "Where do I get one of those swords?"

"This one is ancient and unique. I regret we won't find a second one."

Arik laughed. He tapped his hand on the hilt of his own sword hanging at his side. "I guess I can get by without the magical blade, but if we find another one, I'm calling dibs on it now."

"You've got a deal." Jairin said, smiling back.

There was a knock at the door. Jairin turned to see Zael standing there, her pack on her back.

Jairin knew he wasn't going to be able to sneak out this morning without her. He sighed. "Very well. Let's head out."

03 Onward

Benedict and several of the black-robed monks walked with them to the main gate. Jairin had come to them a young man, full of anger and regret. He was still the only man in the monastery who wouldn't conform to their solitary study and was easy to spot as the only one who wouldn't wear the monk's robes. He always looked like he was just there for a visit. Now, his extended visit was at an end.

The light of the large sun and the small sun circling it were bright in the midday sky. Benedict extended his arm to Jairin and they clenched wrists. "You'll be missed, my prince."

"Thank you for everything. You've made me feel at home here, like one of your own."

"You're welcome to come back." Benedict's gaze was unwavering, but he appeared a bit worried. "I wish you good speed. When you come back, make sure you leave those shadows far behind you."

The other monks said their goodbyes and after a time retreated into the solitude and familiarity of their daily devotions.

Jairin led down the path to the road leading north and south, followed by Zael and Arik. Dust swirled lightly in the air as they walked north along the old road.

Arik sped up to walk alongside the young girl. "If we're traveling together, I guess I need an introduction. I'm Arik." He extended his arm to shake her hand.

Zael looked at Arik and smiled. She tapped her throat several times with three fingers and shook her head.

"She can't speak, I'm afraid," Jairin said. He realized they hadn't been introduced so he stopped for a minute to fix the oversight.

"Oh." Arik said. His response sounded automatic, as though he wasn't really processing what he'd heard. He amended his initial comment with an apologetic nod, "Oh, I'm very sorry."

Jairin had come to expect that kind of reaction when he told people about Zael. People felt a need to be sorry that she had a disability. It didn't come across as empathy. Zael smiled with one side of her mouth, shrugging her shoulders.

"Arik, this is my adopted daughter, Zael. She was born unable to speak, but she can hear better than most."

Arik nodded. "It's wonderful to meet you, Zael."

Zael pulled a small chalkboard and chalk from her pack. She wrote with a practiced hand and held it up so Arik could read it: *I'm glad to meet you.*

"I'm not trying to rush," Jairin said, "but we should keep going. I want to get as far as we can before it gets dark."

They continued on through the afternoon.

"Do you worry, Jairin?" Arik asked.

"What do you mean?"

"Do you worry that the shadows are following us? They followed me for the first day after I left my village."

Jairin reached down for the hilt of his sword, pulling it out of the scabbard a bit. The steel was clean, reflecting some light from the suns overhead. "I don't think they've gotten to the monastery yet. In any case, I know they aren't following us right now." He pushed the sword back down.

"How can you tell we're being followed just by looking at your sword?"

"The blade turns blue when demons are nearby."

Arik's eyes widened. "No way!"

"It's an ancient weapon, enchanted to find and destroy demons. Supposedly, the person wielding it can't be killed by the demons, either."

"And you only bought one?"

"It took me five years and a lot of work to find this one. But I'll remember that you called dibs on the next one." Jairin smiled.

Late in the afternoon, they arrived at the crossroads. Their small north and south road crossed a much larger one running east and west. Arik looked down the crossroads in each direction before turning his gaze east again. "Is this the way east to Retreol?"

Jairin nodded, "Yes. It's a two-day journey, mostly through Turak Forest."

Zael tapped Jairin on the shoulder. He looked over and she made some hand signals and shook her head. Jairin translated, watching her signs, "The forest road is known for bandit ambushes. Zael is telling me three men have been killed between here and Retreol today." He looked at Arik and continued, "We should avoid the road—maybe take the river route. It will cut our travel time a bit, too."

Arik looked at the two of them. "How would she know that?"

"She has a sixth sense I've come to trust." Jairin wasn't sure how to explain what Zael could do and why. "We'll go through that. Tonight, on the boat, we should have time to talk."

"We have a boat?"

"We will in a few hours."

Arik removed his sword from its scabbard and scratched some symbols in the dirt near his feet—four circles arranged in a square with diagonal lines drawn through them, intersecting at the center.

Jairin looked over at Arik. "What's that?"

"It's my sign of Willem Ironfoot. Sorry, it's messy."

Jairin and Zael looked at each other with bewildered expressions.

"You guys don't know who Willem Ironfoot is? He's the ancient leader of my people. He invented the steel shoes that go on the feet of horses to let them travel long distances. We scratch his symbol in the ground before a battle to bring good luck. Willem looks to us from beyond this life when we call on him."

"Aha," Jairin said. "I've never heard of that. I've learned something today."

They walked on, passing through the intersection and continuing north. By evening, they heard the distant roar of water. Small patches of trees became more frequent and larger, beginning to line the road as they walked. The western edge of the forest could be seen ahead and to their right. The air, which for most of the day had felt clear and unscented, was now alive with the fragrance of pine and fir trees and the light scent of grass and moss. The increasing volume of overhead branches robbed them of some of the fading light as they made their way along the road now winding around the gnarled tree trunks.

"There are river men just ahead," Jairin said. "Villages north of the river bring their stuff here to float it down to Retreol. These guys are jumpy, living so close to the brigands in the forest, but they should help us if we pay them enough."

"Do we need their help?" Arik asked.

"We need to rent one of their boats."

They walked a bit farther. "Wait," Arik said. He stopped and looked around nervously. "There's somebody watching us!" He pulled his sword from its scabbard at his waist and quickly scratched another Willem Ironfoot into the hard ground at his feet.

A man burst from the brush, brandishing a sharpened stick. His knotted gray hair hung down his withered frame. His skin was pale, weathered, and his eyes bulged uneasily as he held tight to his crude-looking weapon.

Jairin's hand moved to the hilt of his own sword, but he didn't pull it out.

"You've come back to steal more chickens?" The riverman said in a raspy voice. "Don't think for one moment that I won't defend my friends in their coops! You and your friends can face the business end of my staff again!"

Jairin held a level hand back, telling the others to stay calm. "Whoa, no. No. We didn't steal any of your chickens. We've come to rent one of your boats."

"Men don't come from the south to go to the city. Nope, I don't have any boats going down the river this month."

Jairin looked around for signs of anyone else who might have a boat to lease. Nothing. He could see the river running just ahead, but in the immediate area there was only a single dock and shed. Wait. By the water's edge, he saw an old boat turned upside-down on a cart by the shed.

The riverman turned his head, following Jairin's gaze. He scrunched up his face, squinting. "Yeah, that boat is mine, but it's..." He paused and looked back at the intruders. "It's the very best in the fleet. I only lease it out to the most deserving of customers."

Arik chuckled. "Jairin, come on..."

Jairin nodded. "How much?"

"Twelve gold pieces," the riverman replied.

"I can give you two."

The old man shook his head. "I can't let it go for less than ten."

Jairin continued with, "I have nine. That's all I can offer."

"Jairin, no," Arik interjected again. "Are you serious? This isn't worth it."

"Maybe, but we need a boat."

Arik looked over at Zael. "Jairin doesn't seem to understand haggling."

Zael shook her head and smirked as she looked back at Arik.

The riverman stood for a moment, seemingly in contemplation. "Deal. My name is Diller." He extended his bony arm to Jairin to strike their deal, clenching wrists.

04 Nearly Every Ship Floats

Jairin approached the boat. The lack of paint made it apparent that it was made of several kinds of wood—some gray, some brown, some tan, most of it just old. Several of the patches were nailed directly into the hull. "At least you filed off the nails, so I don't get impaled sitting is this watery deathtrap. Hey, does this even float?"

"Yes, yes," Diller said.

"Will it still float with two men and a girl in it?"

Diller looked at Jairin and his companions, then up and to the left, as if he were making some calculations. He eventually responded, "I'd expect so."

With a scoff, Jairin emptied most of the money in his coin pouch into his hand. He counted out nine of the gold coins and handed them to Diller. Arik helped haul the boat cart to the shore. Moving the boat caused a small flock of chickens of various ages to scurry away in random directions. At least the boat didn't have any visible holes. All told, the space inside was about a meter wide and three meters long. It would need to stay afloat for the next two days' ride down the swift river. Diller handed them a pair of paddles and a few rusty nails.

"What are the nails for?" Jairin asked.

"You sounded concerned about the seaworthiness."

Jairin looked at the nails with a frown. This isn't exactly what he had in mind for transportation.

"Heads up!" Diller yelled. He tossed a rock to Jairin.

Jairin dropped the paddles to catch it, barely, before it would have hit him in the chest. Diller chuckled.

Jairin heard the unmistakable tone of a sword being pulled from its scabbard. He spun around to see Arik getting ready for a fight. "You're a cheat!" Arik yelled.

Diller stepped back with a look of surprise, pointing his spear back at Arik. "Hey, you asked for the boat."

"Don't," Jairin said to Arik. "It's the only boat here." After a tense moment, the others put their weapons down.

"The boat may need some repairs when you get to the city," Diller said. "Ask for Matthias at the docks. He'll take care of it."

Jairin looked over the boat as best he could. Hopefully, nothing would go wrong on the trip, or they would be in trouble. His complete repair kit now included a handful of rusty nails and a rock. He loaded their packs and the paddles into the dilapidated vessel and pulled it into the water at the dock. They boarded the boat and started down the river.

"Hey!" Diller yelled as they parted.

Jairin was surprised to hear any more from the old man. "Yes?"

"I remember you. You're from that monk place."

Jairin didn't respond. He'd been to the river before, but all of the river men seemed the same to him, and he'd never leased a boat of his own. Maybe this guy knew him. He didn't think he'd stood out.

"I'll know who to go after if you don't deliver my boat to Matthias," Diller said.

Arik checked the boards, picking and poking, seeming to test their stability as they floated down the river. He looked over at Jairin, shaking his head. "This is a boat?"

"Kind of."

"Barely," Arik said. "By the way, you aren't in charge of making our deals anymore."

The boat creaked and bobbed in the river. Rushing water roared alongside, as the current swept them farther and farther east toward the port of Retreol. After a few minutes, they got used to the rocking of the dilapidated boat. Zael opened her pack and took out a few apples, some cheese, bread, and a waterskin.

"You're a mind-reader! I'm starving!" Arik exclaimed.

Zael shook her head and tapped her temple a few times, smiling.

There was no other traffic in sight on the waterway as the large sun and the smaller sun circling it made their nightly retreat in the eastern sky. The evening snack would have to do for tonight. An hour later, they all drifted off into an uneasy sleep.

Jairin wearily opened his eyes. The suns were coming up. He woke the others. The city of Retreol was still a speck in the distance, but he could see it now. Zael opened her pack and took out three large rolled-oat bars to break their fast. Arik and Jairin each took one, thanking her. They passed around the waterskin and ate their morning meal.

When they'd finished, Arik turned to Jairin. "You were going to tell me yesterday why we didn't go through the forest."

"Ah. I'd forgotten."

"How did she know that it wasn't safe?"

Jairin looked to Zael. "Grab the chalkboard if you want to add anything." He returned his attention to Arik. "Zael has a condition. I'm not sure how to describe it. She faints."

"Okay."

"When she faints, she wakes up somewhere else." Jairin

looked to his daughter to see her reaction. She nodded and started writing on the chalkboard.

"I don't understand."

"It's like dreaming. She faints here, then awakens somewhere else."

Arik turned to Zael. "And you…When this happens you can see things?"

She held up her chalkboard. It said: *My father was a wizard.*

"Bear with me." Jairin tried to explain what he knew. "Zael's mother died before she was full-term—almost died, I mean. Her father kept enough of his wife alive to save the baby."

"But you can't do that!" Arik looked at the girl, eyes widening. "Someone is either alive or dead."

Zael wiped the words from her chalkboard with a cloth. Her eyes hung heavy and she started writing again.

Jairin nodded. "I've learned when it comes to wizards, you can't make any assumptions. He clearly could and did."

"So where do you go?" Arik asked her.

Zael held up a finger. She wiped off what she'd started writing and started writing something else. When she finished, she held it up: *Where my mother is.*

"I thought your mother died."

Zael nodded.

"She did," Jairin said. "Time passes differently on the other side. A week there could be a moment, an hour, or a day for us. It's like living a second life in the moments between this one."

Arik turned to Zael again. "So where is your father?"

Zael looked to Jairin and nodded. She made some gestures and then went back to wipe and write on the chalkboard again.

Jairin searched for the right words. "People don't trust you when you have an ability they don't understand. When she started fainting, the people in her village didn't understand. They called her evil and… Let's just say she was lucky to get away."

"And her father?"

"He was the worst of them. Wizards are lousy parents to begin with. He wanted a child he saw as normal, or maybe one he could even train in wizardry. I guess he decided Zael didn't qualify."

Tears streaked down Zael's cheek. Her hands trembled as she held up the chalkboard for Arik to read: *The third time he tried to kill me, I ran.* She turned around and lifted the back of her shirt partway up to reveal the bottom of her back. It was scarred and welted with old wounds. Unlike the rest of her skin, it was a patchwork of purple and red, slashes crisscrossing the burns.

Jairin added, "The physical damage has mostly healed, but the real damage from her birth father, the damage he did on the inside, never will."

"I'm sorry," Arik said, slowly. "I'm so sorry. Our parents are supposed to love us and keep us safe. Nobody should ever have to go through that."

Zael nodded, wiping her tears with her sleeve. They floated along in silence.

A few hours into the day, they passed the outer entry tower. The river widened and slowed as it neared the city. After a final bend in the water, they passed by an unmanned guard tower perched on the north bank.

"Smeck! We have a leak." Arik shifted position. His pants were soaking wet. He covered the hole with his hand, but it wasn't slowing down the flow of water into their boat. "Sorry for my language." He looked over at Zael.

Zael shrugged.

"We're almost at the docks," Jairin said.

"This is a joke," Arik said. "If I try to hammer some nails into the bottom of the boat, the whole thing is going to break apart. Move up."

They moved closer to the bow of the boat, and the leak seemed to slow a bit. The city wall was just ahead. Two men atop the city wall opened the river gates as they approached. "Inbound," one of them yelled.

"Inbound," an unseen voice answered back from the docks.

They all watched the leaky spot at the stern as water pooled faster and faster in the bottom of the boat. Jairin held his breath as they passed through the gate. He only had a drinking cup to bail out the water, and the rim of the boat was getting closer to the surface of the slowing river.

Arik and Jairin grabbed the paddles and maneuvered the boat toward an open slip. The boat was filling up rapidly now that the weight was no longer all in the bow. Dockworkers threw a mooring rope to Arik and helped pull the vessel into the slip, where they tied it off. The men jumped out and then Arik reached back to help Zael. There the boat sat, mostly submerged. The three stood next to it on the dock, drenched from the waist down.

The river gate swung shut in the distance behind them. Several dock workers walked up, looking at the craft tied to the pier and then at each other. There was a moment of silence and then they broke out in a round of laughter. Zael smiled and then laughed too.

"I wondered what a laugh from you would sound like," Arik said before smiling back at the girl. He and Jairin joined in the laughter.

"Where can I find Matthias?" Jairin asked.

One of the dock workers pointed to a small shack at the edge of the docks. The three made their way along the docks toward the shack, escorted by a pair of the workers. Outside, a plump man with short gray hair sat, watching them as they approached.

"Matthias?" Arik asked.

The short man nodded slowly. "I know what you're going

to say. My brother is sending his boat back here to be repaired yet again."

Another round of laughter rose from the dock workers behind them.

"He does this every year," Matthias said. "It's more patches now than boat."

"We were told to make sure you got it," Arik said.

Matthias shook his head and stood up. "I'll go take a look. Thanks for bringing my brother's garbage barge back to us. You have no idea how much we look forward to fixing this piece of smeck several times a season."

Arik looked meaningfully at Jairin, hands on his hips, shaking his head. "That was all your idea. You paid that crazy old man nine pieces of gold to rent that pile of rotten wood."

Jairin held his arms out and made an exaggerated shrug. "It wasn't my finest negotiation. But hey, we made it here, and aside from a bit of water, we managed it without incident. Come on. Let's find someplace where we can sit down and dry off. We need to draw up our plan." His pack had stayed dry, but as they walked from the docks, the three left an increasingly smaller trail of water that dripped behind them like a snail's trail.

05 Root Cellar Tavern

As they approached the tavern, the weather-beaten doors burst open. A man flew from the building, as if gravity had suddenly switched directions. His flight was brief, and he stopped a few meters into the street, falling face-first on the ground. He groaned and then stopped to retch before passing out. A burly man leaned out the entrance, shaking a fist in the air. "…and you best not come back!" He looked over at Jairin, Arik, and Zael as they approached. "That's just him I was talkin' to. You lot are okay." He turned and walked back inside.

The sign hanging over the door read, "Root Cellar Tavern" in black. It had an embossed, large red oak tree with gold shadows. In the frosted glass windows facing the street, Jairin could see soft lantern light inside, wavering slightly amidst a few moving silhouettes. "So, um, this is our stop." Jairin told his companions.

Arik looked down at the man lying on the ground and scowled. "Gross. Are you sure this is the best place to go over our plans?"

"If nothing else, it looks like they keep the riff-raff out." Jairin smiled nervously, nodding to Arik. The prince entered the tavern. "Come on."

A stocky man stood behind the long bar, drying wet metal mugs with a rag. Jairin wasn't much for day drinking. He really just needed a place to sit down and drip-dry as they planned out their next moves, but it would look strange if they sat down without drinks. Not that a little bit of alcohol was out of the question. It can always be beer o'clock when you're parched.

Jairin made his way over to the bar. Most of the tables he passed were occupied, each with their own strange flavor of conversation contributing to the overall level of background noise that floated through the air.

The barman watched Jairin approach and set down a mug. He dabbed his dirty forehead with the rag and put it aside. He raised his large bushy brown eyebrows up and away from his eyes. "What then can I be getting for you?"

"Three mugs of your house cider, please. Oh—do you also have a sheet of parchment and a pencil?"

The barman looked quizzically at Jairin. He picked up three mugs and filled them from the tap mounted on the wall behind the bar. He set them down and gazed back up at Jairin. "That would be six coppers then."

Jairin pulled out his coin pouch and picked out his last gold coin. He set it down on the bar, holding it fast with his index finger. "Do you have any parchment?" he inquired a second time.

The barman's eyes widened at the sight of the gold. "Aye." He paused. "It's not something I'd be selling, you see. I'll look." He disappeared into the back room and returned a minute later with a few sheets of parchment and a stump of a pencil.

"Thanks." Jairin took his finger off of the coin and then looked around for his companions.

Arik and Zael were seated on one side of a freshly vacated table. They were pushing a small collection of empty beer mugs out of the way as Jairin walked up. He set down the cider, parchment, and pencil, and sat at the open side of the table.

"Thank you," Arik said, grabbing one.

Zael signed to her father.

"You're welcome." Jairin unrolled the parchment and began drawing. As his companions looked on, the shapes began to form a recognizable picture. He drew Retreol at the top center, with the monastery south and far to the west. A dotted line led south from Retreol through a great open plain and then through a mountain pass farther south. He drew in a ridge of mountains there, encircling a second open area. From there, the path turned west into a shaded place near the left edge of the page.

Arik squinted. "I don't get it. Why did we come this far east just to loop back west? The route on your map brings us nearly to the borders of Keld, where I started!"

"The mountains south of the monastery would have been impassable on that side. There's also the matter of a mob of shadows that have taken up residence in your lands. Most importantly, I need to make a few stops before I get there."

"Where is 'there'? What's the shaded area beyond those mountains?" Arik asked.

"It was farmland when I was a child, but I think it's abandoned now. The farmers and workers who tended it were forced out."

"Is that where the—"

Jairin hastily interrupted him with a wave of his hand. "Don't say it, but yes."

Arik looked over the sketch. He put his fingers on the map, tracing the distance from landmark to landmark. Is this to scale?"

"Not exactly, but roughly."

"So how far is it from here to this spot?" Arik asked, pointing to a square drawn atop a low mountain ridge.

"Those are castle ruins. It would take us three days on

horseback. From there we can head west again once we clear the mountains."

"Do you have horses?"

"No. I have some resources here in town, though."

Arik nodded. "Can we take the horses through the mountain pass?"

"We'll have to check on the approach. We'll need to stop for more supplies in the valley. I'd like to keep the horses with us if we can. If it's too steep, we can leave them at the waypoint. There are stables and I think I know the guy in charge. About the journey… I want you to stay behind."

Arik shook his head and pointed emphatically at the prince. "I can't believe you're still trying to talk me out of going. I'm not staying here, knowing you're out fighting without me." He made a fist and banged it on the table. Zael jerked back as the table vibrated.

"This is where you wanted to go. There are good people here, and jobs. You could have a new life. If you leave the city with me, you're in great danger. I can't guarantee that any of us will make it through this."

Arik exhaled and relaxed his fist. "I want to look into the eyes of this monster as I run him through—or die trying."

"I admire that," Jairin said. "I just wanted to be sure you knew what you were getting into. When the time comes, we'll all need to draw on that kind of fire. I don't think you should come with, but if you insist, I won't try to talk you out of it again. We need to—" Jairin stopped, mid-sentence. He noticed that Zael's face had turned white.

His adopted daughter fell forward, hitting the table face-first. Arik jerked back in his chair, scraping the legs across the floor with an "Rrrrrrrrrt…" He stood, knocking the chair over. "Fitch! What just happened? Did I do that?"

Jairin stood and walked over to the other side of the table as he answered. "She's fainted. This happens sometimes. When it happens during the day, it passes quickly." He gently picked her head and shoulders from the table and set her back in her chair.

Zael shook her head and shuddered. She looked around, rubbing her nose, which had taken the brunt of the impact with the table. She signed to Jairin, "What happened?"

"We're at the Root Cellar Tavern," Jairin reminded her. "We drew our map back to Glensong. You fainted."

Zael gasped and hurriedly pulled out her chalkboard and started scribbling something on it. As two strangers approached their table, she quickly covered it with her arms.

The older man wore long flowing robes, the color of deep red wine. His long gray hair was brushed back from his face and trailed down his back like a stream of silver. The lower part of his face was covered by a thick gray mustache and beard that ended together a few centimeters below his chin. The younger man had short brown hair and robes of a neutral tan.

The elder looked over the group and then cleared his throat. Squinting one eye slightly as he fixed his gaze at Zael, he then looked over the group again as a whole. "Excuse the interruption. I am Madigan. This is my apprentice, Smeech." He motioned to the young man standing beside him.

A shock wave ran through Zael. She wanted to get up and run, but her legs wouldn't listen to her command. She knew Madigan, or at least she knew what he was. Fire. Arms that hugged you one moment and incinerated your bedroom, locking you in, the next. She tried to will her legs to work. Stupid legs. Wizards can't be trusted. They lie to you when they say, "I love you." They cause pain. She managed to move one hand from her side to touch her hair. The locks had grown back in time. She froze up, eyes glossed over, and in her mind she was trying to go somewhere else. Anywhere else but where she was. Wizards are not safe.

* * *

Arik had missed Zael's reaction, but Jairin had not. "I am Arik," the horse rancher replied. "These are my companions, Zael and Jairin."

Madigan tipped his head slightly. "Jairin?" He smiled, looking surprised. "I thought you looked familiar."

"Have we met?"

"Your father. I see some of his look in your face. I knew him quite well, in fact. I served as the court wizard at his castle in days long past."

Jairin noticed that his daughter's shock had worn off a bit. She took a few deep breaths and pushed it out slowly. Jairin didn't see any immediate threat from the wizard. "I knew there were wizards at the castle, but I don't remember you, I'm afraid."

"Do you have any brothers?"

"No," Jairin said. It was an odd question.

"I remember when you were just an infant. I had taken leave of the castle long before your father died. Pity. It would have been grand to spend some time with you back then. Life pushes us in other directions, you know."

"Yes. It's funny that you should mention—"

The old wizard held up his hand. "I would wish to stay and speak of old times, but I'm afraid Smeech and I are in great haste. Before we leave, however, I need to warn you of your companion—the girl. She has the scourge."

Jairin was caught off-guard. The wizard's sudden approach made sense now. He felt like his skin would catch fire as the boiling blood rushed through his body. Why would he expect this wizard to understand what Zael was or what she could do? Her own father didn't understand her. It made sense now. They had been drawn to the table during Zael's fainting spell. They could sense her. He told himself to stay calm. "You're referring to Zael's *gift*?" The tone was forceful. He was losing restraint of his anger.

Zael looked over to Jairin and shook her head in

disapproval. Jairin understood the warning. She had a way of expressing ideas that one couldn't express in words. It was an extra sense of strength that she conferred to her adopted father.

The smile faded from Madigan's face. "I don't mean to insult you, personally, Jairin. As a wizard, I don't care for such matters, but commoners have died because of their 'gifts.'"

As he said his last words, Madigan turned and walked toward the tavern exit, his apprentice following, disappearing into the crowd.

"Wizards have died for their arrogance." Jairin said it quietly, but loud enough for Zael and Arik to hear. He loosened his fists under the table.

Arik chuckled nervously, "Smeech… That's a rodent's name." Something seemed to catch his eye. He glanced over at Zael's chalkboard where she had been writing when the wizards first approached. It said, "Beware Madigan."

"Fitch!" Arik said. "How does she do that?"

Madigan looked to Smeech as they walked away from the tavern. "I didn't know Marax's son was alive. I don't know where he's been hiding, but we'll need to take care of him."

"Is he dumb enough to go after the demon?" Smeech asked. "I like the thought of watching him skewered and burned alive."

"Who does that upstart think he is? He's no king." Madigan said to his apprentice. "The people have lived in peace in the city under my watch and protection. We need to step this up a notch. Find out what the girl can do… and have them followed. I'll take care of matters in the city."

"What do we do with Jairin?"

"He reminds me far too much of his father. He, too, will have to be dealt with." The wizard quickened his pace away from the establishment.

"Is it getting worse, master?" Smeech asked. His voice was farther away now. Madigan turned to see his apprentice had stopped walking.

"Have them followed," Madigan repeated. "I will take care of matters in the city."

Jairin set down his second cider. "We need to find a woman named Raven. I need to talk to her before we leave town."

Zael smiled and her whole face seemed to take on a new light. She wiped her chalkboard. "Yes," Jairin told his daughter, "We're going to go find Raven. I promised you we'd meet with her next time we were in town, and I keep my promises."

"Does she own a stable, by chance?" Arik asked. "You said you had a line on some horses."

"No. I don't think she has any horses, but she'll know where we can get some."

Arik nodded in agreement. "So, where's the woman we need to talk to?"

"Raven. I know where she lives, but if she's at work she won't be home for quite a while."

"So where are we supposed to go?"

"Well, let's go track her down." Jairin rolled up the map and stuffed it into his pack. He made his way to the door, motioning for the others to follow. Zael stood up and seemed to stumble a bit. Arik caught her and helped her find her balance.

At a table nearer the door, Jairin stopped. A group of men were seated, drinking and laughing.

One of the men looked up at Jairin, "Can I help you?"

"We're looking for a woman named Raven."

"Wait," the man replied. "Are you the fellow that scared off the old freak?"

"Sorry about that. He angered me."

The young muscular man smiled. "I'm Brandt; these are

my fellows. There's no harm in it. It's better here when he's not sitting around darkening up the place. Is it the theater-type you're looking for? I know of an actor named Raven."

"Yes, that's probably her. We're heading out of town and I wanted to say goodbye."

"The Greensland Theater. You can't miss it."

"Thanks." Jairin and company turned back to the exit.

"Hey," Brandt called out from behind him.

"Yes?" Jairin turned around.

"If you need any armed guards to keep the old guy away from you, come and find me. Work has been slow here."

"We'll be okay."

"I come from a long line of king's knights… well, back when there was a kingdom, anyway."

Jairin looked back at Brandt with a curious smile. "Next time I see you, Brandt, I'll have a job for you."

06 Child Of Sarlima

A man with a gigantic, colorful, papier-mâché head stepped forward, armed with a wooden sword. He reached out and stabbed a tree-man in the heart. The sword actually went under the tree-man's arm. Theatrics. The tree-man stepped back and did something that looked halfway between sitting and falling. The colorful-headed man turned toward the audience. "And never more shall I worry that the night shall hear my cries!"

The actors cleared the stage as the final curtains were drawn in from the sides. A round of applause arose from the audience, some of whom threw copper or silver coins to the stage. Several children emerged from the center split in the front curtain and walked out on stage, bowed, and then exited. Next came some men with various instruments and fake noses. Then another child clutching a pig dressed in children's clothing. More applause and whistles. Next, a man emerged carrying either a doll or a baby; it was hard to tell. The actors took a low bow and then stepped to the left or right, leaving an open walkway at center stage.

From behind the curtain at center, a man emerged wearing a tree costume, wooden sword still stuck under his arm. The actor reached up a branch-covered arm and pulled off the head of the costume to reveal an older gentleman with white, wispy hair. He took a low bow and then moved to the side. He pointed back to center stage, "Ladies and gentleman… Sarlima!"

The actor with the colorful paper head walked back out. The audience stood and continued to applaud and cheer, throwing more coins up on stage. Several children emerged from behind the left and right curtains to collect them.

"I tried to catch up. I just didn't get it," Arik whispered to Jairin, standing next to him.

"I think we missed too much of the setup. That's what we get for coming in at the end of the second half."

Zael had picked up a program on the way in. Jairin noticed she was looking through it during the performance, but with the house lanterns out it was too dark to see.

Sarlima removed his costume head, and a long mane of black hair fell from it. It was a woman. The crowd continued cheering as the actors took their final bow and filed back off-stage.

Jairin elbowed Arik gently in the ribs. "She… is Raven."

After a long period of cheering and whistling, people slowly began to leave the theater, talking excitedly amongst themselves.

"Just, wow," Arik said after some delay.

Jairin looked back to Arik, who was staring at the empty stage. "Easy, friend."

"Are you two… you know…?"

Jairin looked confused for a moment and then it clicked. "Oh, no. No. Definitely not."

They continued to wait as the rest of the crowd exited the theater. Two large men with maces at their sides approached Arik and Jairin. "You need to disperse. The show is over."

Jairin looked over. "We're here to meet with Raven."

"Lots of people want to meet with Raven."

"Tell her Jairin is out here. She'll see us."

With a nod, one of the guards walked backstage while the other began moving the group toward the entrance.

Zael flipped through the pages in her program, smiling and nodding. The light seemed to have helped.

A few minutes later, Raven emerged from behind the curtain. "Jairin! What an unexpected surprise!" She turned to address the two burly security guards. "They're okay. They can stay." The guards quit pushing the group toward the door. One of them sneered at Jairin before they both walked off toward some other stragglers.

Raven ran down the steps into the small auditorium. When she reached Jarin, she stretched up on her toes and threw her arms around him. They embraced for several seconds, then she got back on her flat feet, pulling a small towel from her pocket. Raven began wiping off some of the grease makeup from her face. Her green eyes sparkled in the lantern light of the theater. "Stage makeup. This stuff is like wearing tar."

"But you were wearing a mask…"

Raven raised an eyebrow. "You missed the first half, didn't you?" She smiled. "Anyway…it's been way too long! Are you going to introduce me to your friends?"

"Raven, this is Zael."

"Zael," Raven repeated, her face lighting up with a bigger smile. "Jairin's told me so much about you! I was heartbroken that he didn't bring you with him last time he came to the city. I'm very excited to finally meet you."

Zael paused for a moment, then she curtsied and smiled.

Raven stepped forward, urged the girl back up, and gave her a hug. "There's no bowing here. We're like sisters, or something."

Jairin motioned to his other side. "And this is Arik."

Raven smiled. "The pleasure is all mine, sir. I figured any acquaintance of Jairin's would be a middle-aged, tassel-haired clergyman. He seems to have found a more attractive crowd to run with these days."

Arik paused a moment, smiling back. "Well met. Knowing you are a friend of Jairin's, I'd have not expected such a lovely young woman. I'm glad to see I was terribly wrong in my expectations!"

Raven changed her focus from Arik to Jairin, adjusting the pins in her midnight-colored hair. "Are we friends then, dear Jairin?"

"Absolutely, without question."

Raven smiled back at Jairin with a quizzical look. "I don't suppose you're in town just to see Child of Sarlima?"

"We're heading south—tomorrow." Jairin answered. "I needed to stop by and make sure I told you."

Raven looked even more confused. "Oh… this is *the* trip?" She crossed her arms, taking a step back. "Don't think for one minute that you're going to walk through Retreol and leave tomorrow without me! I'm going with you." Her tone still sounded playful, but she reached out to put her hand on Jairin's upper arm.

"Maybe this isn't the best place to discuss this," Jairin said.

"No." She put her arm back down and loosened up. "Where are you staying?"

"We haven't checked in anywhere yet. I was thinking of going to the Primrose."

"Ick. I'll tell you what. You're invited to the finest inn this side of Barrington."

"Raven—"

"This production is running for another week. I'll talk to the company manager and make sure they prep my understudy. Sarlima wears a costume half of the time anyway. They won't even notice I left."

Zael tugged at her guardian's sleeve. He knew she'd been looking forward to meeting Raven for quite a while. It couldn't hurt to stay with her for just a night before they left Retreol for the south. Her house had plenty of room and he had a very hard time saying no to Zael. With reluctance, he gave in. "We'll stay tonight, but I'm not making any promises when we leave tomorrow."

His daughter smiled.

Raven turned and motioned to the stage door from which she'd emerged. "Give me a minute to make sure my understudy is squared away. That's my only outstanding issue right now. But really, Jairin, you need to start including other people when you make plans that affect them."

"What? You're right, but the thing is, I didn't intend to include you."

"Don't start," Raven said. "You know exactly what I mean…friend. I'll meet you back up front in five." She walked back to the stage door and entered. Stagehands walked around the theater blowing out the lanterns that had provided light for the performance.

Arik broke his silence, looking back over to Jairin. "So, you two aren't a thing, right?"

Jairin looked back at his companion and sighed. "This again? Raven's a big girl. I think your timing here is pretty crappy, but you don't need to worry about me getting in your way if you're going to make a move. I'll wish you good luck, but if you hurt her. I'm going to have to kill you."

Arik nodded slowly. "Okay…that got awkward real fast."

"Yes."

Raven returned through the stage door. "All right, Sarlima is covered until I get back." She leaned over, playfully bumping into Jairin and throwing him a bit off-balance. "You realize I need the money from my performance and the tips to pay my bills, right? This is going to put a financial strain on me. I expect you'll be paying me back for my help."

The smile creeping across her face made Jairin think she was joking. He couldn't always tell. "All right, let's head out," she said.

They left the theater into the streets of Retreol. Outside, a few stragglers from the audience were smoking pipes with two brown-haired cast members. One of the cast members looked up between puffs of smoke. "Raven! Word from Tibbs is that you're leaving us."

Raven turned to face the man. "How has this information spread out the front door before I even left the theater? Yes, I think I'll be gone for at least a few weeks, Ralph. Mileeta will do a splendid job filling in, I'm sure."

"Well," Jairin said, "We haven't actually decided this yet."

"Shush now," Raven replied without looking at him, finger raised in his direction.

"Ah, nobody packs the house like you do, my friend," Ralph replied.

Raven smiled back and made a quick introduction. "I guess this will be your chance to try to shine. Maybe you can carry your own weight for once!" She smiled at Ralph. "Have a wonderful evening, my friend." Raven turned back to Jairin and motioned for the others to continue following her in the direction they'd been heading initially. "My place is down here just a way."

Ralph sat there, silent, as they turned and walked away. When Jairin and company were a good fifty meters down the road, they heard him call after them, "Ouch! Your words sting me deeply, my dearest Raven!"

The actor laughed quietly with her new accomplices. "He's very sweet, but we don't let him do improv."

They walked down the street, gaslights dimly illuminating the road ahead. After several blocks, they arrived at Raven's stone cottage. The front door was flanked on the right by a small square shuttered window. She pulled a key from the belt pouch hidden beneath her long shirt and carefully inserted it into the keyhole in the door. She turned it until it made a satisfying click, unlocking the door.

They followed Raven into the house. She moved to the near wall and lit one of the lanterns, flooding the room with light. "I don't know if you've eaten, but I'm starving!" She opened a few cabinets and pulled out some salted meat, grapes, bread, butter, cheeses, and a flask of wine. She set the food out on the single table in the common room to share with the others. "Help yourselves." She picked up a piece of bacon, ripped off a bite, and popped it in her mouth.

"Thank you so much," Arik said. "I don't think we've eaten all day."

Raven chewed a little faster, finishing her first bite before replying, "You're very welcome. I'm just glad I have the chance to finish up this food so it doesn't go bad when we leave."

Arik looked at Jairin, who shook his head.

They sat down at the table and started loading their plates with food. "I don't entertain a lot of company," Raven said. "I love having people over, but it just feels like I'm always working."

Jairin looked up between bites, "Raven, I don't think you should go. It isn't safe."

"It's late, Jairin," Raven said. "Let's talk about this in the morning after a good night's sleep. I'm glad you're worried about my safety, but that's my responsibility."

They finished their dinner without talking about it further. When they were done eating, Jairin helped her put things away and clean up the table.

"I have a spare bed I can set up in the bedroom," Raven told her guests, "It's quite small, but it would be perfect for Zael and she's welcome to it. It wouldn't do for either of you two, I'm afraid, but I have a few cots."

Arik looked around the small cottage. "It's all right. We have sleeping mats. We'll make do out here."

Raven took out two cots and set them up for the men.

"Good night, boys." She and Zael went into the next room, closing the door.

Arik unrolled his sleeping mat, setting his sword and gear to the side. Jairin checked his backpack and then set it aside as well. When they were ready to sleep, Jairin blew out the lantern and they lay down on their cots, pulling the blankets over themselves.

Jairin stared at the ceiling. Some light came through the window shades from the lanterns in the street. Arik broke into his thoughts. "Jairin, she's incredible."

"Raven? Yes, she is."

"And smart, and funny—"

"You sound like a little kid," Jairin said.

"And beautiful—"

"Arik," Jairin interrupted.

"Yeah?"

"She's my sister."

"What—?!" Arik sat up straight in his cot.

07 A Plan Laid Bare

Dawn came, throwing beams of light through slits in the shades of the small cottage's living room. Jairin rubbed his eyes to thwart the unwanted intruder that stirred him from his slumber. He gently awakened his traveling companion and then went to check on Raven and Zael.

He knocked quietly twice and was greeted with a "Come in" from his sister on the other side. Letting himself in, he found her on the edge of one of the beds talking with, or at least to, his daughter. Zael was making a series of hand gestures and some invisible drawings in the air with her index finger. Every so often, she laughed a little and changed the signs Raven was making with her hands. Zael was teaching Raven some of the hand signs she and Jairin had devised over the years.

"Can you join us in the next room?" Jairin asked. "I want to run through my plan." He walked to the kitchen, loaded and lit the stove, and then returned to the main room.

He opened the shade, and morning light from the large sun filled the room. The smaller sun must be hiding behind the larger, like a child behind her parent. The late spring weather was markedly milder than a few weeks ago. Summer was coming.

By the time Zael and Raven arrived in the living room, Jairin had already pulled the map from his backpack. Arik eyed the diagram and began writing down some numbers on a separate paper.

"How far is this first waypoint?" Arik asked.

"Probably a hundred kilometers."

"You're right about the horses then. We'll need to find decent runners."

Raven sat down and looked at the map. Zael also pulled up a chair next to Jairin and looked on. He had drawn in more of the map now. To the distant south below Retreol was a vast plain with a marking near the southern edge. From there, the path led on as before to the south and a bit west. With his company now all present, Jairin laid out the plan.

"I know you all know parts of what we're up against. But don't underestimate how dangerous this is going to be. There are reasons why I had intended to go alone. I've told Arik he could accompany me."

Arik caught a glimpse of Raven studying the map. He continued gazing at her as he listened to his friend with half an ear.

Jairin pulled a small brown package from his backpack, tied with twine. He brushed some dust from the wrapping before setting it on the table. Reaching back into his pack, he pulled out what appeared to be a small, leather-bound book. With the two items on the table, he turned back to the map, continuing with his explanation.

"The first leg of the trip brings us here to Thadia." He pointed to a tower he'd drawn south of the city. "I'm expecting we'd be welcomed by the riders of the valley stationed at the outpost. Most of all, I'm hoping to find Sagris—a long-time friend of my father."

Arik noticed Raven smiling at the mention of the outpost.

The others were still all looking at the map. He looked down at the map and then back at Raven. He knew where they were going, so the map wasn't interesting to him.

"I don't know if we'll get any reinforcements at the outpost," Jairin continued. "One or two guides or fighters might be fine, but we're better off with fewer people since the goal is to go quickly and quietly."

"So now we're at the outpost. What next?" Raven asked.

"From Thadia, we go south again to whatever may be left of Castle Glensong in the next valley."

"Should we leave the horses at the—" Raven stopped and looked at Arik, catching him staring back at her. He tried to look away but wasn't quick enough.

"Excuse me, is there any specific reason you've been staring at me since I sat down this morning?"

"You, um…," Arik stuttered. *Oh no, she's annoyed.* He broke off his gaze and felt his face flush with heat. "I'm so sorry." He looked to Jairin and then back to Raven, motioning between them with his hands. "You're… you're his sister?"

Raven's hard stare softened, and a smile slowly came back to her face. Turning to Jairin, she took a breath and sighed. "Oh, thank goodness. We're divulging everything now, right? It was kind of weird you didn't tell him ahead of time." She looked back at the horseman. "Yes, he's the long-term, big-plans, secret-keeping sibling. I'm the fun one."

Jairin felt a need to explain. "The timing didn't seem right yesterday. I didn't know if you wanted to be involved yet."

"See," Raven said, smiling. "He's very good at the secret-keeping part."

"When we were younger, we were passed around a lot among distant family members. She's nine years younger than me, and when our cousins said they could take one of us to live with them permanently here in Retreol, I left her here and went off on my own. It was safe here, at least at the time."

"And now…," Raven said, "Since you've come back here to kill the demon, you're going to *let me* come with you, right? I don't need a big brother to come and warn me of danger and then tell me what I can or can't do about it."

"The plan was to leave you and Zael here if it was safe, or to leave you in Sagris' care in Thadia."

Zael straightened up at this newest revelation. She signed something to Raven.

Raven watched the girl's hand signs and shrugged, saying, "I'm sorry. I don't understand." Raven looked back at her brother. "And you… wrong! I'm not going to stay behind either here or in Thadia. Besides, Sagris isn't even…"

"What?" Jairin asked. "He isn't what?"

Raven smiled. "Never mind. Oh, this is going to be fun."

Jairin hadn't expected an argument. "Look, we can get everyone to safety in Thadia. When it comes to the demon, it's my burden. I'll bring Arik, but otherwise this is my task. The demon razed my kingdom, killed my parents—"

Raven's face grew red. "*Our* kingdom. *Our* parents. I worry, Jairin, that your single-mindedness is clouding your judgment. You're not the only one who has lost part of themselves to this beast. Whether I come with you or not isn't a decision that you get to make on my behalf. I can handle myself. I'm amazing with a pair of short swords."

There was a long silence. Zael's expression eased as well. Jairin nodded toward his sister. "Zael was asking that you intervene on her behalf as well. You've done that." He stood and walked to the kitchen. "I'm going to make some tea, if anyone would like some."

Pots and mugs clinked in the kitchen as Jairin grabbed some items from the cabinet. He filled a kettle from the water barrel and then put the kettle on the hot stove. After a few moments, he emerged from the kitchen and returned to his chair.

Raven turned the map to face her. "So from the castle we head west, into the farmland?"

"First, I'm sorry. I've planned this a long time and I personalized it," Jairin said. He sat there for another moment and then continued, "From what I hear, the farmland is ruined. I don't know how or why a demon would destroy cropland. After all, he must have henchmen to feed. I don't think we'll know until we get to Thadia and ask."

Raven nodded and pointed at an open area to the south. "So once we get through whatever is in these farmlands, then what?"

"Gestron is in the caverns south and west of the castle ruins. We'll find a quiet entrance and make our way through the tunnels to the heart of the caves. I played in them when I was little. I don't remember exactly how they all connected, but it wasn't like a maze. It was pretty much smaller tunnels leading to larger ones."

"Will we be able to see down there?" Arik asked.

"It may be difficult," Jairin answered. "We'll need a slotted oil lamp. That'll give us light that we can direct as we need it."

"Then other creatures down there would see us as well."

"Anything living down there would see us anyway. Unless one of you has night vision, I don't think we have a choice." Jairin smiled a little. From the kitchen a teakettle whistled, calling him back to fetch the Ruhling morning tea he had put on the stove. He came back with some fired clay mugs and a matching pot, sending wafts of steam into the new morning air.

Raven took the tea from her brother and began filling cups. Jairin continued, "The lower caverns are completely flooded. Gestron must be somewhere on the top several levels where it's dry."

"Okay, I'll be the one to ask the obvious question here," Arik interjected. "Assuming we find this demon, then what? Is this the part where our legion of mercenaries jump out and kill the demon? You said yourself that he utterly annihilated your father's best knights with his bare hands."

Jairin closed his eyes for a moment, blotting out an ancient memory. He looked over at his three friends and laid out the final stage of his plan. "This thing is big, no doubt—and tough. My studies have led me to what I hope will be a simple solution." He took a long sip of his tea and set it back down on the table, then picked up the small leather-bound book. "Among a half-dozen other ancient writings in this book is a translation of a spell that I've deciphered. The spell calls forth the magic to freeze a single creature in-place."

"Forever?" Raven asked.

"No. Only for a minute, maybe less."

Arik added, "Just long enough to get in a critical blow."

"Probably not," Jairin said. "Even frozen in place, I doubt you can just hack a demon with a sword and destroy it."

"Then what are we doing?" Raven asked.

Jairin set down the book and picked up the small twine-tied package on the table. His friends looked on as he carefully untied the string and removed the burlap fabric that covered a flat, shiny plate. The back was gray, and the front side shimmered like black glass in the morning light coming through the window.

"What is it?" Arik asked, leaning in toward the mirror.

"Whoa, watch out!" Jairin said, throwing both hands over the reflective surface. "Be very careful not to look into it. This is a Mirror of Wills."

Raven smiled and her face lit up. "No way. Those really exist? I thought it was just part of children's fairy stories!"

Zael picked up her mug of tea and blew at the hot beverage. She brought it to her lips and took several small sips. Jairin knew she had heard this plan many times over the years as he designed one solution after another, refining the approach over time.

Jairin continued, "The Mirror of Wills is empowered by the mind of the person holding it. When the reflective side is pointed at another, the magic literally pulls them in. If the holder is strong enough, their target can be trapped inside the glass like a prison."

"And this is what you'll use to capture the demon?" Arik asked.

"That's my plan. I'm hoping it will work."

"What if you're not strong enough?"

"I have to be. If I have even the smallest doubt, I won't be able to hold the demon in."

The group finalized their plans as they finished their tea. Jairin and Zael helped clean up the small cottage. Raven put out the stove and prepared her home to be left uninhabited for the immediate future. She closed the shades in all the rooms, covered the table and chairs, and gathered some supplies into a pack. Jairin put the two packages into his pack and then he and Arik rolled up their bedding.

"Raven," her brother said, "we need the emergency stash."

"I figured as much." She crouched under the table, wrestling with some unseen switch that eventually made a satisfying *click*. She opened a compartment in the floor under the table and drew out a wooden box. Carrying the small box with some effort, she handed it to Jairin, the sound of loose metal pieces coming from its contents.

They left the cottage and Raven locked the door behind them. "There's a stable on the way out in South Town."

08 The First Road South

The company arrived at the stables and tack shop. The sign at the front of the unassuming wooden storefront read Gunnard and Sons. They walked in and were greeted by a heavy, aged man with blue coveralls, eyes shining brightly. "Welcome! What can I interest you in this morning?" As he lumbered over to the newcomers, hand outstretched, a smile crept across his puffy cheeks and his bushy eyebrows lifted to make his eyes seem to grow that much more. The long outward breaths indicated that he had tired himself out just coming to meet them in the short walk he'd made.

Jairin began to reach out his hand, but Arik beat him to it. "Arik of Keld..." He smiled back, shaking the man's hand. "...Lead negotiator." Arik turned to Jairin and said quietly, "I've got this one."

"Gunnard the Horser," the man in coveralls said, serenely. "Oh my, you are quite a ways from home, my friend. What brings you to Retreol and my stables this fine morning?"

"My friends and I need four horses."

Gunnard smiled and took another deep breath. "I have some fine horses for you to choose from. Come with me." He led them to a fenced pasture out back, where a few dozen horses grazed.

"How much are you looking at spending today?" Gunnard asked as they approached the horses.

Arik looked over the animals in the field before answering. "Strong trotters. We don't need anything fancy for racing or breeding. We're riding south, light and quick."

Gunnard picked out four horses and looked back at Arik. "I would part with these for a mere 120 gold. They're not fancy, but they're strong and they'll get you where you need to go without any worries."

Arik walked over to examine the horses and returned after a few minutes. "I have a concern, but it's not a terrible deal, considering you're actually parting with five horses."

Gunnard scratched his cheek. "What do you mean?"

"The gray mare is pregnant. Change her out for another strong horse and then we can discuss terms."

Gunnard took a long look at Arik, then smiled. "You know horses, eh? It must be Trumfar there that's pregnant. That explains her attitude lately. I'm surprised you could tell before I did." The two horsemen found a suitable replacement horse and then continued with their price negotiations.

"Let me see," Gunnard said. "Sixty, eighty-two, one-hundred-seven ..." The round man eventually came up with a sum. "I'll take an even hundred, since you didn't try to cheat me out of the foal."

"Eighty," Arik said, countering.

"I can't possibly sell them for eighty and still keep my doors open."

"Eighty-five."

Gunnard shook his head. "No. I'd love to do business with you, but I can't budge that much on the price. I'll tell you what... I'll still do one hundred, but I'll throw in the saddles and tack. Well, unless the wandering horse ranchers from Keld all carry around horse gear for four in their backpacks?"

Arik laughed. He looked over at Jairin and Raven. "One hundred, all told."

"We can manage that," Jairin said.

Arik looked back at Gunnard. "Deal."

Gunnard left for a few minutes and came back with saddles. He shook hands with Arik, and they closed their deal.

Jairin set the box on a table and turned to Raven. "Is it all there?" he asked her.

"Yes."

He opened the wooden box, counted out twenty pieces of gold, and gave the box with the rest of the gold to Gunnard. The stable owner handed the box over to one of his assistants. "Please go count that."

"Where are you headed?" Gunnard asked.

"Thadia," Jairin replied.

"Ah. If you don't need these horses after you get there, have someone run them back to me. If you return these to me in perfect health within a week, I'll credit you 15 gold each—18 if they have saddles."

"Sounds like a deal. Thanks."

They all said their farewells and led the horses off a ways. They packed their things in the saddle bags and walked the horses the rest of the way to the city wall in Retreol's South Town, then mounted them and headed out the southwest gates.

They traveled ahead on the wide southbound road, the occasional tufts of thatch and weeds in their path a constant reminder that traffic out of the city in this direction wasn't what it once was. Retreol grew smaller in the distance as they traveled. After a while the path split in two. One sign pointed east to the great seaport of Barrington, and the other pointed south to Thadia. There were two worn spots at the bottom of the signpost with some bent, rusty nails to indicate that at one time, it had shown more destinations.

Stopping a few times only to eat rations and drink, they made good time. As the suns were falling in the sky, they broke camp for the night. Arik tied up the horses and helped Jairin set up the two small tents they carried in their packs, taking care to be out of sight of travelers on the road. Zael built a fire for cooking now and heat later as night coolness set in. Raven cooked up some stew with salted meats and vegetables she took from a pouch in her pack.

After they had eaten, Arik looked around at his traveling companions sitting around the fire. "Story time." He poked at the fire with a small stick and set down his food. "I have an adventure to share. When I was about fourteen, my brother Stalic and I went out on our first boar hunt in the woods just north of our village. He must have been about twelve and he'd never been hunting before without our father being with us.

"We followed a boar through the underbrush for nearly twenty minutes. When it stopped to drink from a stream, I pulled out my bow to take my shot. Just as I was releasing the string, something hit my hand and the arrow flew way off course. My hand was pulsing and hurt like it had been broken. I must have yelled. The boar heard me and took off."

"Your brother threw a rock at you?" Raven asked.

"No, Stalic was right next to me. Off by the trees we saw what I thought was a child. He couldn't have been more than a meter tall; no clothes, but fur down his back and on his arms and legs. He just stood there, staring at us. I thought about getting another arrow ready, but my hand hurt so bad I couldn't move it. The next thing we knew, it dropped down on all fours and scurried off faster than a rabbit back into the brush!"

"A kince!" Raven exclaimed, her voice rising. She smiled, wide-eyed. Leaning forward, she looked more intently at Arik. "That was a caretaker of the animals! You saw a kince!"

Arik nodded. "I think so. You know, in the ten years

before and ten years since in those woods, I've never seen anything like it."

"I don't know what to say," Jairin said. "I've never doubted they existed, but I've never seen one. Elves, sure, and dwarves, and parums. I've never even heard of anyone ever seeing kince before."

Arik looked over at Jairin, raising an eyebrow "You have? Elves? Where?"

"At the castle when I was just a little kid. I've seen a lot of things."

Zael smiled. She was more at ease than she had been earlier that day. She'd never seen any elves, dwarves, kince, or any of these things before. Since she'd left her village, the only friendly faces she'd seen had been humans. Arik's story sounded surreal, a welcome change from the mundane events that filled the days and the darkness that haunted her in her dreams. It made her feel connected, wanted.

"I'll take the first watch," Jairin told his companions. "Arik, take the second half of the night if you would."

"Sure." Sometime in the middle of the night, they switched shifts.

Arik tended the fire, adding enough wood to keep the coals hot with a minimal amount of fresh flame. He nodded off several times, snapping back when he caught himself. Dawn came on quietly, but not as comfortably as it had the previous day in Raven's small cottage. There was a chill in the air. The nocturnal rodents had again retreated underground, but the insects were now awake, chirping and squeaking their carefree songs to the rising sun and its much smaller companion. Arik sat, half-awake, shielding his eyes from the morning light. He stood and stretched near the smoldering remains of the campfire and went to check on the horses. He removed burrs from their coats, then brushed them. He brought them to a nearby stream to drink and graze.

They'd be in the open plains of Bravitleer today, land of the horse riders and herdsmen. That gave him some comfort, knowing the people there would be much like his own—he hoped. What lay beyond the plains, into the mountains of the south? His father had told him of a time long past when there had been order in the land and a castle overlooking the distant valley of Draxmore. Looking out at the open plains beyond the edge of the trees, he thought he could see the ancient mountains on the horizon to the south. In these plains and in these woods, life made sense. Whatever lay beyond was the unknown, from which he might not return.

A warm snort near his ear pulled Arik from his introspection. He repacked their feeding supplies and then walked back to camp to awaken the others. When they had all risen, he helped Raven take down the tents and pack up the horses for the next day's ride. They ate a quick breakfast and then rejoined the road, heading south. Tomorrow afternoon they should reach Thadia on the far side of the plains.

As the morning wore on, there were noticeably fewer trees. Grassland emerged on either side of the road, which itself became more a grassy trail and less a road as they continued. They came across a large field of flowers and dismounted to have lunch and let the horses graze. They didn't stay long, opting to move along until they could find another stream where they could fill their water skins and let the horses drink.

As evening again approached, they looked in vain for some cover to use for their camp. When the larger sun began to set over the plain, they resorted to moving off of the overgrown road to at least stop from being stumbled upon by accident. Dinner consisted of some bread and dried meat.

They didn't want to risk starting a fire in their camp, in the open. The warming spring evening air made the camp feel more cheerful. As the night moved in, Raven and Jairin took the first watch and were to awaken Arik again for the second part. After a long day on horseback, Arik and Zael quickly fell asleep.

Raven turned to her brother. "What was the castle like?" she asked. "I've heard many stories, but I'd like to hear it from someone who's been there."

"Do you mean before or after?" he asked. She sensed a sad tone in Jairin's voice.

"Before, I guess."

"As far as castles go, it was pretty modest, but the view was amazing. The river Ardrual splits in two at the edge of a cliff making two waterfalls that plunge several hundred meters to the valley floor. They built the castle between the forks. You can see all of Draxmore Valley from there."

Raven had heard descriptions of the castle before but had never actually seen any images of it. "It sounds beautiful. How much of it do you think is left?"

"I think the towers were all torn down. I can't imagine anyone would waste the time to knock down the rest of it. It wasn't the building itself that was a threat to anyone."

"That's a horrible waste."

Jairin turned to face his sister in the evening light. "About before… It's not that I didn't want to include you. It's just that you're my little sister and you're the only family I've got left."

"I don't plan on dying."

"I know. I won't lie to you about our odds, though, Raven. Anyone going after the demon in those caverns may not come back out."

"When I was younger, I envied you," Raven said, "You got to grow up in the castle, for some of your childhood, at least."

Jairin nodded. "There was definitely a change in the land. After our parents were killed, the whole kingdom just unraveled. Nothing really felt 'right' as long as that demon was free. I can't live that way." He put his arm around his sister.

"When the time comes, you won't be standing alone. You lost a lot, but I lost being able to see my big brother for more than a day or so every couple of years."

"I've tried to do the best I could for you—given the circumstances."

She leaned into her brother's shoulder. "I know."

"Don't underestimate this demon, though, Raven. This thing is evil. Its shadows reached out and destroyed Arik's village out of nowhere. Nobody is safe while it sits in that cavern, unchecked."

"Oh no…" Raven corrected him, "When the time comes, this demon will have *me* to deal with."

Jairin smiled back at his sister, "You know what? I wouldn't want to be on the other side of that stare when you get angered."

Raven playfully pushed her brother to the side and broke a smile. They talked for a while about their childhood and the different roads their lives had taken. The night wore on and they eventually fell asleep.

09 Prisoners Of the Master

The early light of day hit Arik in the face as the suns rose, stirring him from sleep. He opened his eyes a crack and then stretched as he lay on the ground, taking in the morning. There was a strong scent in the air, leathery and musty like animal skin. The odor was familiar, but out of place. He hadn't fallen asleep near the horses. Arik rubbed his eyes and rose to his feet. He heard the *clack-clack* of cloven footfalls behind him and then the unmistakable snort of a horse. He whipped around and stopped.

A man on horseback towered over him in chain mail armor. "Good morning!"

Arik heard voices at the other side of camp, "All right, up with the lot of you. Come with us." He reached for his sword only to find the scabbard at his waist empty. He looked down at it in disbelief.

"About that," the man on the horse said, "we've had to disarm you. I'm afraid we just couldn't allow an armed militia to roam around free on the plains."

The commotion from the far side of the camp grew closer and louder. Six more men approached, escorting Jairin, Zael, and Raven to where Arik and the other armed man stood.

"You were supposed to wake me to take my turn on

watch, Jairin," Arik said, scolding his companion.

Jairin shrugged his shoulders. "I'm sorry. Raven and I were talking. I guess we fell asleep."

The man on horseback spoke again to Arik, "I am Yardin, Captain of the third division of the Thadian detachment of the Bravitleer guard. In the name of the Master of the Valley, we will be escorting you willingly or otherwise to the tower at Thadia."

Jairin stepped forward with his arms outstretched to show he had no hostile intent. "If you please, Captain, that is exactly where we were headed."

"Traffic here from the north has been a bit slow lately," Yardin replied. "What is your business at the tower?"

"My father was a friend of Sagris. We seek an audience with the Master of the Valley. It's most urgent."

"Your father was a friend of Sagris? I regret it would be quite impossible to speak with him, but you can discuss it with the magistrate when we arrive."

With the assurance of no resistance, the third division guards let the party clean up camp and mount their own horses for the half-day journey south to Thadia. The guards numbered twelve in all, flanking the party on all sides.

"What about our weapons?" Jairin asked.

Yardin replied, "Hostile or not, you are still under escort of the tower guard. Your armaments will be returned if and when you are cleared by the magistrate."

In relative silence, the group made their way south on the overgrown road. As they rode, the distant mountains seemed to grow and take shape before their eyes. After several hours they could see the spire of a tower emerging on the horizon. The tower guard pointed out their destination as they approached.

"Why would you make the tower white?" Arik asked the escorts. "That would make it a much easier target to spot."

Yardin said, "Stealth is not the idea. The alabaster tower stands eternally strong, even in these dark times. It is meant to be seen and to show the might of Bravitleer that those roaming these plains know always where they are."

"What's happening in the valley?" Jairin asked.

"Something is stirring in the lands south of us. It's coming from the catacombs far beyond the old mountains. Dragons now patrol the night sky around our tower. They stay in their lofty heights, but it spooks the horses."

"Is that unusual?"

"They've been rare, but not unheard-of in our skies. The problem is that they're flying in groups of two or three and at regular intervals. These are patrols. Dragons are supposed to be solitary creatures."

The exchange died down as they approached the outpost. Against the darkness of the mountains to the distant south, Jairin could see the tower much more distinctly now, extending thirty meters into the sky. In the afternoon light of the suns, it radiated a white light. As they approached, he could see the silver runes carved into the alabaster. He'd never been able to read them. The light reflecting from the silver text added to the sparkle coming from the white stone around it. Despite his familiarity, it was still a wonder every time he approached. He hoped the Master of the Valley would offer them a guide, or at least a warm welcome. Sagris had ever been a great friend to his father.

Yardin pulled a horn from under his chainmail and issued a series of blasts. From an outpost in the eight-meter-high stone wall, a man yelled out, "Patrol returning for entry."

The guards at the great front gates retracted the entry bars at the cry, answering, "Patrol entering."

Reaching the gates, the third division of the Thadian detachment of the Bravitleer guard entered the outpost with their prisoners.

10 Thadia

The patrol and Jairin's company dismounted. Some of the guard took the horses and led them to the stables. Once the compound walls had been closed and barred, the guards removed their helmets and chain armor. Yardin and another guard escorted the prisoners to the base of the tower. An older man in colored robes emerged from the tower, taking slow, deliberate steps through the double two-story-tall oaken doors. The guards flanking Jairin's party bowed their heads slightly and then took a few steps back as he approached.

The old magistrate lifted his bald head and looked individually at each of the prisoners' faces as Yardin approached him. The two conversed quietly, occasionally pointing at one, or several of their prisoners.

The company was surrounded by small support buildings at the base of the tower—one filled with riding equipment, one with workers carrying stacks of soiled clothing in and clean clothing out, one with several men working with iron.

Jairin looked around at the barracks, stables, and various armories. It had changed little over the years. His thoughts drifted to the Master of the Valley. Sagris didn't owe him anything. He might not even remember him. What if there was no welcome for them at all here? Or worse, what if the Master did remember him, but blamed him for not being here all these years to join their fight? He began to wonder if traveling through Bravitleer had been a good idea after all. But the valley was the only way to get back to Jairin's home, so they'd have to take their chances.

The magistrate broke from his conversation and took a step toward the group. "I've been told our patrols spotted you on the road south of Retreol heading to the tower. What is your business in Bravitleer?"

Jairin stepped forward. With a bow, he said, "If you please, your honor, we were crossing Bravitleer to come here, to Thadia."

"Why?"

"My father was a good friend of Sagris. We are seeking an audience with the Master of the Valley."

The magistrate looked over the company for a few moments before speaking again. "Who, may I ask, is seeking an audience with the Master?"

"I am Prince Jairin, son of Marax, the King of Tarquin."

A murmur went up in the ranks of guards near the tower. The magistrate raised his thin arms to silence the whisperings going on around them.

"I will meet with the Master. If you are who you say, you may be granted an audience. It has been a great many years since the name of the king or his family has been mentioned in these lands."

"That was the plan, your honor," Jairin said.

The magistrate raised an eyebrow. "I don't understand."

"I've been gone and I'm sorry. It was necessary that anyone who came looking for me or my family should find nothing."

The magistrate looked Jairin over one more time. "Indeed." He turned around slowly and walked back into the tower, disappearing into the darkness.

Time seemed to Jairin to come to a crawl. He shifted his weight from leg to leg and wiped his sweaty hands on his trousers. All eyes seemed to be looking his way. *What if they won't let me speak with the Master of the Valley? Worse, what if we are held captive here? The valley seems to be free of the demon Gestron's influence, but that isn't something you can just sense the way you'd sense a forest fire. At least my sword will be able to—wait—they have my sword!*

The squawk of an animal far overhead interrupted his thoughts. A few of the guards looked up. Jairin followed the sound, looking for the dragon who had called forth. The guards had already stopped looking. He figured they must not be terribly concerned. *This must be normal now to hear the sounds from the sky overhead. You couldn't see them in the light of the suns during the day, it seemed.* He looked back at the tower, shifting his weight again. A runner emerged from the tower and ran toward the stables.

Ten minutes later, the magistrate emerged from the darkness. He motioned to the guards and they turned and stepped aside with a bow. The runner returned with a leather bundle. He opened the bundle and pulled out their weapons, which he returned to the four friends.

The magistrate motioned for the party to follow him. "The Master of Bravitleer Valley has granted you an audience. Please follow me."

They entered the huge double doors of the great tower and walked through a dimly lit hall with small oil lanterns on the walls toward a staircase on the far end. Zael looked up at the flights of stairs leading into the darkness above them. Jairin reached out to make sure she wasn't going to pass out. She bobbed a bit but didn't fall.

"Don't worry," the magistrate said. "The receiving room is on the second floor."

They climbed the stairs to the next level. The magistrate opened the door and the stairwell was illuminated with daylight from the hallway beyond. The hallway was lined with beautifully colored paintings and vases and statues perched on pedestals. They seemed to be arranged to drink in the light coming through the open windows. As the group reached the far end, a pair of guards opened another set of oak doors; a smaller version of those at the main entrance.

More light. Inside the receiving room, the flickering flames from the oil lanterns lighting the walls created depth and shadow in the great chamber. At the far end sat the Master of Bravitleer Valley, dressed in elegant red robes that shimmered in the torchlight. Cloaked in shadow and clutching a long, gnarled staff, the Master looked like a wizard seated on the wooden throne.

The Master of the Valley rose. "Prince Jairin and company." The voice was strange, unnatural. "What is it you seek in my valley?"

Jairin made a low bow and fixed his glance on the Master of the Valley, the elected general of all the northern forces of what had been his father's kingdom. This certainly didn't look or sound like the kind, elderly Sagris that he had known as a child. "We're seeking Thadia's aid to banish the demon that cowers beyond your southern border."

The Master hesitated before replying. "In these times, only chaos lies beyond my borders."

"I'm going to change that. Once I lay waste to the demon Gestron, I'll rebuild my father's kingdom."

"Now that's the Jairin that I remember!" the Master replied. The voice was different this time. Higher-pitched.

Jairin squinted, trying to make out the face cloaked in shadow. "You aren't Sagris. I don't mean to sound rude, but who are you?"

The Master of the Valley stepped forward out of the shadows, pulling back the hood. A long mane of golden hair fell over her shoulders, framing the resplendent face of a young woman with striking green eyes. "Regrettably, Sagris passed on nearly six years ago." Her voice was soft, but stern. Powerful.

Jairin stood, unmoving, mouth open, staring at the Master of the Valley. Time seemed to stop. His ears rang and he heard Raven speak from behind him, as if he were underwater. "Sorry, Jairin. You have no idea how hard it was not to mention this."

After what seemed like many long minutes, he uttered a single word in a weak voice. "Carmen?"

11 Masterful Reception

Carmen fixed a cool gaze at Jairin. She took a breath and held it in for a few seconds, then slowly let it out before speaking. "We looked for you for a very long time, Jairin."

Jairin felt a chill flowing through his entire body. The sleeves of his shirt could hide the goosebumps, but this turn of events was unexpected. After a moment, he regained enough composure to speak. "I didn't want to be found, but I wasn't hiding. I was studying—training—at the Monastery of the Brothership of Belcronar."

"Hmm," Carmen said. "You would hide even from me?"

"No, never. Not on purpose, anyway."

"That's quite a way to the west. I guess we just didn't search far enough. Why were you hiding?"

Jairin hesitated, wondering how to explain. "I needed somewhere quiet, and a strategy to stop Gestron." He suddenly remembered his companions. "Oh! I need to make some introductions. This is my adopted daughter Zeal, my sister Raven, and our new friend Arik." He pointed to each in turn.

Carmen's eyes widened. "Raven! You were a toddler when I last saw you!" She approached her and embraced her with a cheerful smile. "You should've come to find me earlier. I thought you had escaped with Jairin. We'd have made a grand chamber for you here."

"It's okay," Raven replied. "I grew up in the city. I have no regrets."

Carmen stepped back. Jairin recounted what had been going on and where they were headed.

"You're welcome, of course, to whatever aid my riders and I have to spare," Carmen said. "We'll have a grand banquet this evening to celebrate old and new friends. But you…" She faced Jairin again. "Stay here and talk with me for a bit. We have unfinished business." The Master scowled.

"We thank you for your kindness," Raven said.

Carmen's gaze for the rest of the group softened. "I'll set up some rooms for you to stay in this evening. No friends of Bravitleer will sleep in the grass while they're in my care." She called for the magistrate, standing at the door, to show the guests to their quarters.

Arik took several slow steps toward Jairin. "Would you prefer I stay?" he asked quietly of his friend.

Jairin shook his head. "No. Go with them."

The others left the room. The guards followed them back out and pulled the doors shut behind them.

Carmen approached the prince. She looked him in the eyes for a few moments and then looked away. She slowly looked back up at him, pulled back her arm, and slapped him across the face with a great deal of force. The sound reverberated through the chamber as she pulled her hand back to her side.

Jairin winced, instinctively reaching up to his throbbing cheek.

Carmen let out a deep breath. "I said 'we' but it was a solo job. *I* looked everywhere for you. My fellow rangers said you were dead. I didn't believe them and I never gave up hope." He could see the anger welled up in her, the obvious slapping aside. She took a trembling breath and put her hands on her hips, stepping back. "I'm glad you're okay. I was irate that you left… but I'm glad you're okay. Wherever 'we' are, I need you to understand that I—"

Jairin stepped toward Carmen, inches from her face. He slipped an arm around her waist and the other around her upper back. He pulled her into him and kissed her, gently at first. Initially hesitant, Carmen kissed him back. Charges of electricity danced through every nerve in his body. The goosebumps were back, and any lingering pain he had in his cheek was lost in the flush of blood that coursed through him. She wrapped her arms around him, caressing the back of his neck and shoulder. He inhaled deeply, filling his head with the vanilla and lavender scent of her hair.

Carmen broke the embrace, fighting to catch her breath.

"I loved—I loved you, Jairin. I loved the man who sneaked me out of my father's house to ride all night along the River Andrual. I loved the man who found blood orchids to plant outside my window without boasting that you'd done it. I loved the man who, by the light of a firestorm, asked me to marry him."

Jairin's voice trembled as he responded. "I love you, Carmen. I don't have the words for how much you mean to me. Give me a chance to make things right with my father's kingdom. After that, I'll give you the world."

"You left. You left *me*. You disappeared."

"I sent word to you, explaining why I had to leave. I'll destroy this demon and we can live in peace. I have to do it. It's my destiny. The Oracle said I was the one to destroy the demon."

She shook her head. "What you sent me wasn't enough. You're not a 'chosen one' Jairin. There is no such path, and not for you. That woman you call the Oracle was no seer. She was a crazy old woman who lived in a cave in the hills. She told you what you wanted to hear so you'd go away and leave her alone. I'm not angry about it anymore, but don't do this. It's foolish—you'll die."

"I don't believe that. And what would become of me if I don't follow through with this? Would I stay here? Perhaps I could learn to become a blacksmith? A cook? A farmer?"

"I know you can do whatever you put your mind to. If you want to be a king, be a king. I told your friends I'll contribute what I can, and I will, but this seems crazy."

"It's not crazy," Jairin said. "I can't live in a world that's only a shadow of what I know it can be. With the demon gone, I can resume my father's legacy and proclaim myself King. I'll build a new castle in your honor. I left—it's true— but I've never lied to you. If you don't take me at my word, watch me do exactly what I'm promising I'll do."

"I believe you, and I know your potential, Jairin. You always amaze me, but I hate your stubbornness. Although I think this is a fool's errand, I admire your bravery. It's also the one thing you've ever wanted."

Jairin shook his head. "Not the only thing, but it's something I have to do, and it has to be now. If I don't, this evil will grow unchecked until there is nowhere safe to hide, whether we're together or not."

Carmen's expression softened. She reached out her hand and ran it along the injured side of his face. "I don't think I can talk you out of this. I can offer some provisions and a few men. As far as your new kingdom, I'll tell you this… If the man who proposed to me so many years ago returns from this quest, my answer will be the same. I'll still want to share everything I am with that Jairin. I would settle for no less a man."

She turned and made her way toward the doors. Turning to face Jairin again, she motioned for him to follow her out of the audience room. "You need to get ready for the banquet. You'll be made to speak before all of the rangers. I'll send a seamstress to take your measure."

Jairin looked deep into her eyes with a bright, confident

smile. "I'm still me, my love. When this is over, I'll rebuild the kingdom. All of Tarquin will be yours, and then some."

The house guard led Jairin to the room he would share with Arik. After several days of sparse food and dry rations, anything prepared by a cook would be a feast. He entered the room to find Arik wearing a new set of ill-fitting clothes. An elderly man was taking measurements with a cloth tape.

Arik smiled when his friend entered the room. He stood in a T-pose with his arms wide. "They say we're having a formal dinner party for a guest of some note. I was trying to figure out who had wandered in after us that was—" Arik gestured toward Jairin's face. "Fitch! Did you lose a fight?"

"What? Oh, I deserved that." Jairin brought his hand up to rub his injured cheek. It didn't actually hurt yet, as the adrenaline was still running through him.

"Don't tell me... she's your other sister?"

"No, not quite. We were engaged, a long time ago."

Arik nodded, but looked befuddled. "It seems she wizened up before it was too late. Did you two get everything sorted out? Or do we need to sneak out of here?"

"Oh... no, no. We're okay. For a moment, when we first arrived here, I wondered if this quest was worth pursuing. I was thinking maybe we could part ways and go live out our lives in quiet safety. Then I saw her. The years have done nothing but add to her enchantment. She reminded me of what I wanted. We each have a role to play, and mine is to fix what Gestron has broken. If I don't do that—at least try—I won't be able to live with myself."

"She inspires that in you? I didn't think the Riders of Bravitleer would ever elect a woman as their commander, but it seems like they've found a formidable one."

Jairin nodded. "She has the heart of a dragon. As far as I know, they've never chosen a woman to lead them before." He caught sight of something from the corner of his eye and looked down at his scabbard. "It appears we have a bigger problem." Jairin pulled his sword out. The blade had a faint blue light coming from it.

"What does that mean?"

"Trouble. There is something not right here. I don't know what it is, but the glow tells me there is a demon nearby."

In the women's chamber, an attendant brought in a selection of gowns, setting them atop the rest on the edge of a bed. Raven looked at the fit of the dress she'd just tried on. "Oh, I love this one!" she said to the seamstress. "Can you take it in a bit here, and take the hem at the floor up just a bit?"

Zael signed to her friend: *I'll be happy to spend an evening in some better clothes.* She smiled.

"Better clothes?" Raven repeated. "Exactly. See, I'm getting the hang of this signing thing."

Finally, their dresses were altered to fit, and they twirled in front of the small dressing mirror to admire them. Raven wore a full-length, classically styled dress the color of spring buttercups. Zael's was pure white with hand-stitched lace trim at the neck and sleeves.

The hour for the banquet arrived, and two rangers escorted the women from their chamber to the dining hall on the fifth floor.

They met Jairin and Arik in the hallway outside the dining hall. "You are a vision," Arik said to Zael. He turned to Raven. Her long black hair fell over her shoulders and down her back over the fitted dress. "You look absolutely breathtaking. There isn't anyone here who could deny that you are a princess, Milady."

Raven blushed. "Thank you, dashing gentleman. I will now cover up my embarrassment with my very practiced 'theater smile.'" She smiled at Arik, sticking out her tongue.

The doors to the great hall opened to reveal the setting for a dinner feast that filled the entire level of the tower. Though there was no gold, or silver, or even table coverings, the sheer size of the banquet tables was impressive. The tables were arranged in two long parallel rows joined by a small five-chair section at one end. The party was seated at the shorter table with the center seat left open, presumably for Carmen.

Over the next ten minutes, the rest of the chairs were filled by members of the Bravitleer guard. When the last seat was taken, an announcement rang out from the hallway, "The Master of Bravitleer Valley." All of the guards snapped to their feet at attention, and the four followed suit. Carmen appeared in the doorway and everything else stopped.

She entered the room, slowly making her way to the empty seat at the front. Her long emerald-colored dress draped to the floor and trailed behind her. She walked down the outside of the table as two guards closed the doors. Jairin knew they chose the Master of the Valley for their skill in battle and their wits in negotiations, but she also looked at this moment very much a queen. When she arrived at the head of the table, she took the seat Jairin had pulled out for her beside his. He eased her chair as she sat down, and everyone else took their seat in turn.

Dinner featured venison, quail, pheasant, brook trout, new potatoes, root vegetables, greens, and fresh-baked bread, served with wine from the cellars, all followed by apple pie and raspberry tarts with heavy cream.

After the dessert, Carmen rose. "We will have a short meeting of the guard once the plates have been cleared. Captains, company commanders, and Jairin's party are asked to stay. Once we're done, everyone is invited back to the hall for a dance and drinks into the night." Her remarks were met with quiet cheers.

Servers came through the hall gathering plates, glasses, and the remnants of dinner and dessert. When the last of the dinner had been cleared away, the diners not directly involved in the defense of Bravitleer were politely ushered out and the doors were closed behind them to begin discussion.

Carmen rose. "This will be news for Jairin's company, but as the rest of you know, the shadow in the south has been infecting the lands surrounding our valley. Dragon scouts have been seen flying over the valley more frequently than we have seen in recent memory. I fear this is only a precursor to an inevitable assault on our lands. I don't think it can be held back much longer by our vigilance and courage alone.

"Many of us, including me, have lost fathers and brothers fighting the demon Gestron, who destroyed the old kingdom. It is ruthless and horrifying. As you may have also heard, the son of King Marax has returned to us. If there is a chance of defeating Gestron, this is it."

Some rumblings went through the assembled guard. At the end of one of the side tables, one of the captains motioned to speak. Carmen nodded to him. "Yes, Captain. Please speak your mind."

The man turned to Jairin. "I'm Captain Dorian. How do you intend to kill the demon? According to accounts, Gestron cut down a hundred men, unaided. These weren't farmers, but armored and trained knights of the King. Are we to be a front line for our prince to ride in and slay this demon with a human shield before him?"

Jairin rose to address the rudely worded question. "There's no doubt you are the bravest and strongest group of men in the land. If anyone here knew my father, I assure you I am that same kind of man. I won't ask anyone to join a fight that I wouldn't be willing to join myself. My company and I will head south tomorrow without requesting a single man to accompany us. The four of us, before you now, will leave the tower on our own just as we arrived."

The group looked to each other, speaking in quiet conversation. Jairin didn't sense confidence from the men.

He pulled his sword from its scabbard and set it on the table in front of him with a clang. The blue glow was much stronger now, pulsing with a magical blue light.

"I won't bore you with the history of this weapon, but it will cleave through the flesh of a demon as if it were a melon. When I run across Gestron and its demons, ancient and powerful magic will protect me." The guards looked at each other, murmuring among themselves.

The Bravitleer guards talked more about the land between Thadia and the castle by the falls. They urged Jairin to tell the stories of where he had been and what he had been doing since he'd left the kingdom. But he knew he had to be careful about what he revealed. Somewhere in the tower, there were demons present. He couldn't trust anyone here to know his true plan to capture the demon in the south. He crafted his responses to be vague, but to instill hope in these men. The atmosphere in the room lightened, partly with new confidence in Jairin, and partly in anticipation of the after-dinner dance.

The tables were cleared and removed from the hall to make room for dancing. A company of minstrels entered and arranged their instruments in the corner nearest the doors. After a few moments, more women entered—possibly wives, girlfriends, sisters, and staff. Jairin wasn't completely sure.

Carmen removed the ornamental outer panel of her gown and sent a server to the bar to bring goblets of wine for Jairin and her.

Zael looked over at her father and made some gestures with her hands, smiling. Jairin looked puzzled by what she was asking. "Something seems different about me?" He signed back, "No. I don't think so…"

The girl shook her head, smiling even larger. Captain Dorian approached the young woman and asked her for a dance. She graciously accepted with a nod, holding out her hand for him. Together they walked out onto the dance floor. She glanced back for just a moment at Jairin, still smiling.

Carmen finished her wine and pulled Jairin out on the dance floor.

Arik looked over at Raven. "What's their story?"

"They have a history. He didn't tell you?"

"Not much. He gave me the ten-word version. It seems he likes to hold back details, like the one about you being his sister."

Raven laughed. "They were supposed to be married at one time, before they both left Draxmore Valley. I was very young, but I remember they were always together."

"What happened?"

"Jairin felt fate was pushing him in another direction. You know how he is—duty, secrecy, and the rest. Once he decided that it was his responsibility to destroy Gestron, he withdrew and disappeared. He said it was to keep people safe. I don't see how that saved anyone, but it gave him a chance to plan out his next moves. So far as I know, that was the end of it."

Arik smiled. "I'd say there was something still there."

Raven leaned toward Arik. "Dance with me?"

"I'd be honored." They went out on the busy dance floor to join the others.

Carmen and Jairin sneaked out of the hall to the quiet hallway. "I'm far more worried about you than I let on before," she told him.

"In what way?" Jairin asked.

"That sword is an incredible artifact, but you and I both know that it's not practical to pit that against something of Gestron's strength."

"That's probably true, but that isn't exactly what I'm planning to do."

"Come with me," Carmen said. "I have something I want

to show you. We need to get to the top of the tower." She took his hand and walked toward the stairway.

Jairin looked confused. "Now? Five more flights of stairs?"

"Don't be silly." Carmen opened a small door next to the stairwell. Inside was a small room with a pair of ropes. After they entered, she closed the door and pulled on one of the ropes. The platform rose.

Jairin looked about in disbelief. As they pulled the rope, the platform moved up faster and faster with little resistance.

"Its engineering," Carmen tried to explain. "This is an elevator. They have a counterweight to allow us to go up or down on this platform quickly, and with little effort. Genius, if you ask me."

"Witchcraft," the prince replied, jokingly.

They arrived at the top of the tower, stepped out of the lift, and looked out over the stone wall. In the evening sky, they could make out mountains to the south and the distant lights of Retreol to the north.

"What have we come up here to see?" Jairin asked.

Carmen pointed straight up. There, illuminated by the last rays of sunlight on the horizon, they could see a dragon circling overhead at a great height. "It's hard to see details, but the markings and colors change. There must be several of them, scouts," Carmen said. "Someone or something is keeping watch on Thadia. If anyone else has seen them, they haven't mentioned it to me. Maybe it's because we openly maintain a military presence in the valley."

"Demons and dragons don't mix," Jairin said. "Whoever is sending these scouts, it's not likely Gestron. Have they been hostile?"

"No. We know the weak points and fighting tactics of many types of dragons, but we learn that as apprentices fighting bales of straw. I have never heard of a dragon landing in Bravitleer. At least for now, it's just one more uncertainty. Whatever the reason, it makes your journey out of here harder to keep secret. I'll make sure I send a scout and a ranger with you to get you through the hills. I think the prince marching into Draxmore would generate an unnecessary confrontation."

"Do you think we should cut through the hills rather than take the road to the waterfall?"

"Exactly," Carmen replied.

"That's a good point. I intended to have a small force with me, but I wasn't aware Gestron was looking for resistance from the tower. I wouldn't want to put the rest of the garrison here in danger either. Do you know what lies beyond now in Draxmore?"

Carmen took another sip of wine and set the goblet down on the stone rail that encircled the observation post. "No, I don't know what lies beyond Draxmore. For our own safety, we don't patrol outside Bravitleer. It would spread our forces too thin to defend the valley." The suns had gone, leaving them bathed only in starlight. Carmen looked at her former suitor with the light of the heavens reflected from his eyes. She brushed some stray hairs from his face behind an ear, letting her hand linger there. "I don't know what fate has in store for us. If this evening is all we have after fifteen years apart, can we discuss something other than dragons and revenge?"

At the end of the evening, Raven retired to her room, finding Zael fast asleep. She brushed her hair and washed her face. She looked out the window. Something wasn't right, but she couldn't figure out exactly what it was. In time, she fell into an uneasy sleep.

12 The Second Road South

"Jairin, wake up. Get up!"

"What? What's wrong?" He opened his eyes to see Raven hovering over him with Arik behind her as she shook him awake. Her eyes were wide and she sounded breathless—something had scared her.

"What is it?"

"It's Zael," she said. "She's not waking up. Her breath is slow and shallow. I tried to wake her up, but nothing's working!"

As they hurried to the women's chambers, Jairin tried to explain about Zael's condition. They found her on her bed, very much unconscious. He felt her forehead—cool to the touch. "I never know how long she'll be out like this. She may wake up in a few minutes, but it could be a few hours or a few days. I hate to say it, but this may be for the best. We should leave her here for now. If she awakens later today, Carmen may be able to get her to Castle Glensong to meet up with us."

"I don't want to leave her behind."

"We have little choice. I love her dearly, but I can't justify waiting for her to wake up. She'll be safer here in Thadia than anywhere else. We can't carry her around, and this could happen again on our journey."

Raven bent down and kissed Zael on the forehead. "He's right. I'll make this up to you, Z. We'll have our share of adventures once this is over. I promise."

After a hearty breakfast, they checked on their fourth companion one last time. No change. Jairin, Raven, and Arik assembled outside the tower, waiting on their horses. Carmen and several of her personal staff met them and escorted them to the stables where their horses and newly provisioned packs were ready.

One of the rangers approached, bowing before the Master of the Valley before turning to the companions. "I'm Rhobin. I'm in your service to accompany you to the caverns."

Carmen expanded the introduction. "Rhobin has been a field commander for many years. He's skilled and fearless in battle, and in the past year has become our expert on demon lore."

Rhobin shook his head. "She exaggerates, I'm afraid, but I'm in your service and will do whatever I can to help see this quest through."

Another man was brought forward; a curious, diminutive thing. He stood a meter tall, a child's height—his hair short and almost the color of fire. In his short arms, the halfling carried a thick wooden club. "I'm Berch. The master asked me to guide you through the back trails of the mountains. I don't do horses. I don't do dragons. I'm a parum, a halfling if you like. Anyone calling me a dwarf or a midget will get a painful thump to the knee or to the stomach. I'll guide you as best I can."

"Parum aren't usually known for their scouting and mountaineering," Carmen told them, "But Berch isn't your usual halfling. Nobody knows the trails and these woods better than he does. If my own life depended on his survival skill, I wouldn't hesitate to put it in his hands. He's also the fastest walker I've ever met, considering his size."

Jairin noticed the horses didn't seem to appreciate their guide, however. As Berch passed them, they grunted and backed away.

Berch gave a harrumph. "Like I said, I don't do horses. Apparently they don't like parums, and so I return the favor."

"Can we leave the horses here?" Jairin asked the Master of the Valley. "It'll take a bit longer the first day, but it's probably for the best. Berch doesn't ride, and we'll need to turn them back when we get to the foothills anyway."

There was general agreement to leave them behind, except for Arik's objection. He eventually agreed to let them stay behind. "Can you have someone take these horses back to Gunnard in South Town? He promised to pay us back seventy-two gold on delivery with tack and gear."

"That's no problem. I'll have the northbound patrol bring them when they switch out." Carmen nodded to one of her captains, who nodded back in acknowledgement.

Rhobin and Berch walked ahead toward the gate. As they passed by the horses, the equines let out varying snorts and neighs. Berch turned back to the group. "See? They hate me." He turned to the horses and let out a, "Blickity, blickity, bap, bap!" waving his fingers with his thumbs in his ears. The horses backed up and snorted.

"Come on, company!" Rhobin said with a grin. "We're moving out."

Jairin addressed Carmen, "Please take care of Zael. I don't know how long she'll sleep. She may have nightmares and she may be scared when she wakes up. Remind her where she is and let her know how long she's been asleep."

"That will be my pleasure. We'll take good care of her."

Their company now numbered five, with Jairin, Raven, Arik, Rhobin, and Berch. They made their way south and west to the hills that separated Bravitleer from Draxmore Valley beyond, following Berch through the soft grass toward the trees they could now see in the distance. The land grew rockier as they approached the hills, and by evening, the spire at Thadia had disappeared in the distance behind them. By nightfall, they found themselves at the edge of the woods south of the valley. In the distance, they saw the first peaks of the mountains housing Jairin's childhood home.

Berch slowed down to let the others catch up. He poked around, looking through the grasses and a few trees before returning to the others, resting nearby. "We should camp here for the night. It'll be far safer here at the edge of the woods than it will be farther into the hills."

"How far is it to Castle Glensong?" Raven asked.

"We'll have a full day's hike tomorrow and then arrive the following day."

Jairin was uneasy. "I never thought I'd find myself trying to sneak back into my home."

"I never thought I'd be heading there, either," Rhobin said. "I'm excited about seeing the ruins. The castle is famous, but I worry about running into who—or what—is camped there."

Jairin was saddened by the thought of his childhood home being referred to as "famous ruins," but he reminded himself that nearly everything familiar from his childhood had changed in one way or another.

They all helped Arik set up camp for the night at the edge of the woods. The festive attitude of yesterday's events already faded, Jairin had snapped back into the reality and seriousness of the job at hand.

"The shadows are all over these woods," Rhobin said. "The trick is to know when the shadows will be in a certain place and don't be there at the same time."

Raven looked puzzled. "That doesn't make any sense. How would you predict where the demons are going to be at any given time?"

"I can sense them—how strong they are and how far away. I can also push them, just a bit."

They dug into their provisions and found food they could eat without building a fire. Given the apparent danger, they appointed Arik for the first watch and Jairin and Berch for the second. As night passed the halfway mark, Arik awakened the two watchers for the second shift.

Jairin and Berch sat at the edge of camp, keeping watch in the relative darkness. Arik had warned them that far overhead; the occasional dragon could be seen passing over the canopy of trees in the light of the moons and stars above. Despite the warning, it still gave Jairin goose bumps to see one of the creatures pass by in the starry night sky.

"I hate dragons," Berch mumbled, under his breath.

"They aren't evil. They don't usually fly in patrols like this, but I don't think they'd attack us just because of our presence here."

Berch looked at Jairin. "I'm not afraid of them because I think they're evil… I'm afraid of them because they like to swoop down, pick up small objects, and drop them from great heights."

"I don't think they actually do that."

"Oh yes, they do!"

Jairin smiled. "You've seen this yourself, then?"

"Well no. But you'd think more about those things, too, if you were only 312 centimeters tall!"

Jairin laughed. "Okay, okay. I see your point."

"Some creatures are born to be big and threatening. Some of us are stuck being wee, wickedly clever, swift, and amazingly handsome."

"I like your outlook. We can use every advantage we can find."

Berch nodded. "She likes you, you know, the Master. I don't know what you've done to deserve that, but I'm watching you. You need to prove to us that you're worthy of her affection."

"I will, Dad." Jarin smiled back.

The relative silence of the next few hours was suddenly broken by twigs snapping in the woods just outside camp. Jairin turned to Berch. "Did you hear that?"

Berch strained his eyes and looked deep into the woods beyond their camp. "I see four or five of them, whatever they are. I'll wake the others." He crawled over to where the others were sleeping.

Jairin pulled his sword from its scabbard and stood up. It glowed a brilliant blue in the dim light of night. He moved it around a bit and the light trailed behind the blade's path like a dim blue flame.

"Pssst… over there!" the parum said in a harsh almost-whisper. Jairin turned to see Berch looking at a group of trees beyond the clearing, pointing. Something jumped out with an eerie "Ahhhhhhhhhhhhh!"

Several dark figures exploded from the woods toward Jairin. He pulled back his blade and swung it into the midsection of the first attacking beast as it neared him. With a blood-curdling cry, the creature fell in a heap at Jairin's feet, then exploded into a cloud of thick, black dust.

"Shadows!" Arik yelled, "…I think!" He scratched a hurried symbol of Willem Ironfoot into the ground with the tip of his sword.

Just as the first one fell, another took its place in front of Jairin. The prince took a swing at this one in turn and it, too, exploded into a cloud of dust.

At the other end of the camp, three more ambushed Arik and Berch. Rhobin and Raven staggered to their feet from slumber. Rhobin stepped back and pulled out his bow from his pile of belongings, notching an arrow.

Arik raised his sword and took a swing at the shadow that had descended on him. The blow hit squarely, but there was no blood from the creature as it pulled back in silence.

"These are different from the shadows in my village. These have some meat on them."

Another creature lashed out at Berch, slashing his upper arm with previously unseen claws. Berch countered with a mighty whack on the beast's stomach with his club.

Raven rushed at another one with a short sword in each hand. As it reached out at her, she took one swing and then another. The first blade struck cleanly into the shadow's chest. It backed up—one sword still protruding from the gash—then jumped forward to attack again. Raven readied her other sword and swung again, slashing across its mid-section.

Jairin realized that the shadows that hadn't exploded were getting up again. He ran over to join his companions. He cut down the first of the three shadows in another explosion of dust. Rhobin dropped his bow and stretched out his arms with a look of deep concentration on his face. In a quick motion, he turned his hands over, and the final two shadows let out hideous screams, staring at Rhobin in terror. After a second, they burst into a shower of black dust before the group's eyes.

Everyone turned to Rhobin, but Raven was the first to speak. "You're a spell caster?"

"No," Rhobin replied. "I can destroy a few—some of the smaller, weaker ones. It's a power that's grown in me since I started studying the demons. I don't think it's real magic."

"That's amazing!" Jairin said.

Arik added, "When they came to my village, they didn't have bodies like this. They were more like actual shadows, but they looked similar and the screams are the same."

"Yes," Rhobin said. "They can take several forms. The pure shadow forms spread disease and cause fear, but they can't touch anything—no body. They need to take a physical form to attack you the way these did—and in that form, they're more vulnerable."

"They didn't seem very vulnerable to me," Raven said.

Berch looked at Rhobin. "So, you can just wave your hands and destroy them?"

"It's not that simple. Like I said, only some of the weaker ones, and only in certain circumstances. I couldn't let those two get away once they knew what Jairin was carrying. They'd fear that weapon, and we should keep that secret. I may be able to set a ward, a protective etching, to keep any more from finding us."

"Gestron knows we're coming then, I guess," Jairin said with a somber look.

Rhobin looked at the prince. "I think we're overestimating our importance here. I'm sure he may care a little that we're hunting him down. He'd probably care a lot more, though, if he knew about the demon-slaying blade you're carrying."

Raven joined in. "If we're fairly certain about the demons being gone for some time, maybe we should rest out the remainder of the night? We have all day tomorrow to talk."

With Rhobin on watch, the others went into an uneasy sleep until the suns rose in the morning. After a quick, cold breakfast, they continued on their journey through the hills, following Berch. Several times that day, Berch stopped and waited for the others to catch up. They could see him peering off into the woods, checking the crossing footpaths, looking at broken branches, and peering up at the treetops.

Jairin quickened has pace to talk to the parum. "Something seems wrong. Aside from the attack last night, it's been eerily quiet."

Rhobin came up behind the prince and asked, "What were you expecting to happen?"

"Well… something. I mean, in a full day in these woods, we've seen a few birds in the treetops, but not a single fox, or deer, or even a mouse."

Arik said, "I guess that answers the question of what the demons eat."

The rest of the day passed, the sky overhead all but blocked by a canopy of trees, without any animals in sight. Even the birds were absent as the party made their way ever higher into the wooded hills. As they grew weary from the long march, Berch stopped and suggested they camp for the night. They couldn't see the suns through the trees, but for the past half-hour they'd been losing light.

Arik and Jairin set up the tents. They had to settle for dry rations and warm water from the water skins. With the shelters ready, Rhobin took the tip of his bow and drew a circle around the camp with strange letters and symbols crossing it at various points. Raven came over to see what he was doing.

"It's a ward," he told her. "a circle of protection. Should any demons be around these woods tonight, the circle will keep them from finding us. It creates a blind spot they won't want to venture into."

That night, they slept more peacefully than the previous night, maybe because of confidence in Rhobin's ward, or perhaps because they were now only a few hours' journey from the castle. Berch snored loudly with his feet up in the air. Jairin was the last to fall asleep, watching stars peek through the thick canopy overhead as they crossed the night sky.

He was shaken awake. "Good morning," Rhobin said. It was dawn. Jairin got up and they made breakfast and planned out the coming day.

Berch addressed the group. "We'll arrive late this afternoon at the ruins of Castle Glensong. There's a mix of good and bad news for the hike. We'll lose the tree cover, but we gain light and open air. It's also steeper for the first leg of the trip. We won't need climbing gear, but it'll be a rough haul. Keep your waterskins out. I'll let you know when we find potable sources to refill them. Whether you picked this time of year for the weather or just by chance, it's a good mix right now. A month ago, the woods would have been very chilly. A month from now the climb would be much warmer."

Rhobin scratched out his circle as Jairin helped Arik pack up the camp. They did their best to remove all traces from the ground to cover their tracks and then began their final journey to the castle beyond the woods. As they marched on toward noon, following a rough trail beaten into the grasses at the edge of the woods, the sunlight was welcomingly brighter and warmer through the thinning canopy. They kept an eye on the water supply, filling their waterskins from creeks as they passed.

Their progress grew slower as they made their way higher into the hills. Short grasses and tall undergrowth gave way to large boulders and sparse tree cover. Jairin stopped walking and took a deep breath. He drew his arm across his forehead and shook it briskly several times to let the sweat fall to the ground. "We should stop here for a rest." They took out rations and the waterskins.

"Hey!" Arik said, with a mouth half-full of food. He stood and pointed at a cluster of rocks about ten meters away. "Rabbits!"

"That doesn't make a lot of sense," Berch said. "Why would they be out here in the hills? Those are forest mammals."

Rhobin came to Arik to look. "I don't remember seeing any animals in the woods. The demons may have driven them out. We had a circle of protection last night. I think that saved us a bit of trouble."

When they had finished eating, they picked up the trail leading higher into the hills. After a few hours' march, Berch signaled the party behind him as he climbed a large group of boulders and looked around. The others approached, weary after climbing through the hills. In the distance, they could hear the roar of water.

Jairin looked out at the valley below. He hadn't been home in fifteen years. The sight still took his breath away. He hadn't realized how far up they'd been climbing the past few days. Here, from two hundred meters above the valley floor, he could see all of Draxmore Valley in every direction. This was the highest point directly overlooking the valley. "'If it's not six hundred meters, it's only a hill,' my father used to say. Mountain or hill, I've always loved this view." He was finally going home. Glensong was now only about three kilometers to the west along the ridge of the hill. No more climbing.

As they approached, Jairin saw the battered and broken remains of the east tower. It stood at the very edge of the cliff, dividing a great river into twin waterfalls pouring from the cliff to the valley floor below.

As they approached the castle, Jairin felt drops of spray from the crashing water hit his skin. The view directly below them in the valley became blurred in the mist of the displaced river falling over the edge.

Berch leaned in to Jairin, quietly saying, "Someone's watching us—humans."

"Where?"

"There are two ahead and one behind that I can make out."

"Are they closing in on us?"

"No. They seem to be tracking us, but they're keeping a healthy distance to stay out of sight."

As the group reached the ruins of Castle Glensong, there was still no sign of the people that had been watching them upon approach. Sitting before them in none of its former glory was the broken and neglected castle. The river Ardrual split as it approached the stone structure. At the north side of the castle, a battered drawbridge crossed the ravine, which the force of the river had created in the ancient past.

Jairin crept onto the bridge, listening to the creaking of wood and feeling the give of its partially rotted surface under his shoes as he carefully placed each footfall. It was old and unstable, but so far it was taking his weight. Once he had crossed, the others followed. The portcullis was in better shape. He thought perhaps it was a testament to good construction. It was open. Jairin walked through the entryway of his childhood home, with the others following behind.

13 Homecoming

Jairin looked around the dusty, cobwebbed entrance hall of Castle Glensong. Lost in a memory, he stepped forward, and the surroundings melted away. Several young boys ran about the room playing tag. "You're it!" one of the older boys yelled as he turned to run away. Beautiful tapestries and colorful paintings hung proudly on the white walls of the hall. Light poured in from the open drawbridge as Jairin made his way to the far end of the hall. The smaller boy ran out of sight through one of the hallways leaving the entrance, though he could hear them in the distance. The prince reached out to touch a marble bust of his father on a stone pedestal along the wall.

His hand slipped through empty space. The sculpture and pedestal were nowhere in sight. The pictures were gone, and the tapestries were ripped and neglected. The bright light filling the hall dimmed as the white surfaces grayed in front of his eyes. The boys playing in the hall had disappeared, their voices first a distant echo and then nothing as they retreated into Jairin's memory.

Raven approached her brother and put her arm around his shoulder. "I don't have any memories of the castle. I'm guessing it's not much like you remember it, is it?"

"I thought I'd feel better once we got here, but seeing the castle in this state of disrepair isn't doing anything to lift my spirits. It's only reminding me of people who are gone and things that have been broken." He laid down his sword and pack, sat on the floor, and stared off into the shadows on the wall.

Rhobin came up to him. "Something's wrong, Jairin."

"The men that were following us?" Jairin asked, turning to the ranger.

"That too, but look at the torn wall hangings and the old remains strewn around the room. Now look at the floor."

"Why?" Jairin looked down.

"There have been people here recently," Rhobin said. "There's no dust on the floors. No footprints. Someone has cleaned it."

Jairin swished his hand around the floor beside him and then held it up to look at it. "Are there people living here?"

Berch and the others pulled their weapons out to be ready for a fight. While it made no mark, Arik traced a Willem Ironfoot on the stone floor in front of him. Backpack still on the floor, Jairin grabbed the hilt of his sword and stood up. It glowed again as he removed it from its scabbard. "There's a demon here," he said.

From the shadows in the hallway, several men approached, armed with crossbows. One of them addressed the party. "We'll turn you into pincushions where you stand if need be."

Jairin stepped forward and lowered his sword, "There's no need for hostilities. My quarrel is with the shadows, not with you."

"We've been watching you since you emerged from the woods. Who are you? What's your business here?"

"We know there are shadows here," Jairin said. "I'll answer your question if you tell me whether you work for them or against them."

"You're in no position to place conditions on your answers. Nevertheless, I'll tell you with pride that despite being surrounded by Gestron's demons, we've lived here in defiance of them for over a dozen years—"

"This is so strange," Rhobin interrupted. "Everyone seems to give themselves far too much credit. You seem to all believe yourselves to be far more important to the demons than you actually are. As one who's spent a lot of time studying them, I'd venture to say it's more likely that Gestron simply has no interest in this castle or any of you."

The young militiaman adjusted his crossbow and pointed it directly at Rhobin, then looked back at Jairin. "Your woodsman is quite a nuisance. Who are you and why have you broken into our home?"

The last part of the young man's question surprised the prince. "I'm Jairin, son of King Marax. I have returned to what you will find is actually *my* home."

"That's nonsense. The demon didn't leave anyone behind when it burned through the castle." He paused and tipped his head to speak to one of his companions. "Fetch the judge. He can sort this out."

They returned several minutes later with an old man. He pushed his curly white hair out of his face and behind his shoulder. "Everyone put your weapons down. Nothing can be settled in this hostile environment." Somehow Jairin felt compelled to comply.

The militia and Jairin's company lowered their weapons. The old man walked with a slight limp toward the center of the confrontation. He wore faded purple robes that were covered in patches. With dark, piercing eyes, he gazed at the prince. Jairin felt a strange sensation as the judge looked deeply into his eyes. After a minute, the old man broke his stare.

"He is indeed the son of Marax," the judge proclaimed, turning to the crossbowmen.

Another man from the militia stepped forward, "If you mean to evict us from our home, I'm afraid you'll find nothing but resistance—prince or not. I've lived in this castle since the swamp took my father's farm—my entire adult life. All that time, I've not once seen a king, a knight, or any prince in these halls. There's been nobody but us to protect this castle and keep the demons out."

"I haven't come to deprive anyone of their home," Jairin reassured him. "I am passing through the valley on a quest to capture Gestron in the caverns south of the farmland." As he said it, Jairin wasn't sure if this was completely true. He hadn't decided whether he'd need to make these squatters leave or not.

Some snickers ran through the ranks of the castle residents. The second young man spoke again, "That is all very well and good. Just so you know, what was farmland in my father's days is now the great swamp. Those grim waters separate the bulk of Gestron's forces from Draxmore. Because its demons won't cross the swamp, they come through the surrounding mountains to carry out raids on our lands. That swamp is dark, smelly, and deadly. If you mean to go after Gestron without hiking for weeks through the mountains, you must somehow try to cross it. I fear, however, that it means we should not see you here again—"

"Enough," the judge interrupted. He turned to Jairin. "My name is Barlemicus. I was your father's high court judge. I will serve you in whatever way I can, your highness." Rather than a traditional bow, Barlemicus extended his arm to grasp Jairin's wrist in the manner of knights greeting each other. Jairin likewise extended his own arm, and they greeted with a shake of wrists.

As Barlemicus pulled back his arm, Jairin noticed a tattoo on the underside of his wrist. It was a small circle filled with a tilde symbol. The circle was pierced through the center by an arrow pointing to his hand. Jairin recognized it. "You're a thrull!"

"Yes, sire," Barlemicus replied. "I'm a thrull. King Marax always welcomed my services when he was alive. When the kingdom was destroyed, I had nowhere else to go. I stayed on with three badly injured guards, their families, and some villagers who were burned out of their homes in the ensuing raids. Many of these young men have lived here their entire lives."

"What's a thrull?" Arik whispered to Rhobin.

"I don't know."

Raven turned to Arik to explain. "They're nomads, most of them very intelligent. They used to serve as judges across the lands, but then they disappeared. They went into hiding."

Barlemicus continued telling Jairin what had been happening in his absence. "At first, Gestron's demons relentlessly attacked the villages and homesteads in the valley. When there was nothing left of Tarquin, it sent out the demons to destroy all the surrounding kingdoms to the east and south. After several years, all the lowland farms flooded with murky, vile water and became a great swamp. The farmers died or fled, and the food stopped. Only a few farmers remained behind, driven mad by the swamp or by the demons."

One of the crossbowmen added to the tale. "There aren't many people left, but the shadows still pour out of the caverns south of the swamp. We don't know where they are going or why, but they feed on chaos and fear."

Jairin introduced the others, "This is Arik from Keld; Rhobin and Berch, our guides from Bravitleer; and my younger sister Raven."

"Raven!" Barlemicus exclaimed. "Thank the stars! When we found Serena's body, we searched the entire castle for her infant daughter. It does this old man's heart so much good to know that you survived."

"She wasn't with our mother when the shadows got to her," Jairin said. "She was in the nursery. I found Raven and took her away. I brought her to grow up with our cousins, safe in Retreol."

Barlemicus tipped his head a bit, "Retreol? Hmm... that may not be as safe as you think."

"Why?"

"That's where Madigan built his tower—"

"Madigan? We ran into that wizard and his apprentice in Retreol. I got a bad feeling from him," Arik said.

Barlemicus pointed a long, bony finger at Arik, nodding. "You're wise to heed that, my young friend. There's something about him I don't trust. Marax put a great deal of faith in him, but when the shadows assailed the valley, he was not to be found and sent no aid in our time of need."

"He came up to us at a public house," Jairin said. "He said he remembered me."

"I don't know what kind of magic Madigan practices or what his role is in all of this, but as far as I know, a demon cannot summon itself into this world. Jairin, come take a tour with me. Our guards will take care of your companions, and we'll meet back for dinner shortly."

The militia escorted the rest of the party from the room.

As the two strolled down the neglected hallway, Jairin pulled his blade slightly from its scabbard. The color was very faint now. Any doubt he'd had of his present company was cleared. He put the sword firmly back into the scabbard with a satisfying click. "Something in the castle isn't what it seems. This sword can alert me to the presence of demons. It's been warning me of the presence of something unnatural in the castle."

Barlemicus took a deep breath, looking back. "Hmm. I haven't seen anything, but I can tell you one thing for sure— that ranger you brought with you is hiding something."

"They said in Bravitleer that he's some sort of

demonologist. The shadows attacked us in the woods beyond the castle, and he banished them. With a wave of his hand, they turned to dust."

"He's wearing an amulet. Perhaps that is giving him some unholy power?"

Jairin hadn't noticed.

Barlemicus continued, "I've heard one can bind the spirit of a demon to an object to obtain such power."

"You can bind a demon into objects?" Jairin asked, surprised.

"A wizard could."

Something clicked in Jairin's head, "That may be what triggers the glow in my sword!"

"Maybe. I don't know what connection he may have with Madigan or some other wizard out there. I can see in his eyes he's hiding something, but I can't see what it is. He has a power to mask his thoughts. I don't think that's a power a demonologist could wield. Speaking of demons, are you seriously intending to confront Gestron?"

"I'm quite serious."

"I was there when your father was killed. I saw that demon kill dozens of strong knights, tearing them limb from limb. I fear not only would you need a wizard to fight him, but a very strong wizard at that."

"I know we can't destroy it, but maybe I can contain it." Jairin explained the Mirror of Wills and the containment plan.

Barlemicus scratched his head, then nodded. "I'd agree with that approach. Demons are ferociously tough, almost impossible to kill without magic. Gestron will be expecting wizards or a much larger force if he believes retribution is coming."

"Would the wizards help us?"

Barlemicus laughed. "Goodness, no. Some of our men approached the wizard council many years ago. They were flatly denied. It was something about politics and wizards not interfering in the business of other wizards. I'm afraid in this venture you're on your own, Prince Jairin."

"What do Gestron's numbers look like?"

"He has three demons—commanders—that it directly controls. These three in turn control the rest of its forces. But this creates a significant problem—since your mirror only works on one, you will have to deal with the others directly."

"That is worrisome. We don't have much magic with which to fight these demons."

"What about the ranger?" Barlemicus asked.

"Bravitleer wants him back. He was only supposed to bring us as far as Glensong."

"During the dinner this evening, I'll have one of our men take your friends' swords to the forge to enchant them."

Jairin stopped in mid-stride, impressed. "You can do that?"

"How do you think we fight the shadows? Ordinary weapons disrupt them, but can't kill them. The enchantment isn't permanent, I'm afraid. It'll last a few days, but that may be long enough. We have a small barrel in the forge, a magic elixir given to us many years ago. The blacksmiths polish the blades with the mixture and it penetrates the steel. While they're enchanted, the weapons can strike down demons. The enchanted weapons take on a blue tinge that fades as it wears off."

"My blade is enchanted," Jairin told the thrull. "It takes on a similar color when demons are nearby."

"Guard that closely. There's no doubt that will be useful in the coming days." They continued walking the halls of the castle. Barlemicus pointed out the two towers that had been annihilated. "We rebuilt the east tower overlooking the cliff. That allows our lookouts to keep watch over the approaches and the valley below."

They rounded a corner, returning them to the main

entryway. "Dinner is starting soon. We'll catch up with your friends there," Barlemicus said. They ascended the grand stairs leading to the upper levels of the main building. On the second level, a short hallway led them to what had once been the throne room. It was bustling with people seated at several large tables, sharing stories and passing around trays of food. No longer covered by the original ceiling, it was now a dining hall, covered by several layers of thick cloth with slits cut into them at odd angles. Looking up, Jairin could see glimpses of the sky above through the slits in the fabric panels.

"It's rather ingenious," Barlemicus said. "I don't pretend to understand how it works. It's painted on the top side to match the stonework of the castle. We can see out, somewhat, and the smoke from our firepit passes right through it. The canopy also does a splendid job keeping out most of the rain."

They met up with the rest of the company, and Barlemicus quietly sent one of the young guards to fetch their weapons and deliver them to the blacksmith for enchantment.

For dinner, they shared generous portions of beef, pork, potatoes, and maja root. There were smiles and upbeat conversations around the table. Jairin figured it was unlikely that the dragons patrolling far over their heads could see them, but they no doubt could smell the food and the smoke. After dinner they had a few drinks and continued exchanging exaggerated stories. As the late evening wore on, they retired to moderately comfortable beds, with straw mattresses on which they could lay their sleeping mats.

In the morning, they packed up their belongings and went with Barlemicus to the dining hall for a hot breakfast. As the larger sun rose, they bid farewell to their hosts. Jairin had decided to leave Glensong in the care of its residents, an outpost for the men and women who had defended it. The memories were better than the building. His new castle should be in the valley—accessible to all without a climb into the hills. Jairin tried to lift their spirits with his parting words. "When I return. I'd like to help fix up these living quarters. You have my word that nobody will be evicted from this castle when I reestablish my kingdom."

"Barlemicus," Rhobin added, "I was to accompany the party only as far as this castle. Can you have someone send word back to Bravitleer that I intend to stay with them further? If nothing else, the past few days have shown that they could use another fighter in their group. I dare say we'll run into more shadows along the roads ahead."

The elder judge nodded. "Most assuredly. I'll send a scout back to the border and have them inform the patrol there."

They said their goodbyes, and the company departed for their final destination.

The rest of the party started down the trail and Jairin called to them. "I'll catch up. I forgot something." He walked a short distance from the bridge to a small garden, passing a half-dozen stones set in the ground. Jairin removed his sword from its scabbard and stuck it into the dirt before approaching a large stone marker at the far end. Taking a knee, he put a hand on the stone and bowed his head. On the stone was etched: *Here Lie King Marax of Tarquin and Serena of Greenlyte, Queen of Tarquin.*

After a minute of silence, Jairin stood and walked back to his sword. As he slid it back in its scabbard, the blue tinge was so slight that he almost missed it. "Hmm…"

Jairin ran back down the other path to catch up with his companions. As he arrived, he pulled his sword a few centimeters out of its scabbard. The blade was much brighter now. Whatever it was, it was following them.

14 The Statue Garden

Several paths diverged beyond the bridge. They followed one of the major trails leading southwest, a worn track beaten into the cracked, rocky ground. While several other routes led to switchbacks down into the valley below, their course kept them at the top of the cliff. Soon the castle behind them faded in the distance and after half an hour, only the top of the rebuilt east tower could be seen. Farther along, it too faded into the background.

"I've grown accustomed to your company," Rhobin told his companions. "I'm not the kind to take an interest in others, but I think I'll miss you when we part."

As they continued, Berch said, "Shortly, we'll reach the old statue garden. Beyond that, we descend into the valley to the south, which has turned to swamplands. Once we see what that route looks like, we can decide how to move forward."

Jairin repositioned his heavy pack. "Rhobin, I was told that Gestron has commanders that directly control the rest of the shadows."

"It's a hierarchy. Powerful demons can summon lesser demons. The summoner is the dominus, the master. The summoned are the servus or servorum. Gestron pulled three servorum from the void to be his generals, slaves to his will: Gernon, Gebdur, and Gerrok."

Arik smiled. "That's cute. That sounds like what you'd do with children—inheriting similar names."

Rhobin harrumphed. "You wouldn't use the word 'cute' if they rolled over Draxmore or Bravitleer—or even Keld. Their true names from the world where they dwell are completely unpronounceable in the languages of men, parum, or even wizards. They are given these names by the dominus they serve."

"They're named by whoever summons them?" Arik asked.

Rhobin nodded. "Exactly. Wizards who summon demons and demons who summon others become intricately connected to them, giving up a piece of their own spirit to sustain them and bind them to this world."

"What do they eat?" Arik asked.

"Pardon me?"

"Demons eat, don't they?"

"Not like a human or a parum would. They get their energy and power from contention, confusion, and fear. Luckily for demons, when people run across them, that's their usual reaction, anyway."

They trudged through the hills, following Berch for most of that day, stopping occasionally to eat or rest. In the late afternoon, they approached a clearing. Berch scouted the area. "Here's our first waypoint." As they entered the clearing, the party was surprised by what they found.

At one end of the statue garden stood a massive creature carved in black marble. It had four arms, what looked like giant bat wings on its upper torso, and two legs like tree trunks. Scattered throughout the rest of the garden were half a dozen smaller stone creations, some winged, some with clubs, and some with swords. Arik walked over to the four-meter statue at the far end. "Is there a name plate or a dedication on this thing?"

"Wait," Berch warned. "Something's wrong. There should only be five statues—"

"I must depart your company here," Rhobin interrupted. "But before I go, we need to discuss a matter of payment."

Jairin frowned. "You're leaving, suddenly? Didn't Carmen arrange your payment while we were back in Thadia?"

"As a matter of fact, no," Rhobin replied. The ranger backed up a few steps and glowered at Jairin. "You see, I'm not asking for payment *from* you. My payment *is* you." With that, Rhobin's eyes turned red and a glow of fire erupted from his face.

"Fitch!" Arik yelled, stumbling backward.

Rhobin thrust a hand forward, sending Jairin flying three meters backward to crash in a heap at the base of a statue. Rhobin spoke again in a voice growing much deeper and more sinister. "Just for the record, I hate horses, too." Its size exploded to three meters, four, then four and a half meters high. "I also happen to hate humans, parums, quests, and taking on the form of a small, weak human that I extinguished weeks ago!

He turned and yelled back at the statues, "Arise, my vanguard! Today we feed on the souls of humans!"

Jairin staggered to his feet as the others drew their weapons. Arik scratched a Willem Ironfoot into the ground in front of him, his blade glowing a soft blue color.

Crack! Crack! Crack! came from all around them. The company watched in horror as the stone of the statues turned to flesh. The tall winged statue came to life and now stomped toward Arik. With two arms forward and two at its side, it threw Arik aside like a rag doll and then rushed toward Raven.

Jairin readied his sword and saw his sister doing the same with her two short blades. The steel emitting a menacing blue glow, she charged into the fray. Jairin lost sight of her, but two other demons had come at him from the other side. He'd need to fend them off first.

With a swing of his sword, Jairin cleaved the first one in two with a sticky, sloshing sound. Blood flew amid a cloud of black smoke. The other moved in toward him. He heard a deep, commanding voice somewhere behind him in the battle, yell, "Die, bitch!" It was Rhobin, attacking Raven. Jairin held his sword up to parry the incoming attack and glanced back. He couldn't see his sister.

The second smaller demon came at Jairin with a sharp claw. Jairin blocked with a swipe of his sword to the demon's wrist, severing its hand in a cloud of dark liquid. The demon roared and swung with its other claw, gashing Jairin's sword arm above the elbow. Blood leaked from the slash, but there wasn't any pain. Adrenaline was doing its job so far. Jairin dropped his arm, using the momentum to help set his sword back into position for another strike. He swung again, cutting deeply across the chest of the demon in front of him. It fell back, clutching its chest with its remaining claw. Blood flooded from the demon's wounds and it fell to the ground with a hollow thud.

Jairin could see Raven again now, but the demon they'd called Rhobin wasn't there. She was now fighting another smaller demon that stood between her and Jairin, about five yards away. She slashed one sword against its chest. The other sword found its mark under the demon's chin and continued straight through its head to protrude through the top of its skull with a gush of thick blood. She pulled the blade back out and wiped it off on her pants as the demon fell to the dirt amid a growing pool of red-black liquid.

The massive, four-armed, winged monstrosity that had been a black marble statue spotted Jairin and headed directly toward him. It raised an arm to full height above its head. Its claws flared like an intense fire as it spoke at last, "When you cross to the land of the dead, tell them Gernon sent you."

Gernon lashed out at Jairin with a fiery claw as he swung his sword. The demon cut four bloody trenches into Jairin's chest through his clothing. In the same moment, Jairin's blue blade completed its arc, severing Gernon's arm near the elbow. "Ahhhhhhhhhh!" the demon bellowed. Jairin fell to his knees, clutching his chest in pain.

The demon shook its head a few times, looking frenzied. Its three remaining arms flamed up, and it gave its wings a single flap, throwing a tremendous gust of rancid-smelling wind at the prince. Blood flowed from the severed arm, soaking the ground even as it walked through it to finish Jairin off.

Jairin could see the demon that had been Rhobin nearby. He couldn't take on two of these elder demons. If this is the end, he was going to take one of them out with him. Jairin took a deep breath and rose from the ground with a groan. He raised his sword defiantly. "Come and get me, beasts!"

"River of fire!" Arik shouted, across the battlefield. "These things are summoning more demons!"

Berch yelled back, "Then we need to concentrate on taking out the bigger demons!"

"Easier said than done!"

Bleeding from the chest, Jairin exchanged rage-driven blows with Gernon. As the prince made strike after blocked strike on the demon, he saw Raven moving to take on the other elder demon who was closing in fast. Gernon raised two arms to land a crushing blow on the prince. Jairin seized the opening to thrust his blade full force through the commanding demon's abdomen and out its back. Dripping with red-black blood, Jairin gave a great yell. "That's for Marax."

Gernon's body violently exploded in a shower of blood and black dust. The turbulent blast of air carried what sounded like dozens of screams all at once. Everything else in Jairin's field of view was knocked to the ground around him. He repositioned his feet to try to keep himself balanced. His blue sword blade was covered in the demon's blood, but he saw nothing else standing before him. He panted for breath but couldn't get enough air to fill his lungs. A wave of exhaustion coursed through him. The light dimmed as he looked down to check the extent of his wounds.

Raven watched in terror from several yards behind her brother as the other elder demon closed in on him. Its voice was deep and slow, causing goose bumps to rise on her arm as it spoke. It uttered two words as it swung up into Jairin from behind with a great flaming sword. "For Gernon!" Flashes of fire ripped through Jairin's body. The prince let out a quiet, "Ugh…" as the demon's fiery blade pierced him and emerged from the front of his chest. He collapsed to his knees and then fell face first into the blood-soaked dirt. His blade, still glowing a deep blue, slipped from his hand, landing a short distance away.

"Jairin!" Raven screamed. She charged at the towering demon. With flashes of rage, she tore into the side of the demon at least twice with each blade before it even had a chance to react.

The demon turned to face her as Berch came flying in from the side, dagger extended. The parum stabbed the servus in the groin. Landing off center, Berch missed his footing and also fell face first in the blood-stained dirt.

This was her opening. Raven stabbed a short sword into the demon's back with a downward angle and with all of her strength pulled herself a half-meter up its back. She stabbed it higher with her second dagger and again hoisted herself up another half-meter.

The elder demon flipped around and threw its weight left and then right. She wasn't falling off. It bent over and threw its arms back and thrashed and howled. Raven stuck the first dagger in higher, alternating her blades as she stuck them higher and higher, climbing the servus' back.

When she reached its shoulders, she plunged the blades into its thick neck and spine over and over in a flurry of deep gashes. As the demon fell to the ground, blood spurting in all directions, she held fast to her swords lodged in its back.

The demon hit the ground with a sickening thud. Raven cut the last of its neck and pulled its head free. "I'm *nobody's* bitch!" She held up the head of the demon that had been Rhobin for only a moment until the entire body of the demon violently erupted into another wave of blood and black dust, throwing her to the ground.

She looked around. The smaller demons glanced at each other. They seemed both angry and terrified. The fiery sword that had impaled her brother faded. The smaller demons popped into clouds of dust and dispersed into the wind and onto the bloody ground. Arik stood and turned in a quick three-sixty. They were battered, savagely cut, and covered in blood and dust, but they had defeated the demons.

Raven forced her breathing to slow. The adrenaline was wearing off. She rose from the pool of black blood on the ground and looked for her brother. "Is he alive?" She ran over toward Jairin's body, shaking back the urge to scream. "Damn it, someone tell me if my brother is fitching alive!" She grabbed his motionless hand for a moment and released it, where it fell back to the ground. She took it in her hand again, tears streaming down her cheeks.

Berch ran up, wiping his blade on his trousers. He put it back in his pouch shand checked the prince's neck with two fingers. He looked back at Raven. "His pulse is weak and his wounds are very serious. We need to get him back to the castle and find a healer or he's going to die. Rip up some cloth to bandage those wounds and get him to Glensong. We can't save him here in the field."

Raven wrapped her brother's wounds and then her own badly injured leg. Berch was covered in claw scratches but managed to bandage Arik's shoulder and chest. With a great deal of grunting, Raven and Arik lifted Jairin's limp body. Berch cleaned off Jairin's sword and laid it across his body. "Hey, it's not glowing." With difficulty, they managed to carry him for a few hundred meters before running into five men running toward them.

The first man from the patrol approached, wearing the colors of the guards from Glensong. "Arik, what's happened?"

"Quick," Berch said, "Get the prince to the castle as quickly as you can. Send someone ahead to find healers."

Raven wiped her tears with her sleeve. "Fitch. Fitch, fitch, fitch, fitch. Don't let him die."

Four patrol guards took Jairin and hastened their pace back the way they'd approached. The other one ran ahead.

Arik put his arm around Raven, and she buried her head in his shoulder. "He's not going to die," Arik told her, "They'll save him."

15 Of Voices and Coins

Meanwhile, in an Other Place, darkness shrouded the gray lands almost completely. Thick fog crawled across the ground, following its highs and lows in every direction. A lost and confused shadow emerged through the haze. Bits and pieces of random thoughts coalesced; a jumbled set of memories and feelings. These thoughts fought each other to come forward and untangle themselves. Moment by moment, the memories sorted themselves out. They were all part of a whole being, an individual account belonging to a single entity. Slowly, the memories and thoughts merged into the shadow as it trudged through the unlit lands, walking along in near-darkness.

As the shadow rambled forward, trying to remember where and what it was, it approached two others. Blurry at first, they came into focus as it drew closer. People—an old man and a young woman. Still many meters away, the old man stopped while the young woman took several steps toward the shadow.

The young woman's voice was calming, melodic. "You've been through the fire, the icy chill, and the dark night. Something drew me here. I didn't know why until I saw you. Welcome to the Other Place."

The shadow strained its eyes, focusing on the young woman. It started to remember specific people. It knew her. More memories flooded back. "Zael?" it said in a weak, disbelieving voice. Something seemed wrong. Its thoughts were still jumbled.

The young woman nodded. "You're in a different world now. In this world, I am whole. Here, I have a voice."

The old man had been standing back, watching silently. He shifted his weight, listening to the conversation. He pulled out a gold coin from the pocket of his dusty, ancient robes, then tossed it up and caught it several times. He looked down at it and then flicked it toward the wanderer, where it fell at the shadow's feet.

"What's this for?" The shadow picked up the coin and turned it over. It had a hole through the center, and markings covered it on both sides, tiny, indiscernible text. The fog had lifted and the shadow could see clearly. Losing interest in the item, the shadow looked back over at Zael. "How can you speak?"

She shrugged. "This is the boundary between the living and the dead. Everyone here is both and neither. The rules are different. This is where my spirit lives, if I can call it a life —"

The deep voice of the old man finally awoke. "Enough. This isn't a social call." His low, raspy voice continued in a slow, monotone stream, "I am Sperin, Sorter of the Dead. Your body on the other side lies broken and destroyed. Despite this, in my infinite generosity, I offer you a choice."

"What choice could you possibly offer me?" the shadow asked.

"No!" Zael blurted out. "Make no deals with him. Follow the river to its confluence. He can't take you. Your name isn't in the Book of—"

The old man raised his hand and silenced Zael.

The shadow could see Zael struggle with a mouth that

wouldn't open and arms that wouldn't move. She couldn't seem to speak or even give hand signs. Sperin must have a great deal of power here.

Sperin continued, "The token you hold is a manifestation of your soul. Give it back to me and I will send you back to the living world." He put his hand back into his pocket and jingled what sounded like a cache of other coins.

"Or…" he added, "perhaps this option will interest you… Zael has been in constant turmoil her entire life, passing from the world of the dead to the world of the living and back. Imagine falling asleep in one place only to awaken in the other, with people out to harm you in both. She will never be at peace. How could a father stand by to see his daughter in such pain? Keep your token, stay here willingly with me, and I will send Zael back. She will be whole and live a life as any other in the living world. Would a loving father do anything less than that?"

Zael's eyes widened, and she shook her head. She was trying to speak, but Sperin still held her immobile.

"What if I reject your choices and find my way back without your help?" the shadow asked.

The old man stood silent for a moment. His expression sharpened, and he looked back into the shadow's eyes, unblinking. "You won't get back without my help. Nobody can leave here and do as they please. I am the sorter of the dead, and I suggest that you make your choice. Your next decision will decide the future for both of you."

The shadow looked down at the token. Sperin must be wrong. *He is trying to trick me.* Zael said something about following the river. Maybe it could get out of the Other Place without making a choice? The shadow approached the old man, looking at the token and then back at Zael.

She shook her head again. The old man's expression eased. "What will it be? Keep the token and send Zael back to the living? Or give me the token and save yourself?"

The shadow paused. Wizards had tried to kill Zael as an infant. They told outlandish stories of the evil of her Gift. They *feared* her. She must hold some secret or power that they either wanted to snuff out or wanted for themselves. All she wanted was to stay by my side when I… Wait. The shadow could remember the rest now, everything. He had a mission to complete. His memories and thoughts had all reunited. He remembered who he was and what he had been trying to figure out since he first arrived in the Other Place. He looked down at his waist and saw a scabbard with a sword. He smiled.

Sperin watched the shadow with interest. "What is your choice? Keep the token and send Zael back? Or give it to me and you return."

The shadow looked one final time at the token. "No. I'm making my own option." He closed his hand around the token, turned, and ran. He ran faster and faster, as fast as his legs could carry him.

The old man screamed. "Thief! You will never make it back across the barrier! Nobody leaves this place!"

With Sperin distracted, Zael found he had released his hold on her. She could move her arms and open her mouth. "He'll get out. He was never yours to take. It's not his time and you know it."

"Hrumph," Sperin said with a grunt. "He's taken his token. Bring that back to me."

"His body was broken?" she asked. "What happened to him? Why was he here?"

Sperin looked at Zael and then back at the shadow running toward the river. "A battle. That demon would have killed him, but he was carrying an enchanted sword that prevented it."

"It worked? He said that sword would keep him alive."

"There are plenty of ways to die. Everyone's name is in

the Book of the Damned. He's just on a different page."

As the shadow grew smaller in the distance, Zael smiled and took a deep breath.

Sperin looked at the young woman. He pushed her, and she stumbled backward, hitting her backside on the ground.

Jairin's spirit came across a wide river. He recalled Zael's advice about following the river to its confluence. He ran downstream alongside it for several minutes before slowing to a brisk walk. He followed it endlessly along the banks, ever east toward the setting suns. Night after night and day after day he walked through shadowy, empty lands trying to reach something real, something that wasn't soft and blurry like the surrounding landscape. Smaller streams joined the river every few days, making it wider, deeper, and faster. After nearly a hundred days, another large river merged into this one. He followed the joined river for a short time and then spotted a building on the horizon. The two-story stone building was more than familiar. He wondered if it could possibly be what he thought it was.

Though he'd walked continuously for months, he just now felt exhausted. He had to stop and rest. As he approached the monastery where he'd lived for many years, several more rivers joined it from several directions. This made no sense. Where was the water going? Jairin entered and was met by a familiar old monk, who helped him to a familiar bed. Jairin collapsed on it with a sense of unimaginable depletion.

16 The Journey Home and the Journey Away

Raven turned the page in her book. "Ugh, this is so incredibly boring. I wish they had some better books here to read." She hadn't intended to read yet another volume of Lockthorne's *History of Dryads*, but since her captive audience still wasn't able to object, she read on in the flickering lantern light. "While the semi-aquatic Dryads of Naymia will often prefer water free of sulfuric compounds, the oxygen-rich springs seem to temper—"

A moan from the bed at her side interrupted her reading. The patient sat up. He wrapped his arm across his chest and winced. "Owwww…" The prince blinked a few times and then looked around in the dim evening light.

"Jairin? Jairin!" she yelled. She ran to her brother and hugged him.

"Where are we?" Jairin asked his sister in a weak voice.

Raven stepped back. "We're back at Glensong. We didn't know if you would make it… until Azil…"

"What's an Azil?" Jairin asked.

"Easy, Jairin. It's nighttime. We'll go through everything tomorrow morning when the others wake up. Try to rest through the night tonight. You have no idea how happy I am you've returned to us!"

"Where's my mirror? My sword?" Jairin asked in a weak voice.

"I have them. Just rest tonight. You've been through a lot."

Barlemicus and one of the castle guards ran into the room. "What's happened?" Seeing Jairin awake, he relaxed and smiled. "Oh, I'm so glad to see you're with us again!"

"We all need some rest," Raven said. "Sleep, brother. We'll come back in the morning." She laid the book down on the small table with the other tomes she'd been reading to him and walked Barlemicus and the guard out of the room. She returned to Jairin's side to bid him good night. She was so relieved that he would recover. She leaned over to blow out the lantern but caught a glint from the corner of her eye. She looked back at Jairin and noticed the gleam had come from an odd-looking coin he was holding. "What the...?" He hadn't been holding any coins a moment ago. She would have remembered that. Zael had mentioned something about a coin in the message she'd sent back from Thadia. Raven couldn't remember exactly what it was. She'd check in the morning.

Jairin awoke to an, "Ahem," from Barlemicus at his bedside. Raven was there as well, with Berch, Arik, and the old judge. Jairin's chest was sore. He looked down to see heavy bandages.

"I'm overjoyed to see you awake and alert," the thrull told Jairin. "When you arrived, we sent for Azil, a diviner and healer, to enlist his magic to heal your wounds. He worked on your injuries for several days, after which you healed unnaturally fast. I scarcely believed when he said you'd be up and walking within a week. But here you are!"

"What happened?" Jairin asked. "I remember demons, in the statue garden."

Barlemicus nodded. "They nearly killed you. I suspect you know that the sword you were carrying was forged millennia ago for the Kings of Satravan. They designed and enchanted several swords to fight the demons that plagued their lands."

Jairin nodded. "Yes. Your diviner told you this?"

One of the guards entered the room, carrying Jairin's sword in its scabbard.

"Not only that," Barlemicus said, "this sword, in particular, was rumored to protect its wielder even from death at the hands of demons. It appears you've proven that rumor true, though you left us for some time."

Jairin perked up. "How long was I unconscious?"

"Nine days," Berch replied. "Your sister kept watch over you almost the entire time."

"Only nine days?" Jairin said, startled. "I—I was gone for months! I wandered the length of a great river in the Other Place. I talked to the guy who watches over the dead. He tried to convince me to stay."

"What?" Raven asked.

"Zael met me there. She spoke to me."

"She's not dead, Jairin. Zael's with Carmen. Riders from Bravitleer sent us word that she'd awakened a few days after we left. She was angry that we left her there, but I think she understands." Raven stared off in thought for a moment before returning her attention to Jairin. "Oh, she sent a message with the riders: 'The token is real—don't lose it.' I saw you were holding a coin, but I don't know what that means."

Jairin looked down at his hand. "As far back as I can remember, Zael has talked about being torn between this world and the world beyond. I saw her there, along with an old man, then wandered through the Other Place for months, following a river. Finally I reached a familiar-looking building, and it turned out to be the monastery where I used to live. When I woke up, I was here. How did I get here?"

Raven looked at the others, frowning, and then back at her brother. "You were always here, Jairin. You didn't leave."

"But I did. It was so real. I found Brother Benedict at the monastery. He brought me to my room and I collapsed on my old bed, exhausted. I woke up in this bed with Raven reading some horrible book about sylphs."

"Dryads…" Raven corrected him, smiling. "It was the third book in what's possibly the world's most boring account of some amazing woodland creatures. After I read you four hundred pages, you got the entire species of the stories wrong?"

"We have some news, Jairin," Benedict said. "You and your friends destroyed two of Gestron's servorum. That means all the demons they controlled were destroyed with them. Gestron lost most of his minions, but he has more power now to wield directly. If he wasn't aware of you before, he is now. He'll be stewing in anger and hatred when you find him—or when he finds you."

"They found Rhobin's body," Raven added. "The *real* Rhobin. His riders found him in a shallow grave in Bravitleer. He'd been dead for several months. The body of the demon that took his place turned to dust with the others at the statue garden. It was a horrible fight, but we're all still here—thanks to your courage and Azil's healing."

Raven felt her brother's forehead. "Your temperature feels good now. The sweats and chills seem to have stopped. We'll help you get out of bed and into a warm bath. We can probably leave the bandages off as well."

They spent the next several days helping Jairin rise and walk, eventually on his own. He would bear the three-clawed scar for the rest of his life, but thanks to Azil's healing talents, the deep wounds healed with little trace.

Once he and the others were all well enough, with all their battle wounds healed, they restocked their packs and plotted a fresh course to the swamps with Barlemicus' help. They had their weapons brought back to the forge for a second enchantment.

They carefully crossed the bridge and left Glensong behind for a second time. Berch led them on the new path, leading southwest and descending to the valley floor rather than following Rhobin's original fateful mountain route. They hoped with fewer demons roaming the land that the valley would be less dangerous. Time would tell. They arrived at the valley floor and walked through the afternoon and evening, eating rations and making camp for the night. Berch took the first watch and then traded off with Raven in the middle of the night.

17 Water Water Everywhere

Raven slashed with one sword and blocked the incoming blade with the other. *Clash!* She grunted, sweat dripping from her brow. Jairin gripped the handle of his sword with both hands, pulling it back into position after blocking his sister's first attack. "There is a proven technique," he told her. "Weapon masters have shown..." He took several shallow breaths as he got into position for another swing. "...shown that a single weapon with two hands is more effective..." *Clang!* His sword again hit his sister's. "...than a pair of smaller weapons."

"That's probably true," Raven said, "if the wielder is a big, slow oaf such as yourself." She caught the blade of his incoming sword with her own and redirected it with a corkscrew motion. They both stepped back and took a moment to wipe the sweat from their brows. She raised her short swords back into attack position. "I don't have your raw strength, but I've got you with speed and I can use your movement against you."

Jairin raised his sword and shifted his weight to his back leg. Fighting flared the pain in his chest, but he couldn't skip training. He needed to work through it. From the makeshift table, Arik joined the conversation. "Strength is important, for sure. But if your opponent is faster than you, all the strength in the world isn't of much use." Jairin lunged forward. Kerang! Raven's sword caught her brother's, and she sent his arm swinging up and out of the way. She slashed out with one sword and then the other in a blur.

The prince stopped and stepped back. "Hey, hey. This is practice. Are you trying to cut me up?" He lowered his sword and looked down at his shirt, cut up in four places.

Raven caught her breath and lowered her own weapons. "Sorry. I was in control of the swords. You weren't in danger of injury."

Arik made his way to Jairin's side and picked at the tears in his shirt. "Damn!" Arik looked over at Raven. "You are deadly with those knives."

"Short swords," Raven corrected him. "I'm sorry, Jairin. I wanted to prove my worth in a fight."

Arik nodded. "Last time we were fighting, she took down one of the big guys with those swords. She climbed up his back and cleaved his head clean off."

"We all owe you a great debt, Raven," Jairin said. "No harm done, and I'm glad to have you with us. I don't want to get on the wrong side of those blades ever again." He smiled and sheathed his sword. Jairin walked back to the boulder serving as a table where they'd eaten breakfast. Taking off his shredded shirt, he made sure he wasn't injured. Just his pride, maybe. He saw the claw scars on his chest from the demon attack. He was eager to dispatch these demons once and for all.

"The scars show off your ferocity," Raven said, smiling, "but I promise not to tell anyone that you were bested by a girl."

"I let you win. Don't get a swelled head now!"

"Sure, you did!" she said, rolling her eyes and grinning.

"Ahem," Berch said. "Your tea has grown cold. If the two of you are done playing warrior, we can take down camp and head out. We're heading west today, into a swamp. Whatever is in there, it's enough of a problem that the shadows don't even enter it. We need to be on alert!"

Jairin put on a new shirt and then they packed up camp. They walked until midday when large thunderclouds gathered overhead, darkening the sky and threatening rain. "I see shelter ahead," Berch told the others. He pointed out an abandoned building, just off the rough path they were following. "Hopefully there's still a roof on that homestead that could help a little."

They made their way to the shelter—a small homestead with the remains of a thatched roof. Lightning flashed and then, *BOOM!* The delay confirmed that the heart of the storm was still far away. Arik and Raven set up a lunch of breads and salted meats and cheese in a corner of the deserted home, uprighting some old barrels and crates to sit on so as not to get covered in the dust and dirt on the floor.

Strewn about the house, they found remnants of shattered furniture and personal belongings, long-since abandoned. The former residents had apparently left in a hurry. The property appeared to have been ransacked. Anything of value had either been taken by the fleeing owners, destroyed, or stolen. Arik found what looked like an old jewelry box. He opened it to find a few rusted hairpins in a child's size.

After several hours, even though the rain wasn't letting up, they decided to continue their journey. Donning their heavy cloaks with hoods, they headed out. The rough path turned southwest. As they trudged along, the short grass gave way to taller, wet weeds.

At first, Berch used his club to separate the grasses in front of him. For the others, the grass came up to their waist, but for their guide, it came up to his armpits. He switched from his club to a sharp knife which he wielded as a machete to cut through the grass. The rain had stopped and the clouds overhead gave way to a sunny sky, but that didn't change the spongy feeling of the ground beneath them. At the edge of the swamp now there was a definite splash from every footstep the company put down. Jairin noticed that their pace had slowed to nearly a crawl. The water at their feet was a bit murky, but they could still see their shoes just below the surface.

"This is the perfect reason to have a horse," Arik said.

Berch looked over with a chuckle. "There's never a reason to have a horse. I'm biased, though I do wish we had something to keep our feet dry. We're going to have to make sure we camp on a dry patch this evening so we can dry out our feet and our boots. Otherwise, we'll end up with swamp foot, and this adventure will be over before it starts."

Jairin joined in between splashing steps. "While I'm not thrilled about the thought of having to walk waist-deep in this stuff, I doubt the horses would have a much easier time in it."

"Hey Jairin..." Raven said. "Where do we sleep if we don't find some elevated ground?"

"This was all farmland. There should be high spots that rise above the water level—or maybe even another building we can take shelter in."

Night was closing in when they found a large area above the waterline. Arik cut down patches of grass to make a clearing, then spread the cuttings for them to put their sleeping mats on. They set their boots by a small fire where they could dry both their footwear and their feet during the night. Jairin volunteered to take watch tonight, but feeling the relatively peaceful surroundings and being in the middle of a large swampland, he fell into a light sleep for most of his watch.

"Aheeeeeeee!" Jairin awoke with a start. Was that a scream? He jumped to his feet and looked around into the darkness.

"Aheeeeeeee! Aheeeeeeee!" He couldn't see a source for the eerie, high-pitched scream. The hairs on his arms stood on end.

The screech had awoken the others as well. Berch frantically searched around him, picking up his dagger and club. "Banshee!" he yelled.

"What are they?" Jairin took his sword from its scabbard. No blue glow.

"A spirit," Berch said. "It's the restless spirit of a magic wielder that died a sudden, violent death. They seek out the living—killing with a touch, I've heard."

In the distance, Jairin could see a light gliding above the surface of the swamp. It grew larger as he looked on—the size of a person now.

"Aheeeeeeee!"

Jairin's eyes followed the glowing figure. Raven kicked her brother in the back of the leg. "Cover your ears, dummy!" Jairin glanced over to see his companions huddled together with hands clasped over their ears.

Jairin crept toward the light, despite pleas from his friends. "Are you just going to sit there?" he asked their guide.

Berch shook his head without removing his hands from his ears. "This is your fight," Berch said. "Only magic can do any damage to those things. All we could do is run out into the dark swamp!"

Jairin raced to the edge of the clearing, readying his sword with two hands. He could make out the rough shape of the banshee now. Still some ten meters away, it was closing the distance quickly. Tattered robes and hair flew wildly as it drew closer and closer, eyes black and sunken. It had the face of a corpse—twisted, partially rotten, and hate-filled. It emitted an eerie glow. "Aheeeeeeee!"

Slowing as it came upon him, the banshee reached out to Jairin with gnarled, ashen fingers.

Jairin's ears rang from the screams of the night terror. Fear stabbed at him, but he tried to fight it. Covered in cold sweat, he struggled to hold his sword steady as he trembled. Jairin looked into the dead eyes of the banshee and imagined it was Rhobin coming for him again. He swung his sword. "Dieeeeeeee!" The screaming banshee reached out a finger toward Jairin, but it wasn't fast enough. The prince's blade struck the banshee first. There was a sickening sound of cloth and flesh ripping—a heavy, sharp object cutting something mushy and bloated. The light from the banshee disappeared at the edge of Jairin's sword and they were surrounded by darkness. After a few moments, Jairin's eyes adjusted to the dim light of the nighttime stars above. The creature was gone, at least for now. He lowered his sword, trying to slow his breath and calm himself.

He heard footfalls behind him. Jairin turned to see Berch hurrying up. "It must have lived and died near here. Banshees don't travel far from where they were killed in life."

Raven approached her brother. "We need to get out of here!"

"No," Berch said. "If it isn't destroyed, it knows we have magic now. It won't come back… not tonight, anyway."

"Not tonight? That's not very reassuring," Jairin said.

"You need to trust that I know how they think. The undead are looking for a weak foe to terrorize. This one won't be coming back just to be struck down again. If it comes back out tonight, it'll be off in another direction looking for easier prey."

They settled back down by the fire to try to sleep, and Berch took watch.

Morning came and nobody had much of an appetite. They ate the last of the biscuits and apples they'd taken from the castle. From here on, they were limited to the few rations they carried in their packs. The campfire and early morning sunlight had dried out their boots and trousers a little. Their boots were warm and damp instead of cold and wet. "We'll need high ground with a fire again tonight," Berch warned. "If these shoes don't dry out more this evening, we may need to stay put for a while. Mildew and swamp water will ruin them, and eventually our feet as well."

He looked around and pointed off into the distance. "I don't see any landmarks, but we need to head due south today. It's going to be slower. Yesterday we were walking in the edge waters, but to get to the caves without taking a week, we need to head through the heart of the swamp. It'll probably get deeper, muddier, and smellier before today's done. We may need to build a raft tonight."

"Ugh," Raven said.

Berch headed out first, with no further words, followed closely by Jairin. They didn't talk about the banshee or what had happened the night before. Jairin tried to convince himself it had been a nightmare. The others still seemed shaken by the events. The swamp didn't look like it would get any less hostile. Arik and Raven tagged along behind, distracting each other in trivial discussion.

"Calisham Tea is amazing," Raven said. "It has a natural flavor, nearly like apples. If you boil it in water, you'd swear that you were eating the most delicious fruit."

"Well, except that it's a liquid and it's hot." Arik smiled.

"Yes. There's that." Raven replied, punching him in the shoulder with a light laugh.

They waded through water coming up well past their knees. Berch balanced his pack on his head, keeping it in place with both hands. The feeling of the gray liquid encasing their legs felt gross—a stagnant, smelly mess. Between intermittent discussions, the overall silence was broken only by the cawing of birds in the distance and the occasional rustling of overhanging tree branches.

Jairin looked up at the branches, spreading like

smothering arms above their heads and blocking out more and more of the sun. "These aren't the trees that used to grow here. These are thicker and darker—and I don't know of any regular trees that grow in swamp water."

"They're linderwood trees," Berch said. "They love this kind of climate. They'll grow to nearly their full height in just a few seasons." He paused for a few minutes to check his bearings and then headed off again in the same direction.

The sky was eventually blocked almost completely by the canopy just a few meters above their head. They saw nothing clearly alive in the murky swamp, but it didn't have a feeling of dread or death either. It was gray, wet, and thick.

As evening rolled on, they spotted smoke rising through a break in the trees about a kilometer ahead. "A fire!" Arik exclaimed.

"Should we find a route around it?" Jairin asked the parum guide.

Berch peered through the branches. "It's not a wildfire. It looks like a campfire."

The company furtively approached the rising puffs of smoke. After several minutes they saw a small hill protruding from the swamp they had spent their day wading through. They could now hear the faint sound of a man singing at the fireside.

Rambling on, the winds doth blow,
Through summer's eve beneath the stars.
Tattered flag of emerald march,
O'er water's flow…
Watch them go…

The man stopped singing mid-verse. The company cautiously climbed the hill, breaking from the murky water. It was roughly square, no more than seven meters on a side. In the center was a campfire and a small hut. Next to the fire sat an elderly man wearing muddy, tattered rags. His short white hair stuck out from beneath a cap about three sizes too small, pulled at the seams to fit his head. The grizzled man turned his head in the cool evening air, squinting to make out the figures crouching at the edge of the swamp. He put down the stick on which he was roasting what looked like a squirrel over the campfire. He scratched his cheek, just above the top of his scraggly beard. Tipping his head to one side, he nodded while a gap-toothed grin crept across his face. He patted the ground next to him and said in a raspy voice, "Come here. Join me by the fire. You're late!"

18 Silence Unfolding

Bang, Bang, Bang! It was louder this time. Benedict looked up from his desk. "Why doesn't anyone answer that blasted door?" Through his arthritic pain, he stood up from his desk, grabbed his staff, and achingly made his way down the hall. Clicking and clanking came from the front entrance. Someone had finally opened the entrance for their guest. He decided since he'd taken the pain of getting up, he might as well be there to greet them.

Next came the familiar clanking and banging of the door closing and the locking bolts sliding back into place. He heard two men speaking as he rounded the corner into view of the entryway. Shimmering light from the lanterns along the walls helped light the path before him, flickering slightly in the breeze as he passed them. In the light of the swaying lanterns, Benedict recognized his fellow monk.

"Ah! Welcome back, Brother Raolic. Thank you for taking on my request. What news do you bring from our patron in the East?"

"It's somewhat as you'd suspected," Raolic told the senior monk. "I checked in with some patrols in Bravitleer. I can tell the others what I've learned."

Benedict motioned to the monks who had opened the

door. "Gather the brothers, please."

In the main meeting hall, Benedict addressed the assembled monks. "Raolic has returned with news from the east. The sudden departure of the shadows from our very door made it clear that something substantial had happened. I sent Raolic to Thadia to investigate."

"There is good news and bad news," Raolic said. "I've talked with riders from Thadia and from farther south. It would seem that our departed brother, Jairin, was correct in his assessment of the shadows' origin. They were extended from the hand of Gestron, the demon who has taken up residence in the plains south of the great mountains."

"What's happened?" another of the gathered monks asked.

Raolic continued, "Gestron had several servorum under his control. We've learned that two of the three commanders have perished in an assault on Jairin's company outside Glensong."

A murmur went through the assembled monks. He continued. "Attempting to destroy the prince in a preemptive attack, Gestron dispatched the commanders to ambush them. In a surprising defeat, the small group vanquished his strongest minions."

"Jairin? Does he live?" the monk Darius asked.

Benedict took a step forward and addressed his fellow monks. "Several nights ago, I had a dream in which yet another shadow approached our sanctuary. This one was different from the others. It seemed familiar and didn't have the darkness surrounding it as the others had. As it approached the monastery, I recognized the shadow as our own brother Jairin. I let him in and brought him to his old room, though he seemed terribly confused. He claimed he'd walked for months in darkness only to find our monastery at the end of several raging rivers. I bid him lay down to sleep. When I checked on him many hours later, his room was empty. I realize this sounds crazy. There was no sign that anyone had been there. The sheets were still tucked as if no one had slept there."

"It must mean something," another monk replied. "You know that dreams originate from the Other Place. There is some half-truth that crosses from there to our minds in our dream states."

Benedict nodded. "It could be, but I've had plenty of dreams with no truth to them whatsoever—as far as I know."

Benedict stepped aside and Raolic once again addressed the gathered monks. "I must add some ill news. Jairin was seriously wounded in this battle, nearly a week ago. They brought his body back to the castle ruins, and the last we heard he was alive but in a coma. I don't know anything further, but there is rumor they expect him to recover, despite the seriousness of his wounds."

"What of the wizards?" Darius asked.

Benedict fielded this latest question. "The wizards, including our great benefactor, have made it abundantly clear that the issue of the shadows is a problem the commoners need to deal with on their own. He's made no mention of whether he will come here this season."

Like most people, Benedict hated being referred to as a commoner. It wasn't an endearing term and it showed no respect to his brothers who were here in the greater service of the wizards. He knew the Kalari, as the wizard council called itself, had reasons behind every action they took and every action they didn't take.

Murmuring broke out in the hall. "We're commoners when they don't need anything." "They don't value us until it suits their needs…" "Do what they ask and don't ask questions back…"

"Enough," Benedict said. "None of us would be able to live here in solitude if it weren't for the resources and protection of the Kalari and our benefactor. You had all best remember that before you speak ill of the wizards who give us a place to live, meditate, and serve. They may not answer all of our questions, but there isn't one of us here who can say that they've neglected us. The Kalari has a purpose for our monastery. We have to keep faith in the magic we serve."

Raolic cleared his throat. "Though the imminent danger seems to have passed, Gestron is still as powerful as he ever was. Indeed, without having to sustain his whole army of shadows, I dare say he has far more direct power now."

"Are we seeing just a lull before a larger storm?" another monk asked.

Benedict stepped forward again. "We can only hope that the campaign in the south succeeds, whether or not Jairin survives. If Gestron can be contained, it will give us some breathing room. I think there is a raging tempest coming our way. My dreams tell me that Jairin still lives, but for now I think we're being told to sit and wait until a path is revealed to us. We must trust that our benefactor will keep protecting us. We have little choice right now."

19 Swamp Encounters

"Late for what?" Berch asked the old man, arching an eyebrow.

"To drain the swamp, of course," the grizzled old man said. He turned the spit to roast the other side of the small animal over the fire. As he grinned, his mouth revealed more gaps than teeth. Jairin wondered how he could even chew meat. The few that remained were twisted and discolored. There was a fog over his dilated eyes, but he gave them a quizzical look. "I'm Toff, of course. I'm the one who told the dim man in the tall boots to send some workers from the castle to fix my water problem. I heard you sloshing through the swamp for fifteen minutes like a pack of hippos."

Jairin nodded, the odd smell of cooked squirrel trailing past his nose. His father had often told him to value the eccentric. This man seemed to fit the description. "Toff, we're here from the castle. What exactly do you need us to fix?" It was *technically* true, at least.

"You don't see a problem here? My home is surrounded by an enormous swamp! You know, the one you had to wade through to get here."

"Yes, of course. This is quite a sizable wetland. Are you expecting that they have sent us here to get rid of the swamp?"

Toff turned back to the spit and gave it another quarter turn. "Well, I have a problem with this. It wasn't a huge issue at first. A little bit of water seemed to help the trees grow taller, but now the trees block out the suns, and I think it's obvious the effect they've had on my crops!"

"You're a farmer? There's no land here for growing," Raven said.

"Was. I *was* a farmer. These days I'm just a sitter." Even as he spoke something seemed to change in Toff. He set the spit with the roasted squirrel to the side and stood up. He was a bit shorter than the company, save Berch. His frail frame was draped in a dirty, tattered cotton shirt. The film cleared from his eyes and he looked around the company with more awareness in his face. "You aren't castle handymen. You're crossing through the swamp to destroy the demon hiding in the caverns to the south."

Jairin grew pale. Glancing at Arik and Raven, he could tell by their expressions he was not the only one caught off-guard. He looked back to Toff. "What do you mean?"

"I've been alone in this swamp for many years, but I know what was happening around me when this started. The king is long-dead. Chaos spread through the land as shadows loomed overhead. There was one among the shadows much greater than the others. He moved into the catacombs in the south and dammed up the rivers running into the valley beyond to create this death trap of a swamp."

"What happened to the other farmers?" Jairin asked.

"Some escaped to the cities or just fled as far from the shadows as they could. The others were killed by the shadows of the great demon."

"You're alone here?"

"Far from it. If you're asking if I'm the only living person in this swamp, then maybe. There are small animals that live in the trees, but if they get close enough to my home, they're simply dinner. There are a few swamp animals living in the water, but everything else in this swamp is quite dead, I'm afraid."

Silence. After a minute, Berch broke the quiet. "We ran across a banshee—rather, it ran across us."

Toff shook his head. "How many of your party did she kill?"

"None," Jairin said.

"You should consider that to be a rare bit of good luck. If you stay still in the swamp, a banshee will come back again and again until you are all sent to the gray lands. Banshees are spirits, ripped from their bodies as they die. They won't travel far from where their life ended. I don't think I've seen any near the house in all the years I've lived here. I've seen them in the swamps, though. The evil here is in the water. You're much safer on the bits of land that rise above it."

"What about Gestron's demons?" Jairin asked.

"The undead spirits—like that banshee—in the swamp are angry and vengeful. They'll attack anything alive, just out of spite for the living. But as angry as they are, they have a special hatred for the demons that killed them. The spirits in the great swamp are strong enough to keep even the demons out. Once in a while you'll catch a glimpse of a dragon high overhead, but you'll never find a demon in the swamp."

The firelight faded a bit as the remnants of a log broke in half and fell into the coals below. Toff stood and turned from the fire. "I'm going to fetch some more linderwood logs." He had a meager pile of split wood next to his house and a large tarp covering something long and slender next to it. He picked up a few pieces of wood and carried them back to his fire. The older trees growing overhead blocked out most of the sky. "This stuff is like weeds. The trees grow a meter a year to fight for a bit of sunlight overhead. They take forever to dry out once you cut them and they burn quickly. Evening is coming on. Stay here and rest."

They huddled around the fire for warmth. As the suns dropped from the sky, the night air bit at their skin. The company pulled out their lined cloaks and wrapped themselves in them.

Toff retrieved the spit for the company. "Have some dinner… I know, it's squirrel. It's not much, but it's all I have today. I also have water boiled pure from the swamp. If you turn down my hospitality, you'll wish you hadn't when you are eating salt pork and drinking dirty water filtered through a sock!"

"I'd love some water, but I'll pass on the rodent," Arik said.

"We have salted meats," Raven added. "You can keep the squirrel. It's only enough for one person, really."

Jairin wasn't hungry enough yet to think that a large-eyed swamp critter was a tasty alternative to fresh rabbit or similar fare. He pulled out his sword and checked the blade. No color. They each ate some dried rations from their packs, except for Berch. The parum seemed content to have some of Toff's cooked squirrel-thing.

"I have some ale," the older hermit told the company. "It won't dehydrate you, but it helps keep away the bad dreams. It's also about twenty times better than drinking plain water." He pointed off to a still over by the house. They all opted for the water. It was surprisingly clear, considering it had originated from the swamp.

Toff fell asleep first, then the others, one by one.

Jairin was awakened by his sister. The air this morning felt warmer and drier. She led him to the tarp near Toff's cabin, pulling it back to reveal a pile of logs. "Toff said these are too wet to burn, but we could take them for a raft. He said he has more logs that he can dry out before these would be missed."

Toff emerged from his small home, sharpening a

spearpoint with a small knife.

Jairin turned to face the old man, "Will they float?"

"They're very buoyant. They'll float well enough, even when damp like this. I cut them down all the time, but they keep coming back. I've got more than I know what to do with."

Berch and Arik fashioned the logs into a raft, tied together with some of the pliable vines they found climbing the black trees of the swamp.

The old hermit sat down by the fire with Jairin and his sister. He picked up a stick and scribbled a small map on the ground. "This here is the southern edge of the swamp," he said, scratching some wavey lines in the dirt. "There is an entrance to the catacombs here. I don't know how dry the caverns are, but it shouldn't be too bad… they've dammed up the rivers that used to fill the lower levels with water. Hence the swamp. I don't know how much more water can be down there anymore. It's going to be dark, though. You'll need some dry wood for torches, and what I have here is all damp. You'll likely fill the caves with smoke if you try to burn this."

"We have a lantern," Raven said.

Toff nodded and looked over at the men building the raft. "Stay out of the water as much as you can. There are a lot of things in this swamp far more deadly than that banshee. I also need to ask you—if this demon is as tough as he's made out to be, how are you planning on destroying him if you ever find him?"

Jairin pulled the sword back out of its scabbard. Toff shook his head. "I know I'm just an old farmer, but I was here when he screamed through our lands with a wave of destruction. He made quick work of the best and strongest knights in the land. If you mean to take him on with a sword, I think you've been in the swamp too long. The swamp messes with your head—changes you, I'm told."

Berch approached. "We're finished with the raft." He held out his hand to Toff. "We owe you a debt, my friend. Thank you!"

Arik brought the raft to the edge of the water and stepped aboard. On it were two long branches he had stripped to use in steering the raft.

Toff stood and shook hands with the parum. "I fear you're all a bit daft to charge after those demons like this. If you insist on continuing on, just head straight south through the swamp. The water should be shallow enough for quite a while to push yourself along among the trees. Watch the branches overhead. Snakes and other predators will drop on you from above. More than anything, don't linger in the water. I can't emphasize that enough. When you—"

Toff stopped mid-sentence and slouched a bit.

"When you what?" Jairin asked. He looked over at Toff and his heart sank. The farmer again had a cloud over his eyes. He seemed again like an old man, lost in his own confusion.

Toff lifted his head, shaking. "Tell the man in his fancy boots to be faster next time. I'm still going to report the delay to the king... and I know some knights in the court. I'm not to be ignored!"

They quietly boarded the raft and pushed off to the south, away from the farmer.

"Goodbye, Toff," Jairin said.

"Yes," the old man said. "Toff. I'm Toff." He walked away to his firepit.

Jairin watched as the old man paced around the fire, head down. "I'm not sure what's worse," he said to Raven, "living in a world that has forgotten you, or one that you've forgotten."

Toff's house and eventually the smoke from his small fire disappeared in the distance as they pushed their way through the swamp. They manned the poles in shifts, guiding their raft through the dark water. Watching several notches on the poles, they tracked the depth of the water as they continued on—sometimes half a meter deep, sometimes up to three meters deep. When Jairin and Berch tired of the endless propelling with the thick branches, they traded off with the others.

"I have a confession," Arik told the young princess as they advanced ever south through the water. "When Jairin and I first ran into you in the theater, I was quite envious. I thought there was something between the two of you."

Raven pulled her hair back out of her face, tying it in a ponytail. "I could see that. If he were there, I think even Toff could have seen it." She smiled. "I wish we'd met before running off on a quest. I bet you'd be fun to spend more time with. You're a refreshing change from that stick-in-the-mud you brought with you." She glanced at her brother, then back at Arik.

Jairin shook his head. "Do you two need a separate raft?"

She stood up, leaned carefully toward Arik, and kissed him on the cheek, then sat down again. "Like I said, a refreshing change from that one over there."

"If you knew what the journey would be like when we started," Jairin said to his sister, "would you still have insisted on coming along?"

She paused, looking up through some tree branches, midday sunlight nipping part of her cheek. "I love adventure. There are some things I would have wanted to plan out a lot better, of course. You're my brother, Jairin, and I love you and look up to you. But you seemed to be so singularly focused on revenge that you just skipped over a lot of details. It's a good plan, but you knew there was a small army of demons here. You ran in with just a sword in your hand. It's reckless, this single-minded pursuit. For revenge? You spent so much time planning this life you wanted to live that you kind of forgot to just… I don't know… live."

Jairin didn't respond right away. "I deserved that." He understood. He had never felt a higher calling than to make right what Gestron had destroyed. Maybe it wasn't something that was placed squarely on his shoulders, but he felt the burden regardless. The mirror had to work, or all of this was for nothing. "This is something I need to—"

"We," Raven interrupted.

"What?"

"I said, 'we.' This is something that *we* need to do. This effects all of us, especially the four of us here, right now." She scowled at her brother.

Arik stepped into the exchange. "Okay, campers, everyone needs to calm down. I'm convinced we've been in this swamp too long."

"You know what?" Raven asked, glaring at Jairin again. "Knowing what I know now, yes, I would have still insisted on coming along. Even more so." She turned away from Jairin and moved to the far side of the raft.

They slowly continued south, pushing and prodding in shifts. The water depth stayed relatively even as they moved on through the heart of the swamp. The stray beams of sunlight grew less and less, then disappeared.

The parum closed the blades on the lantern and gazed up through the trees. "If you look carefully," Berch said. "you can see a star here and there through the canopy." After a moment, he shook his head and opened one of the lantern blades again. "This is very unsettling for me. For the first time since we left Thadia, I don't know where we are."

"Let's take turns trying to get some sleep," Jairin said. "Two of us can push the raft ahead while two sleep." They tried that, but nobody was able to sleep on the moving raft. They decided to try to find some land where they could stop and sleep through the night. Up ahead, they spied a small island, covered in tall grass and dotted with trees. They pulled the raft up and out of the water. They ate some rations and drank water from their waterskins. Toff had warned them to keep a light on if they decided to sleep. Berch set a small fire to keep them warm and provide the light. Raven took first watch. In the distance they heard varied cries of unknown animals, but nothing that sounded unnatural or banshee-like.

Arik took the second watch. Most of the sounds were familiar to him from his days hunting in the woods—the night owl, the warning call of a mother crow watching over her young, and the distant sound of a fish poking its head above the water to grab food at the surface. Then he heard something unfamiliar. *Slosh, fruuup. Slosh, fruuup.* He sat up and listened more closely. He squinted and tried to find the exact location of the new sound.

Slosh, fruuup. "Eeeeeeeaaaaaaahhhhhh!" He jerked. It was much closer now, from the east. He whipped around and saw movement in the shadows ahead, but it was blurry in the darkness. *Slosh, fruuup. Slosh, slosh, slosh, slosh.* The sounds were getting louder and closer together. He shook Jairin awake and then the others.

20 Eeeeeeeaaaaaaaahhhhhh

Slosh, slosh, slosh, slosh. Jairin leaped to his feet and yanked his sword from its scabbard. No blue light on the blade. "They're not shadows. It may be more undead—several of them." Raven stood and drew her short swords.

Berch lit the lantern and opened the rest of its windows, filling their small hill with lantern light in all directions. He fell back, scampering for his club.

Soon the splashing and moaning sounds came from all around. Walking corpses emerged from the swamp, clumps of skin and flesh dripping from their pale skulls. The hill where the group had been sleeping was soon surrounded by the undead, clothes torn and covered in mold and muck, smelling of earth and death.

"Smeck!" Raven yelled. "How are these things even able to walk through the swamp?" The blue glow from the enchantment at Glensong was gone from her swords. She charged to one edge of the hill.

"What are they?" Arik asked.

"Ghouls, or maybe saphants," Berch said. "I can't tell for sure yet, but they're nearly the same."

Arik scratched the symbol of Willem Ironfoot into the ground with the tip of his sword and then made his way toward several of the undead. "What's the difference?"

"A ghoul will infect you and leave you for dead. A saphant will infect you and eat you. Either way, you're dead."

"I'm sorry I asked." Arik swung his sword at the closest rotting corpse. It bellowed out a loud "Eeeeeeeaaaaaaahhhhhh!" as its severed arm fell into the swamp amongst a stream of rotting ooze. The stench was overpowering. Arik raised his blade to make another slash, but then stopped. He turned and leaned to the side, emptying the contents of his stomach into the swamp. "Oh, these things are intolerably disgusting..." He spit a few times and then turned back to the corpse, readying his sword again.

Raven took a deep breath and charged ahead. Jairin lost sight of her as she passed behind Arik.

Jairin decapitated the first one he came to. An unidentifiable mixture of liquids poured from its neck as it fell backward into the swamp. He glanced around as he moved on to the next one but couldn't see his companions in the dark. He heard the slashing of steel, the thumping of Berch's club, and then a deafening "Eeeeeeeaaaaaaahhhhhh!" A shambling corpse trudged up the grass toward Jairin with bony hands extended. *Thurp, thurp, thurp,* came the sound it made as it came toward him. The creature seemed to make the air around it cold. Bits of skin and gunk fell from its hands as it reached out toward Jairin's neck.

He ran the sword through the creature's chest. It didn't stop. It reached Jairin's neck and clenched with an icy grip. Jairin was too close to pull the sword out and make another swing. He managed to pull back as the corpse's hands started to choke him. He whipped his arm, clutching his sword in a circle, trying to cut away as much of the ghoul's chest as he could. The smell made Jairin nauseous. He could hear the cracking of bone and the snapping of connective tissue as he rotated his sword wildly inside the corpse's chest.

Jairin felt light-headed as the ghoul clutched his neck tighter and tighter. He continued tearing at the ghoul—too close to pull the sword free from its chest. He made a last attempt, dropping into a crouch to get the extra distance he needed. With a jerk, he pulled the sword free. *Flurp!* Foul insides from the ghoul spilled out of the chasm left by Jairin's sword. With nothing supporting the ghoul's chest, its hands went limp and it fell to the ground. The blade of Jairin's sword was covered in slime and muck. He stood and caught his breath, then looked around, catching sight of his sister.

"I'm tired…" Raven grunted between foes. She ran forward and stabbed the next one square in the middle of the face, blade protruding from the back of its skull. "I wanted to sleep. Am I asking too much?" She twisted the blade and pulled it back out, an eyeball impaled on the edge of the short sword.

The night lit up with sudden streaks of light. A flash sped past Jairin's line of sight, followed by a scream from Arik and then a loud splash somewhere out in the darkness.

"Magic!" Raven yelled, "At least one of these things can cast magic!"

Before he had time to react, another of the undead came after Jairin. He raised his sword and swung, hitting it in the shoulder. The next swing sent it to the ground, unmoving. He made his way to Raven.

Raven's short swords were a blur, ripping open a belly here, cutting shoulder muscle there. She was covered in whatever was spurting out of these corpses as she slashed her way toward where Arik had been a minute before. Jairin and Raven arrived by Arik's side and she turned him over onto his back. He let out a grunt. "Something blasted him. It looked like magic, and it thumped him square in the back."

Jairin could see wisps of smoke rising from Arik's mouth and nose. His eyebrows were singed and his body trembled. Raven stood back up and turned to face more of the undead. One stood behind the others, creating sweeping gestures with his hands and arms in an almost mesmerizing motion. Jairin charged him. A glowing silver ball of light formed in the creature's hands.

The saphant drew its hand back, but Jairin was upon him now. The glowing orb moved as if attached to the saphant's hand, growing in size in its palm. Jairin's sword struck the top of its head and shattered its skull, further slicing its flesh from head to mid-chest as it made its way down. The saphant fell backward into the murk, extinguishing the ball of lightning.

Jairin doubled over, trying to catch his breath. He wondered how Raven was doing, but couldn't see her in the dark. He heard fighting continue for a few moments before it fell quiet. He scanned himself for major injuries. Aside from various cuts, scratches, and bruises, he was okay.

It seemed they'd managed to eliminate all of the invaders. He went to check on the others. Berch and Raven appeared equally battered, but without major injuries. It was several hours before Arik could stand on his own. He still smelled like cooked meat and his backpack was destroyed, though it had probably taken the brunt of the lightning blow meant to kill him. Jairin looked at his companions, exhausted. "This may seem gross, but we need to go back in the water and clean whatever this mess is off us."

They waded in and cleaned off as best they could, then hung their clothing by the fire to dry. Berch finished Arik's shift on guard duty so the horse rancher had some time to recover. When the parum saw a few rays of sunlight break through the canopy overhead, he turned off the lantern and woke the others. They packed up camp, then climbed back on the raft and pushed on, heading farther south—hopefully on their way out of the dark swamp.

Hours passed, and the trees grew thicker, but less tall. The poles were now consistently less than a half-meter deep in water, and soon the raft scraped along the rocks and dirt just below the surface. They had to abandon their transport and continue again on foot. Sloshing through the water, they had made it to the southern edge of the swamp. Other trees grew in addition to the water-born linderwood, but they were becoming farther apart. It was late afternoon and the reduced tree-cover gave them more sunlight. By early evening, they were walking again through damp grass instead of grassy swamp. The foothills rising above the underground caves slowly came into view to the south. They weren't far off course.

As night fell, they found a tree to camp under. Jairin hoped that their proximity to the swamp would deter the shadows from finding them. Berch warned them to stay alert. He took the first watch and traded off with Arik during the night.

Morning came, and after a quick breakfast of rations and water, they made their way into the foothills to the south to find the entrance to the catacombs. As they approached a large cavern, Jairin recognized it at once. He had played here as a child. Though the fields and farms were gone, the area around the hills was not much changed. "Take a last look at the sun. From here on out, we're underground in the catacombs."

21 Into the Depths

Jairin finished rearranging his pack in preparation for their descent into the caverns below. Half their food was gone, and he discarded the shirt his sister had shredded. "Raven, can you check the oil in the lantern and make sure it's topped off?"

The parum approached her with a sealed jar. "I've got it." Raven unscrewed the cover on the side of the lantern and peered inside, then filled it and put the cover back on. She pulled out a small stone from her pack and poured a splash of oil on the stone and then sealed the jar, returning it to their guide.

Raven examined her short swords. "The blue tinge is completely gone now." She looked at the edges of each blade and worked them over with the whetstone she'd oiled. "Barlemicus said the enchantment would only last a few days. He wasn't exaggerating. If we run into shadows down there, Jairin, you may be the only one who can kill them."

"I'll be careful not to get separated from the rest of you," Jairin said. "We're a team"

Arik walked over to Raven and picked up the lantern. "Is it safe to keep the lantern lit down there? We'll be announcing our presence to every creature within a hundred meters of us."

Berch shrugged. "If we run into orcs or ogres, they'll see us whether or not we have the lantern on. Turning it on and opening the shutter blades just enough to light our path—that's our best bet."

Jairin checked each of the blades on the lantern. The nine shutters all opened and closed easily, each covering a forty-degree angle around the light. When all were closed, it emitted almost no light at all. Satisfied, he approached the rough-hewn entryway into the catacombs and carefully opened a single blade on the lantern, just enough to shine a small beam ahead of him. He passed through the entrance and looked around. The walls dripped with cloudy water, and the stagnant air reminded him of body odor and mold. "Breathe through your mouths. This isn't going to be pleasant."

Berch followed Jairin into the cavern, sniffing the air. "There are undeniably creatures living down here. This would normally be a home for orcs and maybe gnolls. But with the shadows in residence, they could have any number of creatures down there with them. We need to be ready for anything."

Jairin waited for Raven and Arik to enter the cavern, then he moved ahead. Once they'd progressed a hundred meters and rounded a bend, the dim light from the entrance disappeared. The path was now only illuminated for about five meters by the small beam of lantern light. He dared not open the blade any more for fear of attracting attention. Jairin stepped aside in the corridor and passed the lantern back to Berch. "You're in the lead, good parum." Jairin drew his sword a few centimeters from its scabbard. If there was any blue light coming from it, he couldn't see it.

Berch led on through the dark hallway, slowly at first, letting their eyes get used to the diminished light. The nauseating smell of moldy rot seemed to fade, or else they just got used to it. Jairin recalled playing in these ancient caves as a child, but they seemed to have been cleaner then, not so pungent. Maybe the mildew was from swamp runoff. The lowest of the caverns were flooded and wet, but the upper levels had always been dry.

They inched farther down the main corridor, guided by the gently flickering lantern light. Their footfalls echoed in the quiet hallway as Jairin, then Raven, then Arik followed the halfling through the maze of tunnels. A dark rat scurried between Berch and Jairin. "Rodents!" Berch said. "Watch the floors!" As they trudged on, the silence was broken only by the occasional squeak of small critters at the edges of their path, or brave enough to scamper across.

Jairin reached out and scraped two fingers against the dirt and rock of the wall. "At least it's dry."

"Do we need to be so quiet?" Arik asked in a hushed voice. "We've been tramping through the caves for an hour and haven't seen anything but rodents, bats, bugs, and worms. What are we expecting to find here—aside from, you know?"

Jairin pointed down the hallway. "If I remember correctly, there is a split ahead and we need to take the passage to the left. I think that brings us to some stairs cut into the rock leading down."

They kept pushing on to the left fork. As they grew used to the darkness, Berch closed the blade on the side of the lantern halfway. They walked on for several minutes, following the parum.

Berch put up his arm. "The floor here is slanting." He looked around for a few moments and pointed ahead to an alcove. "I think we've found Jairin's stairway down."

"That's it," Jairin said. "They're rough and uneven. Watch your step!"

Berch opened two more blades on the lantern to illuminate the steps ahead and slowly crept down the rough stairs. Steep and crumbling, the descent made for several tense minutes as the rest of the company followed the parum, with flickering shadows on the ground their only guide to where they could safely step. At one point, Raven slipped and broke a bit of stone under the edge of one of the steps, but Arik caught her as she fell forward into him. They arrived at the bottom without further incident.

The air here was more humid, but a bit less rancid. Berch looked at the walls. "We're below the natural water table now. I'm not sure how, with the swamp to our north, the tunnels here can be dry enough for us to walk through. Something has changed the waterflow." He closed the two extra blades on the lantern, cutting light to the walls at their sides.

This level was broader than the one above. Berch pivoted around, pointing to each of the four walls as he said, "North, East, South, West."

"To the west are larger caverns and a river," Jairin said. "The lower levels were flooded when I was a boy. Unless Gestron can breathe underwater, he must be on this level somewhere." He noticed a small, round rock on the ground just a few centimeters wide. He kicked it ahead into the darkness, where it bounced off a wall with a satisfying *clack*.

They headed west, creeping forward in the lantern light. Suddenly, Berch halted, and Jairin nearly ran into him. "I thought I heard something."

Grunting sounds came from the tunnel ahead. Berch closed the last slit on the lantern and they stopped where they stood in an uneasy stillness. The grunting drew closer. "Orcs," Berch whispered. "It sounds like three or four. We need to avoid them or take them down quietly. There may be other patrols nearby."

As the foes drew closer, the party readied their weapons. Flickering torchlight came from around the bend. "There's nowhere to hide," Jairin said. "Let's take them." Berch cracked open one shutter on the lantern and set it down, facing the wall, giving them a soft light to see by. Several nonhumans came around the corner just ahead of them, carrying torches. Jairin sprung at them.

Though caught off guard, the orcs raised crude blades. With only the bounced light from the lantern, Jairin could see a muted blue light emanating from his sword. It was too dim to have been triggered by these orcs.

The two front orcs snarled, their tusk-like teeth protruding from their mouths. They were roughly human height, but much heavier and broader, with dark skin. They had the same odor as the caves around them. Wearing thin leather armor with matching tunics, they appeared to be in the service of an army, rather than a band of random creatures wandering through the caves.

Jairin stuck the first orc mid-chest. It let out a shout and stumbled aside, clutching the wound. The other orcs sniffed and grunted as they closed in on the human intruders. The injured orc motioned with its other arm and blurted out something Jairin couldn't understand.

Berch faced the second orc. It snarled, sticky saliva dripping from the corners of its mouth at the tusks. It let out a low guttural roar and took a swing, striking Berch's dagger and knocking him back.

The third orc made its way around to Raven and Arik, swiping at them with its sword. Raven pulled out her short swords and took a defensive stance against the much larger foe. The orc slashed out at her, but Arik leapt to her defense, striking it.

Jairin ran to the orc he'd injured and stabbed it in the chest a second time. It grabbed its chest as blood poured through both of its wounds. Its hands were now covered in blood and it dropped to the floor with a hollow thud. The prince then turned to engage the orc that had attacked Berch. He was relieved to see none of the orc patrol yelling or fleeing to fetch reinforcements.

Even as Jairin closed in, the second orc advanced on Berch. The parum swung again with the dagger he'd retrieved by his foot, giving a hasty warning to his companions. "This is just a small patrol. We can't let them sound the alarm!"

Jairin attacked the second orc, sticking him in the side with his dim blue blade. The orc let out a loud series of grunts as Berch also cut into his chest with his dagger. Weak and injured, the orc scanned for an exit from the fight. With his blade still deep inside the orc, Jairin pulled the handle up and opened up the side of the creature beneath the increasingly bloody leather. It fell to the ground in a pool of blood.

The third orc swung its heavy blade at Arik, who was able to dodge the blow, but only at the cost of moving perilously close to it. The orc's huge arm muscles tightened as it stopped its sword mid-swing. It dropped its shoulder to take a sweeping slash at Arik's leg. Arik tried to dodge the blow with a jump, but the orc smashed him with the broad side of his sword in the process. There was a sickening *pang, crunch* sound. Arik cried out and fell to the ground, dropping his sword and clutching his leg.

A metal point burst forth from the orc's chest near its heart and then another came through its bowels with a fountain of blood. The orc suddenly stopped, eyes closing, and fell to the ground. Raven ran past it the other way. She tossed her short swords down into the dirt where they landed point down. "Arik!" she said. "No, no, no!"

Arik grunted, rocking side to side on the ground. "Aaaaaaagh!"

As Raven tended to Arik, Berch checked for any more orcs or other creatures bearing down on them. It was quiet. He turned the lantern around, illuminating the battle site, and then stamped out the torches the orcs had been carrying.

"Arik is down and injured. We need to act quickly before he goes into shock." The parum opened the side pocket of his pack and pulled out a pouch.

Arik's eyes were closed. Berch slapped his cheek lightly. "Stay with us. Stay with us." He checked Arik's lower leg, moving his hand gently up the front and down the back.

"Aaaaaaagh! Fitch!"

"Shh… I know that hurts. Try not to scream here." Berch said. He turned to Jairin, shaking his head. "This is bad. The Stable Bone is shattered and the Strong Bone is at least cracked. We're at least two days from anywhere, and he's not going to be walking."

Arik opened his eyes meekly. "I'm too heavy to carry. Make me a splint and I can manage."

"You certainly can *not*."

"I'll use my sword as a crutch!"

Berch looked thoughtful. "Maybe we can do something. Jairin, bring me those orc swords."

Jairin did as Berch had asked, handing the crude swords to their guide. Berch cut up one of the orc tunics with his dagger and laid the swords on either side of Arik's lower leg, binding them with the tunic strips. Berch looked at Raven and Jairin. "He won't be able to put weight on this leg. Whether we bring him back to Glensong or to whatever lies ahead, we'll need to carry him."

"The fitch you will," Arik said, defiantly. He grabbed his sword and started propping himself up to stand on his good leg, clenching his teeth. He failed miserably and landed on his backside again with a yelp.

Berch shook his head. "Always trouble, with you folks." He opened the pouch he'd retrieved from his pack and pulled out a large pinch of crushed leaves. "These are leaves from the Soulbloom flower. They aren't as potent as the flower extract and they may make you more tired, but they'll deaden the pain for a while. Put them in your back teeth and grind your teeth together. Don't swallow any of it."

Jairin took Arik's sword and helped him up. "We're fortunate in one way," Jairin said. "None of the patrol escaped to report back that we are here. But the noise might have alerted anyone nearby, so we'll need to stay alert." He put Arik's sword back in its scabbard at his waist.

Raven moved to Arik's injured side and he leaned against her. They made their way down the corridor, but before they'd walked another hundred meters, they came across a stone archway marking a stairway down to the next level. Berch approached the opening. Leaning in, he closed his eyes and put his finger to his lips. *Shhhh.* He stood there for a moment before speaking. "I can hear water down below— and some faint clanking sounds."

"Is it worth looking through this level before taking the stairs?" Jairin asked.

"That depends. This level has been completely dry. Water could indicate an encampment or congregation spot. I'd advise that we go down first and make our way back if we get to that point." Nods signaled an agreement among the other company members.

Click, click, click! A bat brushed between Arik and Raven, flying through the arch and down into the darkness. Raven swiped it, too late. "Ick! We're following flying rats!"

Berch smiled. "Down the steps it is." He led them through the shadows flickering in the lantern light, down twenty uneven stairs to the next level, Arik descending carefully with Raven helping him on his injured side. There they found themselves in yet another stony passage stretching off into the distance.

Water trickled down the walls to form small pools on the floor. As the pools filled the dips in the ground, they overflowed into channels leading to other pools in a continuous cycle—rivers and lakes in miniature. They slowed their pace to accommodate Arik and made their way down the passage. The sound of water running in the distance became louder with each passing step. Jairin pulled his sword up a few centimeters from its protective scabbard. The blue glow was now significantly brighter. There were demons just ahead.

"We've got company," Jairin said. "Can we dim the lantern a little more?"

"Got it," Berch replied. He closed the blade almost completely. The remaining light gave them a softly illuminated sphere around their immediate area. Ahead, they could hear running water with a noticeable echo.

"Sounds like a large cavern up ahead," Jairin said. "I don't remember any caverns or underground rivers. Then again, I was very young, and this whole level may have been flooded. I don't think I was ever down this far."

Arik jerked his head and put his hand on his hair. "What the…?" He rubbed his fingers together and then raised them to his nose. "Oh great. First demons and now the caves are dripping water on us that smells like orc crap."

"Yeah," Jairin said. "I'm sure the caves always dripped. The demons—that's new."

The group approached a large underground cavern. Berch whispered, "This doesn't feel right. Move with caution, quietly." Jairin checked his sword again, verifying they were getting closer to demons ahead. He sheathed the glowing blade but kept his hand ready at the hilt.

The cavern opened up into a chamber about ten meters high and twenty meters wide and deep. At the far wall they could see the source of the watery noise. Water trickled down the rock walls, creating a symphony of sound as it snaked its way through the rough surfaces. Small drips and larger flows merged all along the wall, flowing into a pool at the far end of the cavern. As they were taking in the site, something moved. Jairin pulled the sword out again, just a few centimeters.

Unseen at first, small creatures glided effortlessly against the far wall with wooden buckets. Twenty or more, the shadowy beings scooped water from the pool below and seemed to float up along the stone wall, disappearing into the darkness above. Moments later, they emerged with their buckets emptied.

Jairin pulled the sword farther out of its scabbard, but Arik grabbed his wrist. "Don't. They either haven't seen us, or they don't care that we're here."

Jairin nodded. "You're right. I'm still a little jumpy." He pushed the sword back in and checked to see that the token still hung on the chain around his neck.

Berch stepped to the front with Arik and Jairin, surveying the pool. "There's a small army of these demons. They're working as if singularly focused on emptying the water from the pool." The parum looked at several other shadows as they scurried up the wall. "Hmm."

Jairin furled his lip. "What kind of creature would be content to spend an eternity emptying water from a pool over and over?"

"It's not for us to judge," Raven said. "A fish may spend its entire life swimming around in a bowl."

They made their way slowly toward the back wall, looking for another way out of the cavern. Still unseen by the demons emptying the pool, they decided Berch's assessment was probably correct. After traveling through the caverns all day, they were growing tired. "We should camp here," Berch said.

"In the cavern?" Raven asked. "That's crazy. They'll kill us in our sleep!"

"Not at all. Because there are demons carrying out a simple project here, there's no reason for Gestron to send patrols through. Also… these shadows don't have legs or eyes. They're just here to move water from that pool for all time."

Jairin grew less skeptical. They had to camp somewhere. It made sense to take their chances here, where nobody would expect trouble. The others eventually agreed. If nothing else, they would get off their feet. Berch gave Arik the bag of Soulbloom leaves. "Please ration these. They have to last until we get out of here, or you'll wish that orc had finished you off." Jairin sheathed his sword, knowing tonight it would be nothing more than a blue nightlight that pointed any possible passers-by to their location.

They huddled in the corner farthest from the water and ate some rations and drank from their waterskins. It was good to rest their weary limbs in the quiet babbling of the water, but they had difficulty dozing off, in constant fear of being discovered after their encounter with the patrol earlier in the day.

When they were finished, Berch turned off the lantern and they were cloaked in darkness.

Raven's eyes had grown accustomed to the night as she watched over the others. At one point, she noticed that Jairin had fallen asleep. She brushed a stray lock of hair behind her ear, exhaling gently. There was a light chill in the air here where the sun didn't warm up the stone during the day. She looked over at her brother, asleep and crunched into a ball a few meters away. *I know you think this burden is all on you. You're not alone in wanting your revenge, and I'll prove it to you. I just hope you understand why I'm doing what I have to do.* She rearranged a few items in her pack, putting the salted beef at the top for easy access when they needed to stop and eat again. She looked back at her older brother again. *I'm sorry.* She rocked uneasily a few times. *I'm sorry.* After several more minutes, she, too, fell into an uneasy sleep.

22 Spheres

A gray rabbit hopped from the rocky path onto the sparse patch of grass. The vegetation was sparse, but enough for a lone rabbit. It twitched its nose in the light breeze and hopped to a patch of clover growing at the edge of the stunted grass. It nibbled for a while and suddenly looked up, scanning its surroundings. Its fur stood on end and the grass straightened, pointing to the sky. The rabbit bounded back to the path and up the hill from which it came.

The air crackled and buzzed with static electricity. A shimmery line several meters tall split the air, distorting the light passing through it. A tear in the fabric of reality. The line widened until it was as wide as it was tall. A man emerged from the portal amid sparks and the snapping of electricity.

Vruthian strode through the portal. He was tall and narrow, with thick brown hair pulled back behind his shoulders. He wore green robes, and carried a staff as he took several steps away from the portal. He waved his finger, and the magical gateway rippled like waves in a still lake. It faded at the edges until it was again just a line, then the tear closed up completely.

Vruthian examined the clearing. Small hills dominated the landscape below the low trail. The valley below plunged into the land like a gash. Down the path ahead, there was a rough tunnel cut into the hill and a dried riverbed that appeared to have been a waterfall by the wearing in the stony ledge. He needed to go the other way, up the path. As he turned and walked up the ledge, he pulled two worn stones from his pocket, one light gray and other nearly black. They looked ordinary enough, though polished smooth. He turned them over in his palm several times and then put them back in his pocket. He stopped his ascent to listen to the path ahead. Someone was coming.

Another man, dressed in red robes, walked briskly down the path toward him, seeming not to have yet noticed that Vruthian was standing there. The newcomer looked up and Vruthian recognized him from the description he'd been given. It was Madigan's apprentice. Smeech's expression changed from focused to annoyed as he looked at Vruthian. As anyone trained to read magic, Vruthian could identify the strength and type of magic Smeech wielded from the aura surrounding him. "You need to turn around and leave here."

Smeech said, "You're a wizard of the Kalari, but I don't know you, ecomancer—*apprentice* ecomancer. And you're in my way."

Vruthian could see the magic flowing around and building in Smeech. In a much deeper voice, the ecomancer said. "I'm Vruthian, apprentice to Tannis." He pulled magic from the air around him as well. He'd hoped he could turn Smeech away from this path without a fight, but it looked like the situation was about to escalate.

Smeech shook his head. "Vruthian, apprentice to Tannis, you're a long way from Barrington, and as I said, you're in my way. Step aside, I have business in the caverns."

"I'm quite sure you don't, Smeech."

Smeech tightened his gaze. "You know me? I'm

apprenticed to Madigan and a free wizard. You're not allowed to interfere in our business."

Vruthian nodded, but brushed off the claim with a wave of his free hand. "Yes, yes. There lies the problem, I'm afraid. I have a vested interest in this valley and in these hills behind us. I have sworn not to interfere with your business so long as our paths don't cross. The nature of this agreement binds you to the same limitation. You're not to interfere here."

Smeech raised his staff with the thick end pointed at the ecomancer. It began to glow with an eerie white light. "I'm here on an errand to check on my own personal property. I need you to step aside and let me pass."

Vruthain stepped to the side, out of the path. He raised his own staff, but it did not glow menacingly as his opponent's had. "You have no property here, Smeech. You can't claim something that belongs to your master as your own. I'd tell you to summon Madigan here to control his own property, but we both know that he's no longer able to do that. He's wasting, Smeech. You know that he's only going to get worse."

"Lies!"

Vruthian reached into his pocket and pulled out the stones again, holding them out for Smeech to see. "You've arrived at your crossroads, Smeech. Your master was given a choice to join the Eastern Domain and join the ranks of his brothers."

"We choose freedom. We choose to follow magic and not the men who wield it!"

Vruthian nodded in understanding. "Look what this has wrought for your master. You have time to think this through. Madigan made his choice a millennium ago. You can choose the same path, or you can choose a different path —Smeech's path."

"You value ritual over the beauty of magic." Smeech

broke his gaze and stepped forward to continue down the rocky path.

"No." Vruthian raised his staff and it burned with intense fire. "Whether or not you choose to join your brothers, Tannis and the Kalari will not allow you to interfere with this demon."

Smeech raised his staff to meet Vruthian's. Sparks flew from the gnarled wood as flame and lightning crossed. Smeech's face strained as he flexed and thrust his staff against his fellow wizard. A drop of blood dripped from the younger wizard's nose as he continued to drive against Vruthian's staff. He grunted and strained. After a minute he stopped and stepped back. The last of the sparks trailed off and fell to the ground beyond them to either side of the trail. He scowled. "Fitching Kalari! You're supposed to stay out of this!"

Vruthian shook his head. "He's not your servus, Smeech. He'd destroy you and he'd destroy me as well if I confronted him. He's even killing your master from hundreds of kilometers away. Why do you think Madigan sent you here? You're bait!"

Smeech's chest heaved as he took several deep breaths. Vruthian could see that the magic the younger wizard had gathered was exhausted.

"Think on this," Vruthian said. "I am not giving you your crossroads today. You started on your journey with Madigan, but your fate is not entwined with his. We will serve you the stones later. The Kalari would welcome you and never demand that you sacrifice yourself just to ease our path. Go home. See Madigan for what he is and make your choice. Take the stones, from whomever they are offered, and decide which is Smeech's path."

Smeech turned and walked back up the path, away from the entrance below.

23 Unusual Denizens

"How long were we sleeping?" Jairin asked. Looking around wearily, he realized he was the last one to wake up. Berch had relit the lantern and opened one blade enough to light just the area around them.

"There's no way to tell," Berch replied. "Maybe four or five hours. Nobody's seen any shadows or creatures in the area—well, except for those little guys hauling endless buckets of water out of the cavern. I'm not sure if that counts."

Jairin helped Arik up, and they quietly packed up their sparse gear. Arik spit out the pinch of Soulbloom he'd been chewing and put another pinch in its place. Raven passed out servings of salted beef from the top of her pack. "Are you able to keep going, Arik?" she asked.

"It's throbbing, but the leaves kill a lot of the pain. I think I can make it."

Jairin paused between bites. "We should reach the far end of the cavern today. Whatever we're going to find down here, we'll be running out of tunnels soon."

Berch left his pack and opened several blades on the lantern just enough to luminate the corners of the cavern away from the water in a dim glow. "I'm going to look for exits." He watched the water-bucket demons for a minute and then examined the far walls around the cavern. After several minutes he returned to camp. "It looks like our way in is the only way back out. We'll need to backtrack, probably back up the stairs."

The parum closed the extra blades so they again lit just the path ahead of them. "Am I the only one who feels like we're being watched?"

"There!" Jairin said, pointing to a small shape that scurried off. "I just saw a shadow from the corner of my eye. I thought I saw one yesterday, too. I wrote it off as a trick of the lantern light, but now I don't think so."

Arik looked over at Jairin. "I didn't see it, but the shadows that attacked us in Keld were human-sized or bigger—and very aggressive."

Berch nodded. "I think it's foolish at this point to believe he doesn't know we're here. Wherever Gestron is lurking, we're probably meant to find him—and we won't have the advantage of surprise."

Jairin pointed. "It went that way, the direction we came from yesterday."

"I don't pretend to know all of the exits and turns down here," Berch said. "We turned at a 'T' when we first entered these caverns and then descended the stairs to this level before we camped. We have food and water for a few days, but I'm more worried about Arik's leg."

Arik ground his teeth a few times. "No, I said I'm good. I've got this."

Raven brought the water flasks to the near edge of the pool, drinking a mouthful from her hand before filling them and bringing them back to the others.

"Let's head out," Berch said. He entered the corridor and moved the lantern from side to side, looking at the walls. The others followed, leaving the chamber and the water-bucket demons behind, with Raven supporting their injured companion.

They walked several minutes before Jairin saw another small stone, perfect for kicking. He gave it a whack with his foot and it bounced ahead into the darkness. *Click, floop!*

Berch swung around to face him. "I was going to lecture you about noise, but I think you may have found something." He turned and crept ahead, scanning the floor. After walking about thirty meters, he stopped and studied a section of the wall ahead of him. He turned back to the group again, with a smile. "Well, I've been following orc tracks leading in both directions. But I see something interesting here." He pointed to the ground, calling attention to several sets of footprints. One set approached a wall and disappeared. "It looks like we've discovered either some orcs that can walk through walls or a wall that orcs can walk through. I wasn't looking for this on the way in."

The others watched as he approached the wall. He pulled out his dagger and slowly moved the tip to the section of wall he'd been looking at. The dagger point touched the wall and continued through it. The area around the dagger point rippled out in waves like a stone dropped in still water. The illusion shimmered and calmed as Berch pulled the knife back out. The others looked on with eyes wide.

"Magic!" Raven exclaimed. "Real magic! I've seen demons and I've seen healers close wounds. I've even seen blades that glow when shadows are nearby." She looked at Jairin and smiled. "But this is free-standing art!" Berch stuck the tip of his dagger back into the illusion and moved it around. Again, the image would bend and shimmer where the blade interrupted it. The image moved to flow around it as if it were water. It even made ripples like water.

Berch pulled the dagger back out again and extended his other hand to the rippling flow. He thrust his hand into the illusion and again it rippled out like waves. He stepped closer and his fingers, hand, and then forearm disappeared into the illusion. "It just feels like air. If there are orcs on the other side, they aren't attacking. "I'm going to go through. If I don't come right back, get out of here!"

He took a deep breath and stepped forward, his entire body disappearing out of sight into the shimmering magical tapestry pretending to be a wall.

Arik ground his teeth on the leaves. Several moments passed as they waited for something—anything. The tip of a blade broke through the visage on the wall, swirled several times, and then disappeared back into the wall. As the waves in the image settled down from the earlier disruption, Berch's head popped through. "It's good. Don't stand around. Come through, but watch your step on the other side." Jairin followed, and then Arik, still leaning on Raven.

As the others emerged through the illusion, Berch cautioned them, "This ledge isn't very wide." They found themselves on a rocky shelf, one and a half meters wide and three meters long. Jairin walked to the edge farthest from the wall and peered down. He couldn't see anything but darkness. The air was wet and the smell of mildew had returned with a vengeance.

Berch walked to the other edge that ran along the wall and looked down. "There are steps on this side. One side butts up to the cavern wall and the other is open without support. This is our way down." The others walked over to Berch and peered over the edge with him. The rough steps were hewn from the rock and continued down into the darkness beyond the lantern's illumination.

"We're already well below the water table," Berch reminded them. "If Gestron is down here, he must have more of those demons who carry the water out. I'm thinking it's going to be wet down there." He opened a second blade on the lantern and held it over the edge at the steps. "I can't see how far these go down." He took his first step down the rocky stairs.

Jairin stood next to Arik as they cautiously made their way after the parum. Leaning on Jairin, Arik winced and spat out some juice as they took their second step down. Raven followed closely behind them. Water trickled down the wall, running into a channel cut on the inside edge and spilling down from step to step. The grooves kept the steps from getting slick with standing water.

At times, the stairs would come to a small landing and then turn this way or the other. After three landings and a half-dozen switchbacks, Berch stopped. "I can see the bottom now. There's water down here, sure enough." He descended the last few stairs to the edge of a pool below.

Berch took several steps out into the water. It came to his knees. Jairin looked back at where they'd come from. Steps extended up one wall of a great cavern back into the darkness above. "How far down do you think we are?" Jairin asked. He thought for sure he would have remembered such a deep stairwell in the caves from his youth. He tried to recall now if he had played two levels down or three. Jairin was quite sure the caves had been completely flooded by the third level. He had no idea if this passage had been here back in those days.

"One hundred twenty-one," Raven said.

"What?" Berch asked.

"I was counting the steps. We walked down one hundred twenty-one."

Berch shook his head. "Why would you keep track of that?"

"Sorry. It's just something I do. We've also passed thirty-eight rats and seventy-one of those spiders with the thick, furry legs."

"Okay. The rat and spider counting doesn't help us. The step count is good, though. We must be at least fifty meters below our entry point." He took a few more steps in the water and it didn't seem to get any deeper. Raven followed the parum, with Jairin helping Arik. The stench of mildew continued to swirl about them.

Arik spit out some juice from the leaves in his teeth. It hit the water with a *sploink*. He checked the pouch to see how much was left. "The leaves are almost gone. I wish I had taken some rum from Glensong before we left. I may need it."

Berch shivered. "I'll be happy when we're out of here. I've had quite enough of wading through water. I feel I've become half fish over these past several days!" He walked ahead, testing the floor before him with his club before taking each step. It gradually got deeper, slowing them down a bit as Berch sloshed through water coming close to waist level.

"I'll tell you one thing," Arik said. "The cold water and pressure are helping dull the pain in my leg."

"I've got you, buddy," Jairin said. "We'll get through this together. There can't be much more ahead of us."

The cavern extended beyond the light of the lantern with a width of over twenty meters. They waded through the water for several minutes before Berch motioned to them. "I can see an exit on the far side of the chamber, flanked by two pillars." A moist wind blew toward them from that direction. Jairin peered toward the exit, but couldn't make out any details. Berch waited a bit as the others drew closer.

When they were all together, Jairin turned to his sister. "Can you help Arik? I don't like the looks of this. I'm sensing an ambush." He put his hand on the hilt of his sword. As the others continued on, he slowed down and took up the rear of the party. Jairin turned and looked back every few meters. At the far end of the cavern, they could now see the exit. There was an opening in the wall with a bright light flickering erratically beyond. The pillars Berch had seen turned out to be stone statues. The exit was flanked by two six-meter sculptures. Jairin's skin felt cold and sweaty. The last time he'd encountered statues in the garden outside the castle, it'd nearly cost him his life. He drew his sword, only to have his fears confirmed. The bright blue glow cast a sheen in all directions, nearly as bright as the lantern Berch carried.

"No, no. We're in trouble!" Jairin yelled.

"What is it?" Arik asked.

"Blue light. Demons. I don't see them yet, but they're close!" He reached for the chain around his neck to reassure himself that the token was still there. He was relieved to touch the small golden coin, his new good-luck charm. He tucked it back under his shirt and gripped the hilt of his sword tightly with both hands.

Jairin kept his eyes on the statues as they cautiously made their way ahead. Berch continued probing the ground as he walked. Jairin could see the flickering light intensifying from beyond the chamber exit. It looked like a fire—a large fire—beyond this room.

"Keep your eyes peeled," Berch said. "The water, the walls, the ceiling, the statues. I'm sensing danger, too, and I can't tell where it's coming from."

They made it past the center of the chamber, all on high alert. Jairin took a step, and then another, and then another. He wondered if it was the statues, or if they were sensing whatever was in the room beyond the wall. He took another step. The next thing he heard was Arik. "Jairin! Behind you!" He swung around.

Several shapes were emerging from the water just behind Jairin. They popped through the surface as though they had been lying in wait below the waterline. They were the size and height of a man and appeared to be made completely of liquid—unarmed and nearly transparent. Jairin stood his ground and readied his sword. The nearest one attacked him with unhuman speed. Jairin unleashed a full swing, cleaving it cleanly in half. Both halves transformed into shapeless water in the air and fell back to the pool. Jairin looked around for the other water creatures.

Before his eyes, the one he had dispatched was rising again. Again, it took on nearly human shape and size. Jairin stood, stunned. An unseen second creature jumped right in front of Jairin and punched him squarely in the mouth. The prince dropped to his knees as his mouth and throat filled with water. One hand clung desperately to his sword as his other hand instinctively went to his throat. He closed his eyes, desperately trying to cough up the water that blocked his breathing. Jairin's ears rang and he started losing strength. While not under water, he could feel himself drowning. He coughed—nothing. He coughed again. Several eerie moments passed, and he finally expelled a sizeable amount of water. He could breathe again, weakly. He was on all fours past his elbows in the pool and opened his eyes to look around.

"Smeck!" Berch yelled as he waved frantically to Raven. "They're made of water. We can't hurt them. Take Arik and get out the exit by the statues—and cover your faces!"

Raven grabbed Arik's arm. "Sorry, Arik. This may hurt." She pulled him ahead faster than he had been hobbling on his own. "Don't look back. This will be quick."

Jairin saw two of the water creatures running after his sister and friend. Occasionally, one would swipe at them from behind, but they didn't slow down. Raven and Arik passed between the two statues and disappeared into the next room.

"Let's get out of here, Jairin," Berch yelled. "We can't kill these things." Jairin ran toward the exit, with one of the water creatures racing after him. It smashed at Jairin's feet as he waded as quickly as he could. He realized that if these creatures couldn't get at his face, they didn't have much power to harm him. It struck out, hitting Jairin in the back. He didn't slow down. Another strike. He felt splash after splash. It wasn't having any more effect. The other water creatures dissipated into the pool. The splashing behind him also stopped.

Berch had been wading ahead and now passed into the next room. He turned back to Jairin. "Come on! We've got this—"

At that moment, a heart-stopping scream filled the chamber. "Eeeeeeeeeeeeeeeeeeeeeee!" *Crack! Crack!* The walls shook.

Jairin stopped, eyes wide. He was alone in the chamber—kind of. The watery creatures were gone. He looked around to find the source of the scream. He couldn't see anything in the chamber now except for the water and the statues. *Oh no!* Unlike the garden ones, these massive stone statues did not transform into flesh. They now flanked the sides of the exit, massive stone clubs in hand. Small chips and sand fell from their joints as they moved toward him. They trudged forward slowly and purposefully, blocking the exit. Jairin looked around. There was nowhere else to go except back to the steps. Watching their fists and clubs, he knew he had to somehow get around them or dodge between their legs to get out of here. One of the stone statues swung an immense rocky club at Jairin. The prince jumped aside, landing in the water with just his head breaking the surface. He thrust himself through the water toward the massive creature and smashed at the leg of the stone guardian with his glowing blue blade. There was a thunderous crack, but just a bit of rubble broke off the stone leg.

As he wondered how he could survive this, Jairin thought of his companions. Were they safe? Could they hear this? Why didn't they come back to help him? These giant stone statues were colossal and apparently unbreakable. Could this be the end? So close to reaching his goal, would he be crushed and broken by these colossal stone beasts in this wet and mildewed cavern? Finally, he wondered what his father would have said about his life, his quest, dragging his younger sister with him on this fool's errand. As he fought to get back on his feet, he saw the other stone statue swinging its club down on him. As Jairin tried to dive out of the way, he heard several loud cracks and felt an intense pain.

Then darkness took him.

"Rise, young one," the elderly monk said to the prince. Jairin looked up at the face of Benedict. The monk reached out his hand with a look of urgency on his face. He spoke again, "Take my hand and follow. You're not going to an eternal sleep here in this pool. Take my hand. Take my ha—"

"Take my hand!" Raven was yelling to her brother. Foggy-headed, Jairin grabbed her hand and rose to his feet. She held one of her short swords, most of the blade broken off. One stone guardian was bearing down on them while the other stood nearby, hand and forearm missing.

They scampered the last few steps through ever shallower water until they passed through the exit door. A loud, low rumble rang out from the guardians in the next room as they froze in place, out-of-position, no longer guarding the exit. Jairin exhaled as they emerged safely on the other side and he saw the backs of Arik and Berch. His relief didn't last. The lantern lay on the ground next to Berch, tipped over and shattered, with the oil light extinguished.

Jairin looked over at his sister. She, Arik, and Berch were staring at something to their left, in the center of the chamber. This must be what the guardians had been protecting. Jairin's skin again grew cold and his heart raced. All four now stood transfixed. Jairin's arm went numb and the grip of his sword hand loosened. Jairin nearly dropped the weapon, but then reflex kicked in and he clenched his grip with renewed strength.

24 Great Hall

Jairin slipped back a step and his blood ran cold. He'd known this clash was imminent, but nothing he'd done had prepared him for the shock of the moment. In a shaky voice, he named his foe. "Gestron!"

The dark figure towered over the raging cauldron, about three meters tall and black as night, even against the light of the enchanted fire. Great wings like a bat's were furled behind his back, tips thrusting another two meters above his head.

All four of the company stood frozen, transfixed.

Through the flames leaping from the cauldron, Jairin could see another massive demon beyond Gestron, among the host that stood in waiting. Jairin hadn't felt so small since he was a child. The last time he'd seen this demon, Gestron had crushed his father like a bag of dry twigs. Jairin clenched his teeth and pushed the memory of his father aside for now. Hatred and the desire for revenge would serve him, but could cause him to make mistakes. His fear might keep him alive. Jairin held his sword tight, the blade pulsing with an intense blue flame, like a living blue heart.

The arched ceiling towered over their head, but for Gestron it looked like a tight fit as it tapered to meet the rough-carved walls around the edges of the chamber. The moldy air filled the room with the nauseating stench of rot, sulfur, and decay.

The great demon stared them each down. Those transfixing eyes. Black pits in the center surrounded by a sea of yellow. He looked lastly at Jairin. The prince's mind ran away with doubt—*I shouldn't have come. I need to run.* The thoughts in his head weren't his own, but they hit him like a hammer all the same. He looked at Raven, Berch, and Arik. *I brought them here to their death. We aren't going to leave this place. This was an incredible mistake. How can we take on a terror of this size?*

As if just a glance induced panic, Gestron looked unassailable, invulnerable. The demon spoke, revealing sharp teeth the size of Jairin's hands. "You've been an inconvenience to me, human. At times I wished I hadn't spared you. Tell me, how does it feel to watch those you care for die before your eyes? I should like to know, as I'm going to do it again. When you see a titan of a man die before your eyes, watch the blood gush from his face and ears, do you feel scared, powerless, or just…small?"

Jairin felt like he was in the center of a swirling storm. Voices in his head screamed at him, *Leave them here. Save yourself. We're going to die.* He shook his head, "Argh! No!"

Jairin raised his sword, blue flame licking and hissing the length of the steel, sending electricity up through his sword arm. He tried to speak again. Nothing. He felt the energy running through his arm and it empowered him. "Why do you hide here in these caves? Are you a coward, Gestron? You retreat to your warm fire, depending on your minions to do what you can't. You grow fat spreading plague and fear among my people." *This is a waste of time. Drop the sword. Let him finish you off. No!*

Arik limped a step forward with his blade outstretched. The other colossal demon shook the cavern floor with a step toward him, hands erupting in flame as a smile grew on his face. Raven grabbed his other arm. "Don't. Wait for Jairin. Attacking them now would be suicidal." Arik stopped and retreated, releasing a deep breath.

Gestron turned his staunch gaze to the others, then returned to Jairin, snorting. "Your people? I looked for you when I saw fit. I'm very good at finding a mouse in a forest when I put my mind to it. You matter so little that it didn't even bother me that you eluded my gaze. I saw nobody who spoke for the insignificant humans of these lands. Where is the son of the mighty king when it really matters? I told you to tell everyone that I would sweep the lands like a great plague. Did you tell *anyone*? You're nothing but a disappointment, to me, to those you call 'your people', to your father. That's right, I know who you are. You're no prince. Who here is the coward?"

A scowl burned across Raven's face. "Those weren't just Jairin's people!" she yelled at the demon. "You've slaughtered hundreds. You destroyed the lives of thousands more. You're nothing but a pernicious swine!" Arik and Berch stood transfixed, listening to the exchange.

Gestron studied Raven, then turned back to Jairin and let out a hideous laugh. "Ha! This one has ten times the spirit you have, little prince. You should have given her the glowing stick. Ha ha!"

The prince glanced at his sister to see her pull something from her pack and draw her remaining short sword.

As Gestron laughed again, small bits of stone broke free from the walls around the chamber with the echo of his deep, throaty bellowing. "I hear you've been preparing to fight me. I find that most curious. You aren't half the man your father was, and I know you saw how that turned out. While I'd like to see this play out, I think I may just kill you and be done with it."

The voices in Jairin's head continued urging him. *Run!*

Jairin forced himself to pull back to center and take a deep breath. He recalled some of his training from the monks. *Think. Feel. Only then, do.* "You'll pay for what you've done. You'll pay for all of those innocent people you've killed. I will give them retribution."

The enormous demon snorted, bits of snot flying from his great nose. "I'm afraid your information is quite incorrect. While the shadows that serve me do bring disease and death, I have no need or desire to kill those who aren't in my way. They—I—feed on the fear and despair I bring upon my land. I get stronger feeding on the people and their life force. Nothing is gained by wantonly killing my own flock. I grow more powerful, expand, and cause more fear with every despot I keep alive."

Now Jairin was confused. Hundreds of people had gone missing since Gestron had appeared, not including those who had died of disease and plague.

Gestron stamped an enormous leg, moving closer to Jairin. "Are you going to destroy me today, little prince? Maybe slash me to pieces with your mighty blue stick?" The demon took a few steps toward Jairin, raising his arms toward the prince. "I'm finding this conversation very tiresome and unfulfilling."

Several demons around the far wall smiled and cheered on their leader. They didn't make a move to interfere. Berch, Arik, and Raven looked from one demon to the other, ready to spring.

Jairin quieted the chaotic voices in his head. He'd missed it before. *Gestron may have a weakness.* A new fire started burning in Jairin's core. *I chose this path. If I am going to die today, it will be on my feet and not like a coward.* "If you aren't powerful enough to kill all those missing people, maybe it was the work of your master?"

The demon stopped. "Aaarrrggghhh!" Gestron's face contorted in rage. He pulled his arms in, clenching his fists at his massive chest, and flexed a ferocious set of sinewy muscle. He whipped open his wings. The enormous full frame of the demon was now revealed in front of them, about five meters from wing tip to ground and from tip to tip. His massive black wings spread out like sails on a ship. The gust of wind from opening his wings fanned the arcane fire. In an ominous, booming voice, he spoke, shaking the walls of the cavern and the very ground on which they stood. "I am Dominus. I have no master!" His words echoed through the cavern. Demons on the far end of the cavern who had been listening intently now glanced around, eyes wide. Through the rumbling, the walls cracked, and more bits of stone fell to the floor. Gestron reached out and ripped away Jairin's sword by the blade with one hand.

Jairin stumbled back in surprise, hands empty. Gestron made a motion with his other arm. Like a rag doll, the prince was thrown without contact to the near wall and held in place by some invisible hand. Ten meters away now, Gestron still clung to Jairin's sword by the blue pulsing blade. Sparks fell to the ground from the enchanted weapon.

As Jairin struggled to release himself from the wall, Arik quickly scratched a Willem Ironroot in the floor and then hobbled, unaided, to Gestron's side. With a dying blue tint in the blade, Arik's sword arced through the air and struck Gestron in the back of his leg. It hit with an empty *thud*, like you would expect when swinging a sword at an oak tree. The demon was cut and he bled, as the light faded from Arik's sword.

Berch charged in, stabbing at the demon with his dagger. Gestron seemed to be ignoring both of them. His wings moved slightly, fanning the blaze in the cauldron and blowing smoky air around the cavern.

Unable to move from the chest down, Jairin fumbled to reach his pack, crushed between him and the cavern wall. The demon had his sword. Grasping it by its pulsing blue blade, Gestron seemed unfazed and certainly unharmed. Blue flame and sparks continued to fall from the cutting edges. The demon turned his attention to Arik and Berch. Thick, black blood trickled from several small slashes on each of the demon's legs as the pair continued their attack.

Jairin finally worked his arms free and retrieved the spell book and the wrapped mirror from the top of his backpack. He opened the small tome and found the page he'd dog-eared containing the spell of holding. He called out,

"tenere utas motum anasa rey munda de amei..."

Several words into the incantation, Gestron engaged with Jairin. "You're wasting your time." Without looking, the demon reached out a massive arm and picked up Berch by the shoulders, then tossed him in a heap across the chamber. Raven moved in next to Arik, taking the parum's place in the fight. She lashed out at Gestron with her short sword. Desperate to help his companions, Jairin continued reading the spell aloud. This was his only chance to contain this terror.

The other demons looked on with jeers and laughter. Gestron crunched up his hand into a fist and turned to Arik. He struck the horse rancher, knocking him back onto the floor. "Aaaaaagh!" Arik's yell and the thump of his body hitting the ground echoed through the chamber.

The demon turned back to Jairin. "You're a fool. You and your friends will die now for your infantile incursion into my lands." He held up Jairin's sword, still grasping it by the blade. The blue fiery heartbeat suddenly flicked off like a torch tossed in the water. Gestron laughed and the blade exploded into a pile of dust. Its body gone, the bladeless hilt fell to the ground with a hollow *tink* sound as Gestron continued his raucous laughter.

Jairin felt fear welling up in him again. *This won't work. I need to run. I'm going to die here today. No!* He continued his recitation out loud. Gestron scowled and again raised his arms and wings to full height. As Jairin reached the end of his incantation, Gestron's movements slowed to a snail's pace. He crouched, reaching for Jairin as his movement continued to slacken. He bared his monstrous teeth, uttering in slow motion, "Fooooooool!" then froze like a statue.

Free of the demon's hold, Jairin fell to his knees. The voices in his head ceased and the dread abated. He hoped he had maybe thirty seconds before Gestron broke free—probably less. He grabbed the wrapped package and hurriedly opened it. He felt the side facing up to see if it was the smooth glass side or the wooden backing side. Wood. There were precious few seconds left. With the wooden side facing him, Jairin held the object up in the face of the frozen demon. He yelled the command word, "Foresake!"

Nothing happened.

Jairin felt panic. *No, no, no…* He looked down at the mirror. It wasn't right. This was the wooden side. He flipped it over in his hand and saw the other side was just wood as well. He'd been tricked. The voices in his head started again. *Run! You're finished!* Gestron would soon be free and they would all be massacred. *Who would do this? Why? Was it Toff the crazy swamp man? Benedict? One of the other men from Glensong? It couldn't have been the men in Bravitleer—not Carmen's men. Rhobin! He was working for Gestron. Had I shared the plan with Rhobin? Berch?* Panic was setting in. His mind began running in all directions at once.

Jairin wasn't sure now, looking back. He had shared his plan with too many people. He looked back up at Gestron. A smile crept over the demon's face. Gestron began to relax his muscles and his appendages creaked back to life. He had broken free of the spell.

Another great four-armed demon was nearly upon Jairin. Based on his size and build, he appeared to be Gestron's third servus. The demon approached the prince with claws drawn, fire building in its fingers. Jairin broke out in a cold sweat. *This is it. These are my final moments. The mirror has failed.* His sword was destroyed, and he had been betrayed. He was going to die now in the tunnels where he'd played as a child. He glanced over to see Berch still in a heap on the other side of the cavern. Demons were hollering and cheering from across the cave. Raven was at Arik's side as he lay prone on the floor. Jairin backed up into the wall with a *thud* and the servus demon bore down on him with claws radiating flames. Jairin's chest ached as he felt his old wounds anew.

Gestron was free and lumbered toward the prince, claws out. The colossal demon smiled down at Jairin. "Now… you're done."

A yell rang out from behind the two gargantuan demons. "Forsake…!" It was a loud but calm voice, a strong voice, a woman's voice.

Gestron and his servus demon stopped and spun around. Raven held her short sword in one hand, dripping in black blood. The other arm was outstretched, holding the reflective end of the Mirror of Wills directly at Gestron.

"No, no, NO!" Gestron yelled. "Aaarrrrggghh!" His body warped and contorted as some unseen force pulled at him.

Raven dropped her short sword and held the mirror tightly with both hands. She grunted and looked over at her brother with a piercing, commanding expression. He looked back at her in disbelief, but maybe also in awe. "Jairin," she said, "remember my words this time. He was OUR father, this is OUR kingdom, this demon murdered OUR family. He forced us from OUR home, from OUR life."

Gestron struggled and writhed as he continued to be warped and squished. "Foolish mortals. No cage will hold me. I will make you suffer for this!" As he was compressed, light beamed from the mirror and struck his twisted frame.

A bright white glow emanated from the surface of the glass. The last of the demon's contorted form was pulled into the reflective face of the polished artifact, with the echo of his muffled screams trailing off into silence as the light faded.

The remaining servus demon stood motionless, for a moment, then exploded into a cloud of wet, black dust. In waves, several other demons at the far end of the cavern suffered the same fate. The rest of the minions, a dozen orcs, some large beetles, and various riff-raff, bolted through the archway back into the caverns.

Jairin, splattered in demon blood, fell back and landed on his backside. He was trying to figure out how events had unfolded this way. *Raven? Why?* Raven swayed back and forth, then collapsed to her knees. Clutching the mirror tightly, she let out a long breath and passed out on the cavern floor.

It made sense now. He suddenly realized how much he'd hurt her. For decades, he'd minimized everything she was going through. She had told him before, but he hadn't listened to her. He had made plans for Raven, for the kingdom, for their father's legacy, and for himself. He'd never even thought to ask what anyone else wanted. Raven, Arik, Zael—they'd put their lives in danger to help him. He'd planned to carry the weight of this demon for as long as it took to keep everyone else safe. He didn't need to do that anymore. It was a burden that was no longer his.

Arik opened his eyes and attempted to rise, falling back onto the floor. He spit out a big wad of the leaves he'd been chewing and jammed the last several leaves into their place in his back teeth. He wiped and sheathed his sword and dragged himself to Raven's side. "Raven..."

In the distance, Jairin heard a rumbling and the echoing of falling rock. He looked around nervously. "What's that?"

Berch slowly rose with a grunt. "Oh no! The water demons are gone. Whatever power Gestron used to keep this lair in its state just popped out of existence. We need to get out—now! This could be a catastrophe!"

The walls shook and rumbled as stalactites and broken rock fell from the cavern ceiling. Jairin yelled to Berch, "Help Arik! I've got my sister." Jairin stumbled across the handle of his destroyed sword on the ground, and picked it up. He ran to Raven and slid his arms under her neck and the small of her back, making sure the mirror was still clasped in her hands as he lifted her from the floor. He held her tight and trotted to the opening on the far side.

Berch helped Arik to his feet and wrapped an arm around his waist to give him support. The two hobbled after Jairin. The opening at the far end of the cavern appeared to lead to the outside. Rocks cracked as more and more pieces of wall and ceiling broke free and fell to the cavern floor.

Arik grunted with each step. "What happened? What happened to Raven? Is she alive?"

"Now!" Berch said. "We need to get out of here. It looks like she did something very foolish or very heroic. I don't know which yet. We'll get her to safety."

They ran through a deep rut that sloped down as they neared the exit. Sunlight stuck, blinding them, as they emerged from the cavern into the fresh air of daylight. Berch shielded his eyes, looking at the wide ledge they stood on. "Stay clear of the exit. Water is going to burst from the mouth of the cave at any moment, along with whatever's in its path."

It took a minute to get used to the sunlight. They were on an overlook with a well-worn path leading up and away along the side of the rocks. The scar forming the valley below was barren and stretched out as far as Jairin could see in both directions. The rumbling continued behind them, and the ground shook with the impact of massive stones against the cavern floor. He remembered now. The water had flowed here into a lake in the valley floor. The demons had stopped up the water flow and the lake had dried up.

"Hurry! We need to keep moving up this path," Berch said. "This ledge won't be safe for long." They raced up the path, putting several dozen meters between them and the cave exit as the rumbling and crashing amplified from inside.

With a great whoosh, water burst out the entrance to the cave and tumbled to the wasted scar below. The hole in the stone widened further as water spilled over the edge to form a gushing waterfall. Several orcs bobbed in the water as it tumbled over the edge. They screamed as the expanding torrent carried them off. The rumbling grew louder as the four companions scurried up the path away from the caverns below—one man carrying his sister and another hobbling on one good leg as he leaned on a halfling.

Arik spit out more of the juice from the leaves, mixed with some blood. "I'm exhausted and I hurt everywhere. I need to stop and rest." They arrived at a clearing with a small patch of grass, nestled into the rocks.

Jairin set his sister down and helped Arik off his feet to rest on some large rocks. Berch looked around the site. "There was a small fire here, very recently." He knelt down to examine the burned grasses. "This is odd. There's no charred wood and there are other burned plants scattered around."

Raven remained unconscious. The others ate rations with water from their waterskins. Not long after, Arik passed out. Berch tended to their sleeping companions, wiping brows and checking for fever. Jairin brushed away some animal droppings with his boot and looked over at Berch. "Rabbit poop. It's too bad we missed it. I'd have loved to cook up a rabbit. If it got us out of eating more of these salted rations, I'd even be open to eating one of Toff's…whatever it was."

By the time the suns had set, the river from the caverns had settled into a constant flow. The water danced on the rocks as it fell into the valley below. Jairin peered over the edge and couldn't help but smile. "Toff can rest easy now. We're finally emptying out all that water from his swamp." Exhausted, Jairin was the last to fall asleep to the soothing sounds of the returned waterfall that was cleansing decades of filth from the caverns behind them.

The next morning, they awoke and tended their wounds. Jairin took the last of their rations from his pack and split them up between Arik, Berch, and himself—leaving a portion for Raven, who was still in slumber.

Early in the afternoon, Raven finally awoke, complaining of terrible dreams and headaches. Jairin ran his hand through his sister's hair just above one ear. There was a streak of white where it had previously been all black. He said to her, "I won't pretend I'm okay with what you did. It was stupid—"

"You can fitching—"

"It was stupidly brave. And I'm so sorry—for everything. You weren't supposed to carry this burden, but you have my eternal gratitude."

"I have a stake in this."

"I know. It was wrong of me not to give you a larger part. I'm sorry."

Raven smiled. "Yes, you are."

She took out the mirror. "Look," she told her brother. The surface still had a shine, but it was no longer reflective. The background was like polished black marble. In the foreground they could see the image of Gestron, writhing and fuming with malice. He darted around the surface like a starving shark in a fishbowl. He looked hateful and vindictive.

Raven looked at her brother. "I can feel him. We can see each other's thoughts. He is constantly fighting to get out. It's going to be a struggle to keep him trapped in here."

Jairin nodded. "What you've done is the noblest act I've

ever seen—except for the part where you hid it from me."

"What can we do with the mirror?" Raven asked.

"You need to hang onto it for now. If it leaves your hands, Gestron could break free. I promise you I'll find an answer, even if I have to track down every sage and wizard on the entire continent to do it."

Raven looked back at her brother. "Gestron didn't do it. He did…part of it, but he wasn't directing the shadows that attacked Arik's village. He was summoned to our world. He didn't have any reason to kill so many people. He needed them alive."

Jairin sat next to his sister and put his arm around her. "I know. At the end, I figured it out. We'll fix this."

They finished off the water from Raven's waterskin as she ate her portion of the dry rations. Jairin bandaged Berch's chest to protect several broken ribs. With Berch, he checked the others for other injuries.

"What now?" Arik asked his companions.

"We need to get you healed," Jairin said. "We all need time to rest and regroup. But first, a man who's been a spectator of his own life for a very long time, has pressing business to take care of in Thadia."

Part II - Mirror Blind

25 Renewal

The bedraggled company trudged through the spongy grass. After several days of draining, the swamp now seemed like a distant memory to Jairin, but it was still a tedious journey. He timed his stride to match Arik and adjusted his grip on the horse rancher's waist between steps. "Are you okay? Do you need a break?"

Arik shook his head. "Let's catch up first." Berch and Raven had stopped about fifty meters ahead to wait. They were making slow progress on their trek back to Glensong, but at least they were out of the hills and back on level ground. After several minutes, they were gathered together again.

"I'm so tired," Raven said. While slower than before, she still kept a faster pace than Arik. She clung to the mirror at her side, not looking at it. "We've only been walking a few hours, but I don't know how much longer I can go on without resting. And my hair…" She ran her other hand through her locks, pulling them within her field of view. Wide swaths of white had taken over her mane in the past several days.

"Shhh!" Berch said. The guide turned east, shielding his eyes from the suns' rays. "There are horses approaching."

"I can't do this," Arik said. He grabbed the handle of his sword, pulling it from its scabbard. Turning his head, he spit out a mouthful of chewed leaves. Much to Arik's relief, Berch had sourced more Soulbloom leaves the previous day.

As the horses drew nearer, Berch turned back to the group. "No, it's okay. It's Bravitleer." Arik exhaled and dropped his sword arm.

The first of the horses was upon them a minute later. Jairin realized it was Carmen and Zael. His adopted daughter jumped down as the black horse came to a stop a few meters away. She ran to her father and threw her arms around him, crushing him in her embrace. He returned her affections with a tear in his eye.

Carmen dismounted, smiling. "Thank the stars you're okay!" Two more men rode up, wearing the familiar garb of the Bravitleer patrols, each leading a second riderless horse. Raven closed her eyes and dropped to her knees, clutching the mirror now with both hands.

Carmen's expression faded, "Oh no! Get her up on a horse!" She looked over at Jairin. "What happened?"

"She used the mirror on the demon. Arik's leg was injured quite badly, as well."

"Get her to Glensong!" Carmen ordered her men. "Load her on one of the extra horses, Arik on the other. Tell Barlemicus to fetch the healers. I'll escort Jairin and Berch." The guards rode ahead with their injured companions, while Carmen rode slowly to keep pace with the others on foot.

Jairin sat at Raven's bedside, where she was propped up on pillows. His sister had grown paler and weaker in the weeks since they'd arrived at Glensong. "It's going to be okay, Raven," he told her. "The builders have finished part of the temporary house at the lake. Enough that we can move you down there in a few days. You, me, and Zael. You'll be able to see the geese out of your window as you recover."

She smiled weakly back at her brother. "That will be wonderful. You've been a great help, Jairin, but I don't feel like I'm getting stronger. I've been up and about a little less each day. I tire so easily."

"Does he ever give you any peace?" he asked, looking at the mirror in his sister's clenched hand.

Raven shook her head. "I've got this. I just need to rest a little more. Don't worry about *me*. Have you asked her?"

"Not yet. She is coming tonight to see us. I'll ask her, I promise." Raven smiled, closing her eyes. In a minute, she fell back asleep.

Later that evening, Jairin and Carmen walked along the riverbank, where the twin waterfalls fell from the cliff into the river. He reached out and put his hand on her shoulder and she stopped, turning to him. He peered into her eyes, almost losing his nerve. "I just wanted you to know there are very few things I've ever needed. Things that would make my world whole."

Carmen smiled. "I told you before, you're not a 'Chosen One.' That Oracle was an old crackpot. You have your revenge now, though. You are a King, Jairin!"

"No, no. That's true. She probably was just a crazy old woman. That's not what I meant."

"What is it? Is something wrong?" She cocked her head and looked at him quizzically, resting a hand on his chest.

"I've heard there are many ways to be happy, and I had the great honor of finding my path many years ago. Life's demons and dragons rush through and thrust plans asunder, but never forever. I'm envisioning a forest that started with two trees, growing side by side, aging together and giving each other strength as their roots intertwine and dig into the soil beneath them. You deserve the very best in this world— someone who will push your boundaries and force you to find the pinnacle of your purpose. Someone who will be an equal partner in removing all of the barriers that stand before you."

Carmen stepped back, dropping her hand. She shook her head, covering her mouth as she whispered, "I, I…" Jairin pulled something from his pocket and got on one knee before the Master of Brivitleer Vale. Her eyes glossed over.

"I have loved you since childhood. Though I was ripped away, not one day passed that I didn't dream I was right here, with you, about to ask you this question. You are the better half of me—the fairer half—the half I could never live without. I've loved you vehemently and ferociously from the first day I met you and will until my last—and whatever comes beyond. Would you do me the honor of marrying me?"

Carmen wiped a tear with the back of her hand, looking in Jairin's eyes. "I'm honored by this, Jairin. You were the only boy who ever won my father's approval. You asked me this many years ago, and I told you I would. You made me the happiest girl in the world in those days. I need to be honest with you, though—I'm not the girl I was then. I rose through the ranks to be the first woman to ever lead Bravitleer, and it was only that much harder that I did it on my own.

"I intend to stay the Master of Bravitleer Vale. While you were gone, I was sought-after. Men young and old asked for my hand and I turned them all down. No less than the King of Rasheen promised to give me his kingdom upon my marriage to his son. But I loved the disheveled boy who drove me crazy and taught me how to run free and fight against the rules imposed on me when I felt they were unfair. I was going to marry that boy… and then I was told he was dead. Who are you?"

Jairin stood back up, ring still in hand. "Carmen, I—"

"No. Shut up. Who are you?" She asked, tears welling now in both eyes. "I spent weeks with Zael, talking with her about the stranger that saved her life and took her in as his own. And I see how you've cared for Raven. You also helped Arik heal and secured a place for him in my guard—the one place where he feels at home amongst my equines. You risked your own life to contain a demon, knowing the odds were against you. You are, without exception, the kindest, most loving, bravest man I have ever known. I loved the boy you were, but I love the man you are today so very much more. I intend to stay the Master of the Vale, but becoming the Queen of Tarquin is the highest honor anyone could have ever bestowed on me. Of course, I'll marry you, Jairin. I would marry you a dozen times over and be happier with each exchange of vows. All of my happiest days have you in them, and I need more of those like I need breath in my lungs." She threw her arms around Jairin in embrace. He wrapped his arms around her as well, letting go of hours of fear and tension—nearly dropping the ring he'd yet to put on her finger.

Two months later

Jairin fastened the last button on his shirt as he walked across his room to the window on the south wall. Peering out, he saw a small crew of workers already working in the early morning light. One man held a wooden stake in place as two more walked off paces to the west, holding a rope tied to the stake. Jairin could see Lake Tavril behind their temporary home, but the waterfalls and hills he'd known as a child were too far west to see from this point along the lake. He felt the chain on his neck to make sure the token was still in place, then left his room.

On the wall outside his room, Jairin passed a small shield he'd mounted on the wall, along with the handle of the sword Gestron had destroyed. He paused, looking at the hilt. He'd never intended to use the sword in that fight. Despite its lineage and ancient power, it was too fragile for that. It was a shame and now was ruined. He blamed himself for that.

He walked down the hall to Carmen's room and knocked on the door. He hated the pretense of having separate quarters, but he must keep up appearances even if everyone knew or suspected that it was only a formality. "Just a minute," she said. After a few moments, Carmen opened the door and peeked out. She looked at him with her bright green eyes and smiled. "Hey, good morning!" She wore a dress of deep blue, belted at the waist with a black cord, with a finer, matching cord adorning the neck and cuffs. Jairin decided she looked far less imposing without the robes and staff of her office in Bravitleer.

Jairin smiled. "You look as radiant as ever, my future queen."

She grabbed Jairin by the placket front of his shirt and pulled him through the doorway into the room and against the wall. After three months, this still felt new. He'd loved Carmen his whole life, but they had lost a lot of years. She grabbed him by the collar and pinned his shoulders against the wall. *Maybe she's just as imposing after all.* She leaned in and met his lips with hers.

Something had changed in Jairin. The world felt different. Carmen clearly saw a change as well. With Gestron contained, he'd been able to focus on building—building a kingdom, building diplomatic skills, and rebuilding a relationship with the woman he'd never stopped loving. Several moments later, Jairin gently urged her back, brushing her golden hair behind her shoulder. At that point he noticed that the cord at her neck was attached to a black cloak. Jairin smiled. "Remind me to talk with your tailor. He finds ways to make you look somehow even more stunning. I'd spend the day here with you, but I'm told there are emissaries returning today. Do you want to join me?"

"The honor would be mine, King Jairin," she replied with

an exaggerated smile and a curtsy.

He kissed her again and motioned for her to follow him to the receiving area. Carmen took several steps down the hall as Jairin admired the way her waist-length hair fell and moved against the back of her cloak. She turned and feigned a scoff. She'd caught him again. He knew he was neither sly nor inconspicuous, but he couldn't help it.

Carmen and Jairin stepped up on the dais and sat in a pair of oversized chairs behind a narrow table. Jairin opened a book on the table and checked that his pen and inkwell were ready.

A page entered the room. "Your Majesties… If it pleases the King and Queen Betrothed, the first sentry this morning approaches with word from Gresenbaad to the south."

Jacob, the newly appointed captain of the first guard, entered through the main door to the north. He approached the dais, brushing his brown hair out of his face. Two other guards entered shortly behind him, but Jacob didn't wait for them to arrive before speaking with the king. He stepped forward, handing a small scroll to Jairin. "Your Highnesses, please accept the report from the Council of Elders in Gresenbaad." He cleared his throat and continued. "The former Kingdom of Gresenbaad accepts your offer of protection and patronage. Their lands, having been devastated by the shadows of the demon who now has no name, will join Tarquin in banner. They swear fealty to King Jairin and Queen Betrothed Carmen in exchange for a regular patrol route by the king's troops, full rights and representation in court, three bestowable knighthoods, independent rights for a subject tax of local citizenry, and a noble title of Lord of Gresenbaad, to be bestowed upon Francis of Twight, current chair of the council."

Jairin nodded in agreement and opened the rolled paper. He signed the scroll in several places and set it aside for

Carmen. "As in Marax' day," Jairin said, "we happily bring the independent state of Gresenbaad back into the new united kingdom. Once papers are copied, I will send you the documents to bring back to Lord Francis. Thank you for your work, Captain Jacob. As always, I appreciate your service to your kingdom and to your King and Queen."

Jacob bowed. "My travels took me through the night. If it pleases your majesties, may I be relieved to rest?"

"Of course, of course. You are excused. Thank you, Captain Jacob."

After Jacob left, Carmen turned to her fiancé. "Is that nine lords now?"

"Ten."

"And the taxes?"

Jairin nodded. "My father concealed the location of his treasury. It's remained undisturbed since his death. We have some gold that should cover expenses for a while. The lords can recover their farms and markets for now with local taxes, and we can wait to levy the king's portion. We also have sprawling farmland for homesteaders, now that the great swamp is drained. I won't collect money from my people as they struggle to repair their homes and pay for food. Everyone is in need. The new borders are now twice what my father's kingdom ever entailed."

"Entailments are responsibilities," Carmen reminded him.

"Yes. More responsibility, and more resources to share. I need to travel to Retreol as well. I'd like to see if they intend to stay an independent city-state and at least discuss a trade alliance."

Through the morning, more messengers came and went with news from the nearby villages and the remnants of several other kingdoms to the south. There was little leadership in the region, and people had been living in fear, thirsting for someone to unite them. Poor farmers, ranchers, and tradesmen were all asking to join under the banner and protection of a king. Those who had lived through Marax' time professed a great love for their fallen king. Jairin hoped those feelings were transitive.

Troubling news came from Retreol, however. The wizard Madigan had constructed a new tower near the city walls of North Town and had been exerting his influence throughout the city. The city council had also seized Raven's home and property. Receiving the news, Jairin slumped in his chair. "Can you manage affairs here? I haven't checked on Raven yet this morning."

"Yes, of course. She's still fading, Jairin. We need to call the healer back."

"I'll send for him right after I check on her. I can't bear to see what she's been going through." He kissed Carmen and left the room.

Jairin walked down the hall past Carmen's room and several others. At the end of the hall, he stopped at Raven's door and rapped several times. Hearing his sister answer, "Who is it?" in a feeble voice, Jairin announced himself and let himself in. Along the wall opposite the door, Raven lay in bed, covered with a thick, stuffed quilt.

Jairin sat next to his sister on the bed and looked into her ashen face. Her once-black hair had lost nearly all of its color and now looked like that of a crone. He hugged her gently for several moments, turning his face to hide his deflated expression. He'd watched her grow weaker each passing day. "Raven—"

She waved her hand. "Katherine," she said, in a weak and trembling voice. "I've been a raven since I was smaller than I can even remember. But that nickname doesn't fit anymore. For whatever time I have left in life, I'll be content just being myself."

"My dear, can I bring you anything—food, something to drink?"

His sister shook her head. "No thank you. The kitchen attendant was here an hour ago."

"Katherine," Jairin said, "you know we'll find a way to cure this. We didn't go to all that effort to capture the demon just so he could consume your spirit and be free again."

Raven's expression drifted as she studied her brother's face before speaking. "He's wondering why you no longer call him Gestron. Did you know that isn't even his true name?"

"I don't care. I really don't."

"He was given that name when he was summoned. His actual name in the common tongue is…" She mouthed a long string of what sounded like gibberish to Jairin.

"He talks to me," his sister said, "inside my head, all the time. He has all kinds of new names for you, dear brother. He hates all of us. He has a special hatred for you."

"It would surprise me if he didn't."

Raven tipped her head, not breaking her gaze with Jairin. "You're keeping something from me. Something important."

There was a knock at the door. Zael entered. She signed to her adoptive father and Raven. *I'm here to check on my aunt.*

A small smile crept across Raven's face. "I've told you before, you're my sister. Though I suppose now, I don't much fit the part. Come here!"

Raven gave Zael a weak embrace, holding her close.

"Arik is coming back tomorrow," Jairin said. "He's been on patrol in Bravitleer for the past several days, but I got word he's coming to meet us here tomorrow."

Raven nodded. "That will be nice, though I doubt he'd want to spend time with an old hag such as I am."

Jairin gave Raven and Zael the news from the morning messengers. New lords, new lands, and new knights. He left out news from Retreol. In Raven's state, he wanted to keep ill tidings from her. After, Jairin excused himself from Raven's room and left her in Zael's company. He made his way outside to the stables.

One of the castle guards was going through morning patrol plans with his men. Jairin approached him. "Can you spare a messenger to find the wizard Azil?"

"Sire?" the guard asked.

"I have need of the wizard Azil," Jairin said. "Find Barlemicus in Tower Glensong. He knows where to find him. Azil was here several months ago when Raven first lost her mobility. She's weakening and I don't know how much longer she'll live. We need him again, with all haste!"

"Yes, Your Highness." He jumped on a horse and rode off to the west.

26 Silence Revisited

Benedict made his way down the long hallway with Vruthian. The elder monk thought Vruthian looked much more at ease than at their last meeting over a year ago. Benedict carried a lantern, which lit the hallway in the catacombs beneath the monastery as they walked. Here, beneath the surface of the ground, there were no torches or permanent lights mounted on the walls. Vruthian had arrived earlier that evening, to the surprise of the monks. Since Jairin was no longer with the order, the senior monks didn't have to hide the wizards with visits in the night. Vruthian seemed to prefer night visits anyway, arriving unannounced with a hood shrouding his face at the door.

"We're honored by your visit, Vruthian," Benedict said. "How is our benefactor?"

The wizard's apprentice nodded. "Tannis is well. I think after so many years, he's anxious for me to be on my own. The rules of the Kalari don't allow him to sit on the council while he has an apprentice. I think he misses the power."

"Are you as anxious?"

"It's been a long time coming. After my testing, I told him I'd stay on to oversee construction here at this monastery. Tannis has taught me everything he intends to teach me. The

Kalari values this monastery and the grounds it's built on. It's been an honor to watch events unfold. Oh—Jairin will be coming soon."

"Here?" Benedict asked.

"We expect he'll come to Barrington, but if he comes here first, guide him our way. The Kalari want him, so it's been left to Tannis."

"Of course," Benedict said. "Jairin has always been as one of my own. Are they intending to train him?"

"I doubt it. It sounded like they need something he carries, or more accurately, something he *will* carry. That's all I've heard from Tannis."

Benedict tugged at his short beard. "Besides sending Jairin your way, what do you need from our order? The monks are growing nervous with the shortage of information from you and from Tannis. What's planned for us?"

Vruthian stopped and looked up at the elder monk. "Now we come to it. Here is what I can tell you. Continue searching out the ancient books. The library we're building here was specifically requested by the Kalari, and it must remain secret."

"I understand, but can you share any of the grander picture? Why are we building a library of books, most of which none of us can read?"

"The books are ancient histories and a few books of magic."

"Is this for Jairin?" Benedict asked.

"No. Jairin is a bright man, but he doesn't seem to have any talents indicating he'd be a good practitioner of magic. Tannis said he'd considered Jairin many years ago. There are strong ties to magic in his family, but they seem to attach only to the women. While anyone can learn magic, wizards look for the best candidates. Jairin isn't one of them."

Benedict nodded. "What is the library for, then?"

Vruthian shook his head, "I don't know. I assume the

Kalari haven't shared that with Tannis either, so we play our part and do what's asked of us." He pulled a sheet of folded paper from his pocket and handed it to Benedict. "Construction plans for an addition to the monastery. The builders will start arriving on site in a week's time.

"Tannis will continue to provide some gold to pay expenses. If you need any more supplies, you have only to ask when I return at the end of the season. Most importantly, if Jairin or an emissary from his court arrives to offer protection of the King, you are to reject whatever offer he presents. This monastery must neither become entangled in commoner politics nor become subject to a commoner king. If there are any objections, send them to Tannis."

Benedict nodded again, and they resumed their earlier pace. "Tell Tannis he has our continued thanks. We've only asked for a safe place for quiet reflection and to search for knowledge. He has brought that to fruition."

"It's symbiotic," Vruthian said. "You work to help the Kalari, and the Kalari help you in return. We all get what we want."

Benedict attached the handle of the lantern to a hook in the wall. He opened the unassuming double doors at the end of the hallway, revealing darkness beyond. He picked the lantern back up and held it into the darkness, lighting the way beyond. In the space ahead, they looked into a natural cavern with a rough stairway carved into the cavern wall, descending to the bottom. Tool marks showed where people had labored to straighten the cavern walls in several places. Row after row of free-standing shelves filled the room, enough to hold thousands of tomes. Most of the shelves were still empty, but Benedict looked at those that were full. Books had been found and cataloged every few weeks for the past decade. "As you'd requested," the elder monk said, "we've set out small buckets of rice in each row to control the humidity."

Vruthian nodded. "Most of these works won't need it, but it's better to be safe."

Benedict again hung the lantern and unfolded the papers from Vruthian. Construction notes. He raised an eyebrow and rotated the first page, reading it. The image at the base was their familiar monastery, but something new had been drawn out in the center—in great detail. "The Tower of Midnight? This is an ambitious building project. You've assured us you will have a place for my brothers to stay on here. Once the Kalari have finished construction on this tower and the support structures, is the plan still unchanged?"

"Unchanged," Vruthian said, "You have my word. I have explicitly been told that all of your Brothership are to stay on after construction. Your order will support the tower. The tower will ensure the continuation of your order."

"Can I tell them what we're building?"

"No. Nobody needs to know anything yet."

"What is the Tower of Midnight for?"

"I don't know. I don't think Tannis knows, either."

27 A Journey For Raven

The wizard arrived the next day. As he examined Raven in her room, Jairin embraced Carmen in the hallway. "If anyone can help her, it's Azil."

After what felt like hours, the wizard reappeared from Raven's bedroom. He wore plain clothes of a very unassuming green and brown, with a grim expression on his face as he walked toward them.

"You must be able to do something. What can we do?" Carmen asked. She wiped a tear from her cheek with her sleeve.

The healer pursed his lips. "She'll live for now. She's unusually strong. As a diviner, I'm particularly skilled in healing arts. I can determine what someone needs with just a touch. Every living thing has a life force, an essence, that replenishes over time. Like a pitcher of water, we take from the pitcher and the pitcher is refilled so it doesn't run out. The demon bound to the Mirror of Wills she carries is stealing water from her pitcher. Because of this, her essence is drained faster than it refills. She's contained him by keeping the mirror under her control, but he's fantastically powerful and needs to be sent back to where he came from. If not, she'll die within a fortnight. For now, I can only make her more comfortable."

"Do whatever you can, Jairin. We need to make this right," Carmen said. "Please excuse me. I'm going to sit with Zael in Raven's room to keep her company." She walked down the hallway.

Azil looked in Jairin's eyes. "It wasn't long ago I treated you, King Jairin. Your sister stayed at your side for days, not knowing if you'd survive. Now it's she who is in trouble. Her physical wounds have healed over, but this demon, he's in her head. Awake or asleep, she has no rest from him. He has changed her as well. I don't know exactly what she can do, but I sense that she is learning to read something from people. It no doubt is a side effect from close contact with an overwhelming magic."

Jairin wringed his hands. "This was never her burden. She sacrificed herself to show me something I couldn't see. I promised her I'd make this right—that I would save her. What must I do to banish this demon?

The wizard's eyes widened. "You have no idea what you're asking. It would take an enormous amount of power from a wizard trained in demon-summoning to banish one back to where the souls of demons are forged."

"So how do I convince a wizard to do this for me?"

Azil thought for a moment, "The Kalari wizards are a political body. They decided ages ago that Gestron—"

"The demon has no name."

"Very well. The wizard who summoned this demon maintained it with their own power, until your sister ensnared him in the mirror. That wizard was an outsider. Despite the damage this wizard and the demon caused, the Kalari didn't get involved. The council has an agreement to neither aid nor hinder wizards outside their order. It's one of their highest laws."

"I don't answer to any wizard councils or orders," Jairin said.

"Think what you will, King Jairin. The council cares very little for the affairs of the people that share their land. They're in a circle of their own, with rules independent of governors or kings or emperors in your lands. They look upon men, dwarves, elves, and even dragons as mere resources to fulfill their proclaimed higher calling."

Jairin tipped his head. "But aren't you a member of the order?"

Azil smiled. "Yes, but I am greatly removed from such politics. I leave such efforts to wizards with a lust for prestige and power. I answer to the leader of my order of diviners and to the Archmage of the Kalari. While I am bound by their decisions, I'm not a part of the process to create them."

"Are you also barred from helping me rid the world of this demon, then?" Jairin asked.

"That's true, and I won't go against the orders of the Kalari."

"With the council deciding not to help us, how do I get the power I need to do this?"

"You need magic," Azil said, "and there's no way around it that I can think of."

Jairin's squinted, scratching his chin. "Who summoned this demon?"

Azil smiled. "Ah, the direct question. Now you're on the right path." He took a long breath. "I can't tell you, but I think you already know."

"And would the summoner have the power to banish this beast?"

"Yes. I can't tell you more. Seek out the wizards in Barrington. You'll find help and guidance there. But be careful how you approach them. These are Kalari wizards, and they know who you are and why you've come."

"Will you come back to check on my sister again? In a few days?"

"I will. The best we can hope for is that her condition will be unchanged. Her spirit will continue to weaken until one day she will just fade away. When that happens, the demon will be freed."

Jairin lowered his head. This wasn't any easier to hear the tenth time as it had been the first. If they didn't figure out a way to banish the demon, Raven would die.

Later that evening, as they walked back to their chambers after their meal, Carmen spoke to her fiancé. "You were a world away at dinner. What's on your mind? Raven?"

Jairin nodded. "She's going to die if I can't help her. After being apart for so many years, there's nothing I want more than to be home, with you, but I need some answers. Azil said to go to Barrington. It will probably be a few days in the city, and a few days to travel."

"What's in Barrington?" Carmen asked.

"I don't know yet. I need to talk to the wizards there. For once, I don't have a plan for anything."

She put her hand on his cheek. "Tomorrow is the celebration for setting the cornerstone. Can you stay just to make the announcement?"

"A fortnight. Azil said if she can hold out, she may have only a few weeks left to live."

Carmen's gaze softened as she exhaled. "I love your sister. I couldn't bear to see anything happen to either of you two." She put her arms around his neck, hugging him. "Get some sleep tonight. Tomorrow, ride like the wind. Save Raven."

Jairin tightened his embrace. "Arik should return tomorrow. Keep him here until I return. I'll have need of him again after I've met with the wizards. One last quest."

Carmen nodded.

Jairin arose with the suns and had the stablemaster ready a gray horse with saddle, bags, and some provisions. He took his pack and mounted it on the back of the saddle. He told the stablemaster, "I'll be back in four or five days. Have a carriage ready here with fresh horses and another set of horses for a changeover at Thadia."

The stablemaster tipped his head. "Aye, Your Majesty."

Jairin rode off quietly to the northeast with a new sword at his waist. He urged his gray horse into a fast trot and made his way alone toward the city of Barrington. He estimated he could arrive at the river by tonight to camp there and then enter the city tomorrow.

28 Castle Rising

Carmen awoke with rays of the early morning sun shining through her window. Her view of the lake beyond was much the same as Jairin's, next door. She looked through her wardrobe and pulled out a gray dress, donning it. Carmen buttoned it up and swirled in front of the long mirror by her bedside. It flowed cleanly over her figure, form-fitting, but not inappropriately so. She tightened the waist cord and emerged from her room. Raven's door was open at the end of the hallway, so she made her way down there first. She knocked lightly before stepping inside.

Arik was asleep in an oversized chair next to Raven's bed. She insisted that everyone keep her drapes closed, choking out the sunlight beckoning at the other side of the glass. Carmen shook Arik by the shoulder, waking him. "Good morning, Arik. Are you free today?" she asked, in a whisper.

He smiled back at Carmen. "Yes, Milady. I'm off today, but tomorrow evening I am on watch here at the castle grounds."

"Ah, good. And I'm Carmen," the Queen Betrothed said. "If you insist on this formality when we're in private, I'm going to have to have you flogged." She winked. "How's your leg?"

Arik raised his healing leg with a chuckle. "Well, it's not going to rain today. I can tell you that much."

"That's good to hear. Has Raven been sleeping long?"

"She finally fell asleep about an hour ago," Arik said. "The sun was already rising." He rose and kissed Raven on the forehead.

Carmen nodded. "She gets so little sleep. Jairin has ridden to Barrington to speak with the wizards."

"Has he already gone?"

"Yes, he was leaving at first light."

"Drat. I'd have loved to go with him. I've never been to Barrington."

"You know, I don't think Jairin has either." Carmen turned to leave the room. "Come with me." After they exited, she pulled the door closed behind them. They made their way down the hall to the throne room of the temporary residence.

Several assistants waited there for Carmen, bowing as she approached. "Good morning, Your Highness." The offered her counsel on how and where to stand at the ceremony, which way to walk to the table with the cornerstone, and other details for the morning event.

"You're very popular this morning, my Queen," Jairin said.

She nodded. "This is one day I'd have preferred Jairin be here. I find myself asking if I could get away with stealing a horse and riding off into the fields to be alone. This is important, though. With Jairin gone, it's even more vital that I be present for our people."

Carmen raised her arm to catch the attention of one of her maids. "Can you fetch the stablemaster to the dais at his earliest availability?" The young woman nodded and disappeared around the corner. The queen sat in her chair on the dais and looked over to Arik who stood nearby, looking lost in thought.

"Jairin said to keep you at the ready," she said.

Arik looked up. "Your Highness?"

"He'll be back at the end of the week—four or five days, he said. He wants you to go with him when he returns, but I don't know where he's planning to go." Arik nodded, his face brightening.

Several minutes later, a middle-aged man with a reddish complexion entered the chamber. Carmen recognized Ridgeway, the stablemaster, right away. He brushed the dust from his overalls and bowed. "You summoned me, Your Highness?" There was no disguising the smell of horses and feed emanating from his work clothes.

She missed her patrols on horseback. *Never let them take you away from your horse riding*, she reminded herself. "I trust you saw Jairin and his guard off this morning when he left for Barrington?" she asked.

Ridgeway looked a bit confused. "Aye, Milady. He was alone though, he was. His Highness didn't take any guard with him."

Carmen felt concerned, although she wasn't surprised that he'd ride off on his own. He thought himself to be invulnerable, and had it not been essential to save his sister, she would have vehemently protested to his going at all. "You are quite certain that he went without escort?"

"Quite so, My Queen—bit, bridle, saddle, pack, and naught else."

"Very well," she replied, "Thank you, Ridgeway." Carmen dismissed him and walked down the hall and out the main entrance with Arik. She heard a fervor of voices coming from the water's edge. As they rounded the corner, she saw a crowd gathered.

A hundred men and women had congregated at the lake —farmers, merchants, tradesmen, stonemasons, and others. On a small wooden table, Carmen studied a parchment with a drawing of the layout for the new castle. The stone building was designed to sit on the edge of the lake with posts set deep into the ground to keep the footings solid. There would be two levels, topped by ramparts.

Carmen looked over the design, drawn up by engineers from Gravine in the new south lands. The design mapped out two kitchens, two ballrooms, a throne room, stables, and other spaces with a central courtyard. There were to be twelve bedrooms in the top level, with those on the south side overlooking the lake. It was far larger, though not as tall, as the old castle on the cliffside. It would be elegant and functional, but not the grandiose monstrosity that was the castle at Barrington or Rivensveer to the north. They had agreed that it should be in the center of the valley, near the lake, with views of the falls and the plains. It would stand here to be a monument to the new kingdom and a reminder of the accessibility of the king and queen and the justice that would be given out in the land after so many years of lawlessness. The name plate at the top of the parchment read "Berylsmoor."

The crowd cheered at Carmen's approach. They had known her as the Master of Bravitleer Vale for many years. She was compassionate and loved, perhaps even more than Jairin. Carmen accepted the cornerstone from the master stone mason and held it aloft to reveal the name carved into its mass. Many of the assembled citizens pointed to the stone and looked to each other, murmuring. "Some of you may have known my father. Beryl of Gantry was a strong man, a loving man, a brilliant businessman, and a merchant's guild master. He would be very proud that we are dedicating Castle Berylsmoor in his honor. No man was ever good enough for his little girl, save one. Jairin was the only man to ever receive that blessing from him. My father wouldn't have approved of anyone less than a king for his daughter. Today we look to a time of renewed hope, a time of growth, a time of wealth, and a time of endless possibilities. King Jairin was called away today on urgent business, but he and

I will be wed in four months' time…maybe three. Go out this afternoon and celebrate. Fill the pubs and fill the dancehalls. The king and I will pay the tabs for the food and drinks ordered at the tables within our borders in celebration of this day."

A louder roar ran through the crowd at the proclamation. Carmen turned to Arik, next to her. "We'll have to teach the people, high and low alike, to read and write."

Arik smiled back. "Yes, My Queen."

Carmen adjusted her dress again. "Oh, and Arik…"

"Yes, My Queen?"

"I think we need to bump up the wedding a few weeks."

"Okay," Arik replied. He stood there for a moment, at first looking confused, then his eyes widened. He turned back to Carmen, but she had already walked away with the cornerstone.

Carmen carried the small cornerstone to a spot roped off near the lake. The stone would mark the southeast corner of the new castle. Ropes extended near ground level to mark the outline of the new footings. The crowd clapped as she set the stone in place. Two stone masons passed by Carmen, bowing, carrying trade tools to the cornerstone. She nodded in kind and walked into the crowd to greet those who had taken the time to come and mark the occasion. Back at the planning table, more design engineers came with detailed plans for digging and setting pipes for water catchment and exchange to the lake. Dozens of men were now gathering to begin digging and laying the stonework for the footings. With an initial team of five engineers, ten stonemasons, five carpenters, a dozen laborers, and a handful of runners, the project was starting today. It was the first major construction project in the forming kingdom, lending greatly to the chances of prosperity in the new kingdom—and to the new King and Queen of Tarquin.

29 The Quiet River and the Noisy City

Jairin pulled gently on the reins. "Whoa. Good boy. Let's take a rest." For the past hour, they'd been following a tributary to the northeast that would eventually join up with the much larger Montamar River that ran from Retreol in the west to the coast. He jumped down from his horse and led it to the edge of the water to drink and graze on the late-summer grasses. He took a few swigs from his waterskin and refilled it in the stream before rummaging through his pack for his dinner. The suns were now low in the sky and it would soon be time to camp for the evening.

He was about eight hours ride from Barrington, so he planned to ride a while tonight while the light allowed. Having never been to Barrington before, Jairin had no idea what to expect or even how he was supposed to find any wizards there. He figured he'd just look for something that appeared magical and see where that led him. It was just one more detail he wished he had asked Azil when he had the chance, but he was too focused on his sister's deteriorating condition.

A rustling sound arose from the knee-high grass behind

Jairin. He spun, dropping his waterskin, and reached for the handle of his sword. The grass was still. He pulled out his sword, checking to see if the blade glowed—only then remembering he couldn't do that anymore. He brushed through the foliage with the tip of his sword. Still nothing. Why did he keep feeling someone was watching him? It was unnerving and irritating. Several times today, he thought he'd seen eyes staring at him from the shadows. He didn't trust magic, and he didn't like what little he'd seen of it so far. Several tense minutes passed as he made a few more passes with his sword in the grass. He found nothing but a terrified-looking muskrat that bolted for the water when his cover was blown. He put away his sword and retrieved his waterskin, finally content to sit and eat dinner.

He rode on for several more hours, following the water. The sense of being watched had eased. He could hear the roar of the larger river ahead and decided to camp there for the night, beyond sight of anyone on the river. He found a grouping of trees that would offer some natural cover and a place to hitch his horse. Taking out his bedroll, he set up camp. As he fell asleep, watching the sky, a small white light streaked across the sky. Star flares in the night sky were a good omen.

In the morning, Jairin ate and tended to his horse. The Montamar ahead was now visible in the early morning light. He mounted up and urged his horse forward the last hundred meters to where the tributary merged into the main body. The roaring river was deafening at first, but once he had traveled east with it for several kilometers, it became familiar and he could tune it out. Jairin passed several tradesmen with two-horse carts headed to Retreol and other cities in the west as the harvest season was coming into full swing. Though friendly waves were exchanged, no one stopped to exchange pleasantries. The roar of the water would have made conversation difficult anyway. Several boats also passed by, headed east toward Barrington. Jairin was glad to be on horseback this time. He smiled, recalling his last boat trip into Retreol. It hadn't ended the way he'd hoped, but it was an experience he wouldn't forget.

In the late afternoon, Jairin could feel the sea air coming from the east. He had arrived at the walled estuary city of Barrington. The whole of Tarquin, even if you include the roughly ten thousand residents of Retreol, was less than thirty thousand people. Barrington, the capital of the Kingdom of Rasheen, had about fifty thousand residents just within its walls. His father had brokered an uneasy peace with the King of Rasheen. It was an agreement Jairin hoped to one day renew.

The river now ran much more quietly and turned north, entering the city through an open pair of large steel gates. He could see several guards on the ramparts making rounds to watch over the people and carts coming in and out of Barrington's south gate. Jairin approached the guard post at the road gate of the sprawling city. The wardens wore green and orange, the colors of the king. Two of them looked Jairin up and down as he dismounted from his horse, but Jairin walked past and they seemed to pay him no further attention as he entered the city.

He looked around and suddenly felt insignificant. The city was vaster than he had ever imagined. One- and two-story buildings stretched out as far as the eye could see, a great maze of wood and stone construction. In the distance, he spotted a hill rising above the rest of the city with a large complex perched atop. An official meeting with King Ferris would need to be set for another time, preferably when he could bring an entourage and could represent the populated cities of his lands with unified authority. Barrington was known far and wide as a great seaport, but Jairin couldn't see the docks or the sea from here. He found a stable near the gate and checked in his horse. In exchange for three silver coins, they gave him a numbered token. He thanked the stable hostler and turned back to the street. Flipping the coin, he looked at the marking: 2033. He'd need this to claim his horse when he left the city for home. Jairin put the coin in his pocket and then checked the chain on his neck to make sure his other token was still there. Yes.

He walked down the first large street he came across. A sign on a corner building read Canton Arch Way – 7200, which seemed to represent the street name and the section he was walking through. He passed a candle store, a dressmaker, a few stores selling boating and construction supplies, and a weapons exchange of some kind. The city grew louder as he walked farther into the town center. Ahead he heard the familiar sound of musicians and laughter. Such merriment often accompanied drinking and gossip and was just what Jairin was looking for. Someone must know where he could find the Kalari wizards, or at least could point him to someone who did.

30 Vextagan's

The establishment ahead of Jairin looked grand from the entrance on Canton Arch Way. Two burly guards stood on either side of the front door, but they didn't appear to be checking people for weapons. The one to the left, who looked like he'd just finished a fine lunch of nails and rocks, was the type of guard you would expect at an establishment that was used to dealing with trouble. The other was a bit smaller, but very well armed. He had broadswords in scabbards on both hips and a bow and spiked club somehow attached at his shoulders. Jairin thought the guard looked a bit silly with all of the weaponry, but the large scar running the length of his face indicated that he'd been in at least one serious fight and had come back to work this door. He wondered if this guard had won the skirmish that had bestowed him with such a memorable facial trophy. Either way, Jairin didn't want to get on his bad side either.

From inside he could hear minstrels playing the duet version of "David's Path." The song was comical, but apparently very difficult to play. A fancy sign above the door read Vextagan Rathaway Saloon. Jairin entered the establishment and looked around, surveying the crowd. The air was thick with smoke from pipes and hand-rolled smokable items. Through the gray haze, he could see a stage along one side of the common room where two men sat, still playing the song he'd heard from the street, on some type of lutes. It sounded enchanting for a comical song, seeming strangely appropriate for the gathered crowd.

A provocatively dressed, middle-aged woman approached Jairin, speaking with a bit of a rasp. "Would you care to buy a young lady a drink?" Her brownish blond hair, cleanly braided, fell down the back of what looked like an expensive blouse. The strings on her blouse strained to stop her breasts from breaking free. She arched her back, pushing them even further out. This one is trouble, he thought.

Jairin looked around at the crowd, hoping to find an excuse to leave the conversation. "I'm sorry. I'm looking for someone."

The woman smiled at Jairin. "You've definitely found someone. I'm Madeline." She extended her hand toward Jairin's chest.

He intercepted her and shook her hand, casually. Looking around again, Jairin saw a group of men halfway to the stage talking and drinking around a table. "Aha," he said, nodding to Madeline. "Those are my friends. It was a pleasure to meet you, but I need to be on my way."

Jairin walked to the table of men drinking. Between the three of them, they had two empty pitchers and three large mugs in various states of fill. Several large shells from what looked like clams lay strewn around the table amongst coins and playing cards.

"No!" one of the men huffed to Jairin as he approached the table. "We're playing Mollusk. It's for three men and we're full up. Unless you're here to fill the pitchers, off with ya!"

Jairin introduced himself. "I don't want to interrupt your game. Just smile like you know me, and I'll buy the next few rounds. I'm looking for some information."

The man who'd initially scolded Jairin smiled. "Well, then that's a different story! I'm Franklin." He dipped his head. "Franklin, the Tailor of Lumbard. This is Wylen and Robbis," he said, pointing to the others. "We're in the District of Stars Clothiers' Guild, in the service of King Ferris." Franklin pulled out a chair and motioned for Jairin to sit. "It looks like there may be an extra chair after all."

"Save my spot," Jairin said, picking up the pitchers. "I'll get these filled. Is it a particular brew you're drinking?"

Wylen looked at Robbis and then back at Jairin with a smirk. "Yeah. We've got the one that goes in kind of brown and comes out yellow! Har, har har…"

"Okay, I got it." Jairin smiled back and went to the bar, returning several minutes later with two full pitchers and another mug.

His new friends continued with their game of Mollusk, exchanging cards and moving shells. Jairin didn't know how the game worked, but there was beer involved, and beer always seemed to put people in a chattier mood. He filled his mug and took a swig, watching the game for several rounds as he tried with some success to figure out how the game worked.

Jairin drank another swig and set down his beer. "I'm trying to find the Kalari."

Robbis looked up from his cards at Jairin. "I don't have one."

Franklin said, "Hmm. Well, as robemaker for King Ferris —"

Wylen and Robbis both rolled their eyes. "Oh, not this again," Wylen said. "You are not the royal clothier. Your brother is the one who makes the robes."

"Well, it's my whole family, isn't it?" Franklin said. "You know as good as any that my brother and I both work directly with the royal family."

"Okay, okay," Jairin replied with a smile. "The Kalari isn't an object. They're wizards."

"There's no wizard guild in the District of Stars. I know that much," Robbis said.

Jairin shook his head. "I don't think they're a guild. I'm looking for some wizards here in Barrington. I was sent to find them. I'm just hoping for a shove in the right direction." He picked up his mug for another swig.

"Hmm, let me think," Franklin said. He tipped his head and nodded a few times, staring off into the distance and muttering under his breath. "Rodwen? Kalispell? Darvish? Yep." He looked back at Jairin. "Darvish and Mutton. There's a place on the corner of Darvish and Mutton in the District of Flame. I believe there are wizards there." He picked up his mug and poured the last of its contents into his mouth.

Jairin stood and grabbed one of the pitchers that had been nearly emptied during the course of playing, pouring the last of it into the other pitcher. "A deal's a deal. I said I'd pick up a few rounds." He walked off to the bar and again returned with two full pitchers filled for the clothiers and himself.

After another hour, Jairin started to feel tired. He needed a place to spend the night—somewhere with a warm bed to sleep in. He made his way to the front door, making sure to avoid Madeline, but there was no sign of her. He left Vextagan's and found a moderately quiet inn a few blocks down Canton. For five silver, they gave him private quarters with a promise of breakfast in the morning and a plush bed with soft sheets, woven blanket, comfortably stuffed mattress, and down-feather pillow. It was much more relaxing than the bedroll on the ground last night, but he missed his view of the clear night sky above dotted with white stars. He lay down to sleep on the bed and moments later heard the crier outside, "Evening lamp check. All is well in the city of our honorable King Ferris." Not long after, he was asleep.

Jairin's face was bathed in the morning sunlight as it broke through his window. He dressed and went downstairs and found the small dining area behind the entryway. He was treated with a serving of fresh fruits and cheeses, some hard bread, fruit juice, and fried potato patty. After a good serving, he left and walked back out into Canton Arch Way.

Several short conversations pointed him to the District of Flame, at the western edge of the walled city. He walked uphill most of the morning away from the sea docks. As he continued, he could catch glimpses of the port far to the east. Barrington was the largest seaport for hundreds of kilometers in any direction. It was nestled where the tributaries of the Montamar River met the Aolian Sea.

As Jairin left the District of Stars and entered the hilltop District of Flame, the pace of the city changed. Signs overhead that had been identified as numbers prefixed with "S" were now replaced with an "F." A bustling commercial area gave way to an industrial working area. He passed an immense ironworks where raw metals were melted down into bricks of steel and other valuable metals. The workers here, covered in sweat, had big shoulders and muscled arms, the type of men you would expect to be wielding massive hammers and pushing crucibles around. It looked like a small army of blacksmiths carrying out specific tasks in a long line of production. The air here smelled like sulfur, burning wood, and sweat. Jairin passed a weaver, some book setters, and what looked like a thatcher's guildhall. Eventually, he came across a Mutton Hall Lane running north and south.

Jairin asked a few of the workers in the street for directions to a street called Darvish. "'Tis over ways," a stocky many replied, pointing up the street without raising his head from his forge to look. Jairin followed the street to the north and a few blocks later came by the corner of Mutton Hall Lane and Darvish Street. Three of the corners had small, unassuming homes, but at the southeast there was a two-story ornate brick building. The sign in front had a few symbols he couldn't read, but the door was open. A calming smell of burning Elden root came from the open doorway; something Jairin had a hard time resisting. He called briefly at the doorway, "Hello? Is anyone about?"

31 You Have Been Misdirected

There was no answer. Jairin entered and looked around, calling again, "Excuse me, is anyone here? I'm looking for a wizard!"

The entry lobby looked much like a hotel. An unmanned reception counter stood by the entrance, with a closed doorway behind it. Two large pottery jars sat on the counter, wafts of smoke and an occasional spark rising from them—the source of the burning Elden root scent. Heavy curtains were drawn over the windows in the lobby, blocking most of the light from the street. Several small lanterns around the room added to the eerie light from the jar fires. Jairin noticed an unobtrusive stairway at the far end of the room leading up into the darkness beyond.

The door behind the desk opened and a dwarf, scarcely more than a meter tall, emerged from the back room. He opened a pair of curtains to let more light into the room. "Aye." He walked up to the desk and then jumped up on a crate, suddenly putting him at eye-level with Jairin. He was clean-shaven with short gray hair. While unusually bare faced for a dwarf, he had the usual heavy frame and deep eyes, but they were an equally rare green. Jairin hadn't met many dwarves in his lifetime, but they usually grew long beards as a sign of their stature. They were short by human standards but tended to be plump and tough as nails.

"What can I do for ya?" said the dwarf.

"My name is Jairin. I've come seeking the Kalari."

The dwarf smirked as he studied Jairin's face. After a short pause, he replied, "I believe you've been misdirected, sir. There ain't no wizards near here."

"Odd," Jairin said. "You have some knowledge of the wizards then?"

"Nope, can't say as I do." The dwarf cracked his neck from side to side and then shook his head.

"I say it's odd, because just now I only asked if you knew where I could find the Kalari. I didn't say anything about wizards," Jairin said, smiling.

"I think before, maybe?"

"Are you sure?" Jairin asked.

"Hmm." The dwarf fumbled his hands around the desk and looked away, seeming to gaze anywhere but at the king. Eventually, he looked back at Jairin. "I'm sorry, I cannot help ya. Whatever these Kalami things are, we don't sell them here. This building is just private office space."

A deep voice called down from the top of the stairs. "Who's down there?"

"It's a fellow called, um…" the dwarf said.

"Jairin."

In the shimmering lantern light, Jairin could make out a man coming down the stairs into the lobby. His black hair flowed over faded red robes. He looked to be somewhere around Jairin's own age, perhaps a bit taller, and with light brown eyes that seemed disciplined, penetrating. *It's his eyes,* Jairin thought. They carried a power and wisdom that didn't match the rest of his appearance. The man had a short black beard that matched his dark hair. On the left side of his beard was a longer braid of hair, tied with a small gold bow. The man looked over at the dwarf. "It's okay, Frangle, I've summoned him." He turned to Jairin. "Welcome, King Jairin. I'm Tannis. I've been waiting for you."

"I…" Jairin searched for a reply. "I came here of my own volition. I've received no summon."

"That's not quite true," Tannis responded, with a small laugh. "I have definitely summoned you. I've been expecting you for some years now, but I guess the expression would be 'better late than never'?"

"I was sent here in search of the Kalari."

"In that case, you've been misdirected. The Kalari of the Eastern Domain meet in the Plains of Zimm, a great distance from here. It would take you months to travel there on that horse of yours."

Jairin felt defeated, "I was sent here by Azil the Diviner."

"Aha. Precision is important. You seek an individual wizard of the Kalari. That makes more sense. In the case of Azil, I told him to send you here. Come with me. There are many things we need to talk about."

Tannis gave a wave of his hand and the path up the stairs to the second level lit up like daylight. He started climbing the stairs and turned back to address Jairin. "Come now, let's not waste a moment." The lobby behind them darkened as Frangle drew the curtains closed again.

Jairin arrived at the top of the stairs and continued following Tannis. The wizard opened a door into a surprisingly small room, only about three meters in each direction. There was a clothes rack near the door covered in various robes in red and gray and at the other end sat a cot and a pair of chairs. On a table next to the cot were several jars and a few unidentifiable items. Tannis walked across the room and sat in one of the chairs. "Come, sit down."

"I was expecting a wizard to have grander chambers," Jairin said.

"Were you, indeed? Sleeping chambers are exactly that. You have a table for the contents of your pocket, a cot and pillow to lie on, and a rack for your clothes. This is all I need. But let me greet you more properly. I am the Wizard Tannis, Master Ecomancer, Holder of the Vaxian Nocleum, Commander of Dansmoor's Secondary Guard, Slayer of Liam's Wyrm, and Fellow of the Red Order of Eastern Domain."

Jairin looked on at the wizard, careful to be sure he was done with his introduction before he spoke. "You seem to already know me. I'm Jairin, the King of Tarquin. I'm afraid I have no further titles. May I refer to you by a shorter title?"

The wizard smiled. "Jairin, my friend, that was the short title. You may just call me Tannis, of course. I sometimes forget to tailor my declamations to the audience at hand. Wizards are far more formal amongst themselves."

Jairin wanted to get right to the point. "Tannis, my sister is dying. I need to find out how magic works and I need to get rid of what appears to be a rather powerful and definitely very angry demon."

Tannis nodded. "I have an apprentice, Vruthian. I don't know if you've met him. For the past ten years, I've been teaching him how to properly ask the question 'How does magic work?' He will, if he survives, spend the next thousand years trying to figure out the answer to that question. What you ask is a monstrous undertaking, young Jairin. I could no more teach you what magic is than I could teach you how to grow wings or to live under the sea. What I can do is try to explain the very basic building blocks upon which magic blossoms. Some of these building blocks are vital if you are to help free your sister from the grasp of a demon. Tomorrow, at first light, I will show you what I can of the arcane force that hides in plain sight from the eyes of man."

Tannis cleared his throat. "Magic, despite popular belief, is an integrated part of our world. There are exceptions to every rule, but from birth, all people have the ability to manipulate magic. Some creatures are born to command this force, just as some are born to swim, some to fly, and others to dig. People, unfortunately, need more effort to knowingly manipulate this force. There is a part of your spirit which manipulates magic even if you do not recognize it. That nagging feeling that you would call your conscience is part of that spirit, your avatar. Your mind and your avatar work together in everything that you do. The trick is to make them talk and listen to each other. When you begin to do that, you begin to work in a much different, much larger world."

Jairin nodded. "Some are born with a command of this magic without the instruction of a wizard."

"True enough. The use of magic by the uninitiated is not recognized as true magic. It is largely random, haphazard—dangerous. Wizards refer to those who wield a wild talent as sufferers of the Scourge. While others call it a gift, it is nonetheless the use of a power they wield but do not understand. You can give a child a sword, but it is rough, crude. It will cut, but most often will never be controlled the way such an instrument is to be properly used. Wizards command a force that they can see just as easily as you can see a cow, a building, or a cloud of fog. We have an oath to never show the Scourged how to see the magic they manipulate. It is too dangerous. Imagine if I were to give a crazed man a sharp blade and anatomy lessons. This would produce a killer with lethal tools and skills. Such things do not contribute to the order of our world."

"Can everyone be taught to see magic? Can I do it?"

Tannis took a deep breath. "Magic flows around and through all things. It is a skill anyone can learn with much time and practice. Almost anyone. Some rare few are born without an avatar. They bear no ability to manipulate magic, whether they see it or not."

This reminded Jairin of the man he'd met at the castle, "My father had an advisor, a judge name Barlemicus. He said he was a thrull, whatever that is, and he could see a man's thoughts. Is this done with magic as well?"

"In a way," the wizard said. "The thrulls are an ancient people. They can reach out with their avatars in a way I do not understand, to gain knowledge from others. They use this ability to know when someone is lying or being deceptive. Wizards don't acknowledge this to be magic. More importantly, thrulls are immune to the magic of others. Those who can see magic flowing through the world can see it warp and bend around a thrull, like a boulder in a river. It makes them useful as judges as they are not bendable to the will of magic. But we're getting sidetracked."

Tannis moved a few of the jars around on the desk, picking one up and tipping it over in his hand, thumb holding the cork firmly in place. "Back to magic," he said, returning the jar to the table. "On the most fundamental level, there are four known forces that can interact with each other. Two of these are all around us. The first is Essence, the force of life. All living things contain some amount of Essence they consume and continually regenerate. The second is Vis, the force of magic that flows freely through the world. Vis flows around and through most things, the living and the still. We share this Vis as it flows. I can see this flow, though it is invisible to most. Think of Vis as like the air. You breathe the air and I breathe the air. Neither of us own it, but together we share the resource. It's a connective tapestry.

"Unlike Vis, Essence in our world is contained and doesn't flow from one thing to another. It's more like the blood in your veins—delivering the new and removing the spent life from your body. There is Essence in you and me, your horse, a spider, trees, and any living thing you can think of. Your form has more Essence than a cat, and the cat has more than the spider, but we all have Essence and it's all the same energy, in different containers. Beyond our world, this energy is connected in a great ocean. In an infinitesimal way, the death of that spider affects the cat, and the death of that cat affects you, and so on. Essence is stronger than Vis, and when they meet, Essence will displace it. Neither can be destroyed—they are just displaced, Vis to space around you and Essence to the pool beyond our world."

Jairin raised a finger. "I'm not completely sure I understand. First you said that we generate Essence, but then you say that it's a great shared pool. How can we both create and share a resource from a common pool?"

"You're an astute learner, Jairin?" the wizard replied. A smile crossed his lips and he nodded. "A lesson on Vis and Essence transformation is well beyond the scope of the time we have. For now, let's agree that both Essence and Vis can be contained, altered, and distributed—but not destroyed. They are natural parts of the world around us, and they connect all things in their own ways. Let's move ahead. Tell me about your demon."

"We captured a demon, a very powerful one, in a Mirror of Wills."

The wizard nodded, "Clever… but dangerous. Demons are entities that come from another place, outside of our world. They're not made of Essence as you and I. They sustain themselves in our world by feeding off of Vis if they can find it—or Essence if they cannot. Is this why your sister is dying?"

"Yes."

"Because your sister does not command magic, the demon she carries feeds constantly on her Essence."

Jairin leaned forward, nervously. "Tannis, help me save her. Show me how to wield some magic, no matter how small. Or at least give me the ability to see it. She's going to die. I can't stand by and watch it happen."

Tannis backed away in his chair, shaking his head. "Absolutely not. You have the eyes of a child and you cannot understand what you are asking. I'm not barred from teaching you, but there is no time if you intend to save your sister from a demon of Im'Dalanra Gestron's power."

Jairin's eyes widened. "You know his name?"

"I've kept an eye on you for many years, Jairin, always from a distance. I knew who your father was. I know what happened to Tarquin. It was I who evaluated you at a young age for your aptitude with magic. Your strengths lie elsewhere, and you must believe that I am leading you down the correct path even now to help your sister. Beyond that, you can't imagine the consequences of what would happen if I were to awaken you."

Jairin's shock and anger had lessened, and curiosity got the better of him again. He took comfort in the thought that perhaps Tannis would be able to help him after all. "Awaken?"

"Those who can't see Vis as it flows through our world are called sleepers. When a sleeper is taught to see magic, the process is called awakening. Just as a person who is asleep opens their eyes when they wake up, a wizard's awakening lets them see the world around them with a new set of eyes. This is a long and painful process, I'm afraid. It's not something one can just get up and decide they are going to do on a whim."

"What are the other forces? The third and fourth?" Jairin asked. "If you won't teach me to see magic, are those something I can use?"

"The other two are foreign and rare. Katravis is the dark devourer. It is the life force of your demon. It displaces and disrupts Essence and Vis, feeding on the energy of their transformation. I've been around a great many years and have seen an amazing number of sights. But the fourth force, I've never witnessed with my own eyes. Depending on who you ask, Quintessence is either the divine will of the gods or the eternal darkness of the endless void. What I do know is that it displaces and devours the other three."

"Tomorrow morning," Tannis continued, "we will meet with Vruthian on the road and accompany him back here." He reached down to the table by his cot and picked up a vial of red liquid, handing it to Jairin. "I need you to drink this. Don't mind the texture, I have no way to change it."

"What is it?"

"You want to see magic at work? This is how we do that. You need to trust me again."

Jairin pulled the cork out of the top of the vial. While he held it, the liquid changed from crimson red to orange. It didn't look or smell appealing. He swirled the contents of the vial, watching it swish around inside of the glass. Reluctantly, he pressed it to his lips, tipping his head back. It tasted like metal. Copper? There was something flowery in the mixture as well. He couldn't put his finger on it. After several gulps, the container was empty. His head felt heavy. He could see the wizard stand up, but all of the sounds around him were muffled. Tannis took him by the hand across the hall. The wizard opened the door and ushered Jairin into a room similar to the one they'd just left. "Tomorrow," Tannis said, "you'll see why I've..." The rest became unintelligible as Jairin's ears began to ring.

It's not evening yet, Jairin attempted to say. His mouth had stopped responding. He used the last of his strength to plop himself down on the cot just before the whole world went black.

32 The Fast Road-2

Jairin turned over and hit the floor with a *wham!* The room was still dark, and it took him a moment to remember where he was. With great difficulty, he pulled himself off the floor onto his hands and knees. His whole body felt sluggish and heavy, as if he was in a quicksand. He staggered to his feet and took the steps to his window, where he managed to throw open the shade and bathe the room in light. *That was a mistake.* His eyes burned and he looked away in haste with his hand covering them. Every muscle hurt and the incredible weight he fought to maneuver made the pain so much more intense.

There was a knock at the door. Jairin turned to see Tannis in the doorway. "I'm sorry," the wizard said. "I knocked a few minutes ago, only to hear you crash onto the floor. It's the elixir. We'll be heading out in a few minutes." He turned and walked back out, closing the door behind him.

Jairin staggered out of his room, almost tripping as he fought to move one leg after the other. He found Tannis, dressed in a different red robe, drawing with chalk on the floor, his staff lying next to him. He marked out several concentric circles with some symbols. When he finished writing, Tannis stood up, grabbing the staff. He looked back at Jairin and raised both arms. "Are you ready?" He pointed the staff at the center circle, and a small blue point of light appeared on the floor, about the size of a coin. The wizard began to speak.

beatum teis mohaman Vis a-nul
ret vomus am sidio numra vay
extan vestra bidio

The small spot lifted from the ground, with a ray of blue light still tethering it to the floor. When it had reached over two meters above the ground, the spot split into two, and each of the points fell back to the floor, leaving behind a blue trail. The final shape evolved into what appeared to be a blue archway, high enough for one to walk through. On the other side was still just the hallway.

"Concentrate," Tannis said, "and walk through."

Jairin struggled to move. His muscles fought him with every motion, and he felt like he was trying to swim upstream as he trudged slowly ahead toward the archway. The area beneath the arc grew fuzzy as he approached, turning from blue to green. He felt his body moving as though it were weighed down by stone. As he passed through the arch, the green began to look like grass, then grass with some water, then a meadow next to a swift-moving river. Soon, he began to identify grasses with crickets and small insects darting around. He could feel weight lifting off as his body became responsive again. He was walking into a living, moving meadow and not just a portrait.

He heard Tannis' voice faintly from behind. "Keep going. You're almost through."

Jairin took a final step. Grass. He was standing in soft grass to his calves, near rushing water. As he took several more steps, he realized the great weight and soreness in his body had disappeared. The scene looked familiar. A few moments later, he heard footsteps in the grass behind him and turned to see Tannis stepping through the archway. Beyond the wizard was the fuzzy outline of the hallway they had come from. Tannis waved his staff, and the arch closed back into a center line to the ground and then was gone completely.

Tannis adjusted his robes. "The elixir was a potion of raw Vis. I built the portal and I decided where it would lead, but it was you walking into it that created the rip in the world that bridged my hallway and this meadow on the Montamar. You couldn't do that on your own, of course. The Vis in your body was depleted as you created and then passed through the tear. The Vis also kept you in one piece as you traveled from my home in Barrington Flame District to this riverside, a few hours walk west of the city. We will run across Vruthian shortly as he returns from his errand in the west."

"Why didn't he use a portal?" Jairin asked.

"We like to walk when there's no hurry."

"Is this what wielding magic feels like?" Jairin asked.

"Wizards are taught more slowly, over time. We also don't harness Vis all at once that way. I suppose we feel some of that weight, but it comes on slowly. Over the course of years."

"The stretch of river looks familiar," Jairin said, "I came this way when I rode to Barrington to find you. I felt an unseen presence before."

"Someone may well have been watching before. I don't sense anyone now, though. It wasn't us, I assure you. I have left you to your own devices," the wizard said.

"I'm here to save my sister. She is holding on to the Mirror of Wills that has imprisoned the demon. Azil said she has maybe a few weeks. I need to save her. How do I do it? What happens if I can't?"

"That's complicated. The demon must be feeding from her

Essence faster than she can recover it. A diviner would know how long she has better than I, but it's just a matter of time before she will pass from this world. When she does, the demon will be free. Maybe 'free' isn't the right word. He would be free from his prison but would again be bound to his summoner's will."

"I need to banish the demon. I can't let him return to his summoner."

Tannis shook his head. "I'm not an expert on demons. I do know a demon is much more challenging to banish than he is to summon. The demons don't want to go back to their world in most cases. It's also not likely that a wizard who summoned one of these demons is in much hurry to use the power it takes to send him back."

"Is Madigan the summoner?" Jairin asked.

"I can't answer that, I'm afraid. The Kalari have forbidden discussion of your demon's origins and any insight into who may have summoned it. By that same rule, I can't tell you it wasn't him."

"I don't understand," Jairin protested. "I thought the Kalari was the ruling body of wizards. Why would they be banned from talking about such things?"

"Our vast lands are separated into domains, each with their own Kalari. The wizards in these Kalari are bound together by choice, not force. There are those, however, who are trained in the magical arts that do not join the organized wizards. Some crave the isolation and quiet of having no one to answer to. Others have agendas that do not match those of the Kalari. A great many years ago, Madigan made a choice to be separate from the wizards of the Eastern Domain. He is free to do so, but in that decision, he became ostracized from all Domain wizards. We don't interfere in his affairs and he stays out of ours, lest he face great punishment."

"My conclusion is correct then," Jairin said.

"How so?"

"You said that you couldn't discuss the demon's origins and you couldn't discuss Madigan. I would assume that if the summoner were some other wizard, a member of your order, you would at least have been able to say that it was not Madigan."

"Believe what you will."

"How do I save my sister?" Jairin asked again.

"The demon needs more Essence or more Vis. It's a simple solution, but you'll find it very difficult to implement."

"Can I take the artifact from her?"

"If she relinquishes the mirror, the demon will be set free. If it leaves her possession by any other means, it will also fight to escape. In the end, you'll need to seek out the summoner to save your sister. Only someone with great skill in summoning demons would have the power to send it back. I warn you again that you will find such a summoner quite unwilling to do so."

A man on horseback rode into view from the west. He slowed to a stop as he neared the two men in conversation. Vruthian looked at them and smiled. Jairin had seen him before—a friend of Benedict's, he thought. Jairin hadn't realized who he was and certainly had no knowledge he was a wizard. Looking back, he should have seen some of the signs, but the brothers at the monastery had excluded Jairin from any meetings where Vruthian was present. They'd only shared greetings and the occasional glance in the past.

"Jairin," Tannis said, "May I introduce my apprentice, Vruthian of LeReaux. This is Jairin, recently King of Tarquin —though I suspect you knew that."

Vruthian nodded a greeting to Jairin and Tannis. He brushed his horse's mane lightly and then jumped down, releasing the reins. "Have you taken on a new apprentice, Master? You know the Kalari will only allow you to have one."

Tannis smiled back. "When it's you, one is certainly more than enough. I dare say you're more than any wizard should be forced to handle. Welcome back, Vruthian."

The wizards clasped arms just above the wrist. "We've just come to the fun part," Tannis said to his apprentice. "The balance and the Paradox."

"Ah ha!" Vruthian replied.

Tannis set his staff on the ground and took several steps away from it. He motioned for Jairin to follow him, and continued with his lesson, "There are, of course, limits to what a wizard can do with magic." Tannis pointed at the ground making a swirling motion with his index finger.

Jairin watched the ground where Tannis pointed and saw nothing. After several seconds, a small trickle of water spurted up from the ground. It grew larger, until it was a small fountain in the grass.

"The problem the wizard faces," Tannis said, "isn't in making the water come here where we want it. You must recognize that to bring water here, we are taking it from somewhere else." He waved a hand and the fountain stopped, leaving just a puddle of water to soak into the grassy ground. "If we brought a large quantity of water to this land, we might be creating a desert somewhere else. There is a balance and a flow to both Essence and Vis."

"Where did this water come from?" Jairin asked.

Tannis motioned to his apprentice, while continuing to address Jairin. "Let's walk as we discuss this, King Jairin." Vruthian grabbed the reins of his horse as Tannis continued his lesson. "The water is coming from the river, but *where* in the river? Even if he is only taking a small quantity, a wizard must always be aware of the repercussions of that change. When we create this fountain here, perhaps we're diverting it from the raging flow next to us. Perhaps we're taking it from a spring where it emerges far upstream and provides water for a small village. That bit of water is now missing from where it used to be. We create a small splash with the things we do, but the effects ripple out and expand in all directions in reaction to our action."

"Are these things you can plan or predict when you cast your spell?" Jairin asked.

The wizard tipped his head slightly, nodding. "A good wizard plans these things. Most changes don't create huge impacts, and many are never noticed by anyone at all. But the thing to remember is that all actions have consequences. The ability to command and channel the Vis is only a small part of being a wizard. The much larger job is to anticipate and manage the consequences of your actions. Not doing this can be catastrophic—both to the wizard and potentially to everyone or everything around him.

"Our reality, like Essence and the Vis clouds, is a collective. Whenever magic makes a change in the world, that change propagates to everything around us. A small change is relatively simple, but as the complexity increases the difficulty increases. If a wizard tries to manipulate the tapestry of reality too far, they face unimagined peril. Wizards have been ripped apart trying to push magic too far. The collective reality pushes back. This is very difficult to explain in any way that would make sense to you. Unfortunately, the more you learn of how the forces work, the more difficult it is to understand and predict the mechanics behind it. Wizarding is a tiring and perilous study of things you hope nobody ever notices."

"So a spell of any magnitude changes reality for everyone? The collective consciousness decides what magic can and can't do?" Jairin asked. He was suddenly aware that the footfalls of the horse had stopped. He looked around, unable to spot either the horse or Vruthian. Jairin looked around a second time in disbelief. "Where is Vruthian?"

The air behind Jairin shimmered, distorting the light like a reflection in a still pond that has been stirred. From the distortion, Vruthian stepped forward, still leading his horse by the reins. "Now that you're looking for me," the apprentice said, "The spell becomes much harder to maintain. Make no mistake, magic is real and not just a trick of perception. But it has many limits."

Tannis nodded. "In all things, we are connected. We collectively design our entire existence. I will warn you though; at this point I will not be able to try and explain how the mechanics work. We will need to leave discussion of the balance with the understanding that if you cross a certain line, very bad things happen. Anyone who uses magic must respect this balance or they will be lost forever."

"My sister," Jairin said. "How do I save her?"

Tannis nodded. "You know everything you need, whether you realize it or not. Respect the forces and remember the flows. You have another weapon to wield as well."

Jairin looked at the wizard quizzically. "What?"

"You can fight this wizard with your lack of magic."

Jairin's frustration rose. "I came searching for answers. After the time we've spent, I only have more questions. There is so much more I need to know," Jairin told his wizard companions. "I must make haste to get back to my sister. Is there anything I can take with me, even on loan, that may help me?"

They arrived at the stables by the river entrance. Jairin fumbled through his belt pouch for his claim token. He presented it to the stable worker at the desk, who in turn passed it back to a runner who disappeared into the stables.

"I'm sorry, my friend," Tannis replied. "As you know, I am forbidden to interfere with this effort. I do have something to send with you, however." The wizard opened his hand to reveal a black band, four centimeters wide and half a meter long. He dropped it into Jairin's hand.

"What is this? Will this help my sister?"

"If you are going to Retreol soon, I need a favor. Madigan

made a choice many years ago not to join the Eastern Domain. His apprentice, however, is not bound by that choice. This band is a key. Give it to his apprentice—he will know what it means."

"My sister?" Jairin asked again.

Tannis shook his head. "You have something that can buy your sister more time. Think on this, then confront this wizard you are seeking."

Jairin tried to relax a little. He had a long ride ahead. "Thank you, Tannis. When this is done, I hope to spend more time in Barrington. I have an accord to renew with your king."

Tannis looked back at Jairin, awkwardly silent for a moment before speaking. "I hear you are working on a building project. All of the best stonemasons for a hundred kilometers are tied up at the moment building a new castle in Tarquin. I'll be starting a new project of my own soon. I'm building an addition to a monastery west of here. I'll need the masons when they are finished with your site."

"It was you!" A smile crept onto Jairin's face. "You're the benefactor for the monks of the Brotherhood!"

Tannis made a bowing motion with his head. "Yes. I admit that it was never a selfless enterprise. It's more of a symbiotic effort between the monks and the Kalari."

"And stop in to see the monks when you have the time," Vruthian added. "They haven't seen you in many months."

"I'll send word, in person…and I'll visit the monastery," Jairin said. "But I'm scared. I don't understand what I'm supposed to do next."

Tannis nodded. "My usual advice is not to do anything rash, but in this I don't think you have a choice, Jairin. The summoner you seek may still be reasoned with, but I don't expect that. As you know, I can't tell you how to resolve this. I told you before that your talent lies not in magic, but elsewhere. You have deep wisdom, plenty of compassion, and are finally learning how to compromise. This will serve you long and well as king. The path forward has been laid. You will find it."

The stable runner returned with Jairin's horse and pack. The king stashed the black band in his pack and then shook the wizards' wrists. He mounted his horse and trotted to the gates to retrace his journey back to his humble home by the lake.

Vruthian turned to his mentor. "Do you think he'll be able to kill Madigan?"

Tannis shrugged. "No. Without magic, he has no chance. But he doesn't have to."

"What about the demon?"

"If the demon is released, he will wreak havoc on the lands again. Our plan would change, but it would be of no long-term consequence."

"What if Jairin is killed?"

Tannis tipped his head. "I would miss him a great deal. I received word several weeks ago that protection of the king is no longer required. Whatever his role was in the Kalari's plan, apparently he has already completed it. Capturing the demon? Destroying the Sword of Tarun? Now that I've met him in person, I think I understand what the Kalari needed him to do. Letting him die would be a mistake on their part and would create unnecessary risk. But we must let him figure out what to do on his own. What have the dragon scouts reported?"

"We've called off the patrols for now," Vruthian said. "Trouble is still brewing in the South Domain, but it's only just starting. It may be many years before we even know the name of the wizard who will try to destroy the balance."

"Good, good. When you've lived for thousands of years, what is a few more to a wizard? The dragons will be glad to be free of patrol duty. If Jairin lives through this, keep your eyes on him. Procure an invitation to his castle after the wedding."

33 Houseguests

Carmen sat at the head of the dining table in the hall for her evening meal. She'd requested several house guards and workers join her to help keep her company, but it wasn't the same with all of her new family elsewhere. One of the servers refilled her mug as she set it down. "Sarah," the Queen Betrothed said, "Can you check on Zael again to see if she has awakened?"

"Yes, Your Highness."

The queen had never been at a loss for conversation with her generals surrounding her in Thadia. Staff ate between bouts of joking and telling stories of the day. Carmen listened and tried to stay engaged, but it had been a long day. Arik entered the room, picking up her spirits.

"My leg is mending," he said with a smile. "Since Azil had some time this afternoon, he was able to work on part of the fused bone with his healing spell. He said I may lose the limp after a few more sessions—as time allows, of course."

"That's wonderful! Is Azil still here? How is Raven?" Carmen asked.

"He's attending to some matters at the guard house, but he's coming back this evening for a final check-in with her. I haven't seen any progress, I'm afraid."

"That's a shame." Carmen said. "Jairin should be back tomorrow or the day after. Hopefully, he'll have some news. Join us for dinner."

Arik looked around the table and then sat in one of the empty seats. "Grouse! I don't mind if I do."

Meanwhile, in an Other Place, Zael sat at the table in her dimly lit home. She ran a hand through her long light-brown hair, pushing it out of her face and behind her ear. She turned back to the man sitting across from her. Now past middle age, his hair still clung to some bit of unidentifiable color but was now mostly a sea of white. He leaned forward and continued with his questions. "How has Raven been holding up?"

"Not well. She's been fading for the past several months. Jairin summoned a healer and they had her stabilized last time I checked. They're optimistic. Jairin had set out to consult with the wizards to get some help. We'll see what they can do."

"She deserves so much better than the hand she's been dealt. Give her my best. Are those the wizards in Barrington?"

"Yes." Zael remembered her other news. "Oh, speaking of optimism—Jairin's engaged to be married to Carmen in the spring. That gives us something to look forward to. They've begun working on a new castle as well."

"He's not going to rebuild at Glensong?"

"No. They brought in architects from the south, the ones who can shape even steelstone. It's set on the lakeside in <u>Draxmore</u>. The fields have been turned for planting in the spring, and the new stable was just roofed a few weeks ago. It's starting to feel like a home."

"It's about time," the man said. "I was surprised to hear she even waited around for him to take those blinders off. What are they doing with Castle Glensong?"

"It's a guard outpost now. It wasn't feasible to bring horses up and down the trails all the time. It's being repaired, though. I think it will look wonderful when they've fixed the broken tower. I think they are exchanging vows at the waterfall in Glensong's shadow. Hopefully, once Raven—"

The candle flame flickered, bending the shadows in the room. The door behind Zael opened abruptly and she turned to see someone entering the room. Long white hair trailed down Raven's shoulders and back. She stepped forward, looking apprehensive.

"River of fire!" Zael exclaimed, bolting to her feet, her chair falling backward to the floor. "Katherine, how in the world are you here?"

"Zael? You can talk?" Raven asked. She stood sturdily, looking strong and aware. It was a version of Raven that Zael hadn't seen since they first parted in Bravitleer. Besides the white hair, she looked fully recovered.

"Here, I have a voice." Zael walked over to Raven and threw her arms around her. She smiled and pointed back to the man who had been sitting across the table from her. "Katherine, it would be my great honor to introduce you to Marax—your father."

Raven's knees gave way and she nearly fell before catching the edge of the table with her hand. She ran to Marax and hugged him tightly. "I... I have a million questions." Tears ran down her cheeks.

Marax wrapped his arms around his daughter with a smile. "My heart is filled with so much pride to see you. I've heard amazing stories of all that you've done—of all the lives you've touched over the years. My baby girl."

She stepped back to address both of them, wiping her face. "Not so much a baby, these days, I'm afraid." She chuckled before speaking again. "Okay, tears aside, not such a baby, anyway. I'm overjoyed to finally meet you, though not under these circumstances. I've been looking for Zael for several days. It took me a while to figure out where I was. Nothing here has any color. Things don't move right. Things here don't even stand still right!"

Marax looked back at his daughter. "What happened to your hair?"

Raven smiled. "Until quite recently, It was black as coal, like yours. I was even called Raven by everyone who knew me."

"Yes," Marax replied, "Your mother gave you that nickname when you were just a baby."

Raven's smile faded. "I guess the hair is the least of my worries. I held back a demon for months. In the end it seems like he drained me of everything I had to fight him with. When I first arrived in this world, I panicked. At my death, Gestron would be freed from his prison. I've come to accept that I can't do anything to stop the lands from being ravaged again. I'm sorry I failed you, Father."

Marax shook his head. "You are my pride and joy, Katherine. You didn't fail anyone. I'm sad to see fate has brought you here, but I'm overjoyed to be reunited with you."

"They brought a diviner to look after me. He saved my life, and Jairin's before that. I guess it wasn't enough."

Zael disappeared. Just as Raven turned and noticed, Zael was back again, standing right where she had been before.

Raven's mouth fell open. "What just happened? I *told* you things were strange here!"

Zael took a step toward Raven, touching foreheads with a hand behind her neck. Zael smiled at her aunt. "The demon isn't freed. He's still trapped in the mirror, in your hand, on your bed."

"How can that be? What does that mean?" Raven asked, shaking her head.

Zael took a step back as Raven's image became blurry and

started to fade before her. "You aren't dead, Katherine. Your life force is very low, and it was no longer able to bind you to the world of the living. You're welcome here, but for now—you're going back."

"How is that possible? How is this just happening now after I've been here for so long?"

Zael shook her head. "It has only been a moment. Something is happening in the world of the living. If your Essence grows, even the smallest bit, you will be pulled back."

Meanwhile, back in this world, Jairin arrived in Draxmore Valley, just hours away from home. A rider approached. It was Captain Jacob from his guard.

The captain rode up alongside Jairin. "Welcome home, Your Majesty."

"Thank you. What's the news?"

Jacob shook his head, "Raven is still hanging on. Azil is with her. She's called out for you more than once, but we've all helped to keep her spirits up. Your queen is upset that you left without guard. But more than that, she's worried. Arik has returned after his rounds at Thadia and stands ready as you requested."

"I think I know what I need to do for Raven. Come." Jairin spurred his horse with a *yah*—quickening his pace as Jacob matched it. An hour later, they arrived back at their home. "Take the horses to the stables, please."

Jairin entered his home and hurried to check on Raven, who he found to be asleep with Azil in her care. After quietly consulting with Azil, he followed voices to the dining hall where he found Carmen and Arik eating dining with a small group of guards and kitchen workers.

As he entered the hall, everyone at the table rose. Jairin wanted to run to Carmen, but appearances dictated that he restrain. He walked briskly to her end of the hall and embraced her. "Five days," Carmen said. "You were gone for five days. You're lucky that I love you, to tolerate such absences when there is so much to be done here at home." She smiled. "In any case, you were sorely missed by both your sister and your future wife. Welcome home!"

Jairin smiled back. "You're lovely and ferocious, my dear. I hurried home as quickly as the horse would carry me."

"What about Raven? What can we do?"

"I have a plan. I'm taking Arik and the thrull to Retreol. We can get rid of that demon once and for all."

Carmen raised a brow. "You just got home."

"Not under my care...," Azil said. He put one hand on Raven's forehead and the other on her neck. A soft glow emanated from her body as she lay with her mouth open and eyes rolled back. "Come on, come on, stay with me." Azil had felt her Essence slip away moments before. He positioned two fingers on her neck and felt for a pulse. She was alive, but barely. He reached into his pouch and pulled out a small vial of blue liquid—his last. He swirled it around and carefully removed the stopper. He elevated Raven's upper half and slowly poured the contents of the vial into her mouth, taking care not to choke her.

As the last drops passed into her throat, Raven gasped and sat up, coughing. She lurched forward, taking several deeper gasps of air, and opened her eyes to see Azil seated in the chair next to her bed. Looking confused, she raised a hand and turned it over. "Father?" She looked around the room for a moment and then again at Azil. "Was I dead?"

Azil nodded. "We lost you for a few minutes."

"Minutes?" Raven said. "I was wandering around for days! Oh smeck, Jairin was right. This is crazy!"

"I promise, Raven, it was only a few minutes."

Raven pulled back away from the wizard. "Don't call me that."

Azil nodded. "Sorry. What's important is that you get some rest. I've given you another elixir that should keep you stable for several days while your body stabilizes."

"Thank you. And I'm sorry for snapping. You're a life-saver."

As Jairin exited the great hall with Carmen and Arik after dinner, he found Azil waiting for him in the hallway. The wizard told them what had happened and that he had given Raven an elixir to help her recover.

"Vis?" Jairin asked.

The wizard looked over at Jairin and tipped his head inquisitively. Carmen stared at him in confusion.

"If she is to recover some Essence, she needs Vis to feed the demon so it will not drain her life force."

Azil smiled. "You are full of surprises, King Jairin."

"I was given the short lesson."

"She'll need to rest overnight. The Vis will buy her a few days while she builds strength. It's my last one, I'm afraid."

"We're leaving at first light tomorrow," Jairin said. "I have to meet with Madigan in Retreol. He is the only one who can get rid of this thing for good."

Azil looked concerned. "You may find that difficult. If he was the summoner, I don't expect he'll be in a hurry to help you out when you ask him."

"I have a plan."

Arik glared at Jairin. "Your last plan got her where she is right now."

"She got herself where she is. This wasn't my plan. She took the mirror from me in secret. And at this point, she has nothing to lose if Madigan won't make a bargain. Tomorrow, I'll leave for Retreol with Barlemicus. You can go, or you can stay here. I need to convince the wizard to banish the demon or I'll have to force him."

"I'm going. I need to help make this right for Raven's

sake."

Jairin nodded. "Your help is appreciated, my friend." He called one of the guards over. "Bring a message to Barlemicus at the tower. Tell him we're leaving for Retreol tomorrow morning just after first-light."

"Aye," the guard said. He turned and left.

Zael awoke with a start. She looked around the shadowy room. It smelled like pine and wildflowers and there was a dim lantern beyond the door. She sprang upright with a gasp. After a few tense seconds, she recognized her room at the lake home. Switching between worlds always left her disoriented. *I was having tea with Marax. Raven was there!* She tried to speak—*still nope.* She got out of bed and dressed, grabbed her chalkboard, and walked to Raven's room.

She knocked and Arik answered, "Come in." He stood and offered her the chair by Raven's bedside and looked at her quizzically. "Have you been up long?"

He doesn't know the signs, she reminded herself. She shook her head and then pointed to Raven. Arik nodded. "She's still with us. Azil said she left us for a few minutes, but he's brought her back. It's unnerving. She's such a strong person, but she has to fight so hard for something we all take for granted."

Zael put her hand on Raven's cheek. The princess opened her eyes and looked up. When she saw Zael at her bedside, she smiled. "Was that real?"

Yes, Zael signed, nodding.

"Thank you for giving me a chance to meet my father. It was something I never thought I'd be able to do. The wizard said I was out for just a few minutes. I was in that other place for several days. Is that how the time always passes on the other side?"

Zael nodded. She was painfully aware.

"So when you pass out just for the night, a month can

pass for you?"

Zael shook her head and pulled out her chalk board, writing: *a day, a week, a month…*

"Years?" Raven asked.

Zael nodded.

"I can only guess what it must be like for you. I lived several days in the course of a few minutes."

Zael hugged Raven, turning her head to hide the tears running down her cheeks, and walked toward the door as Arik resumed his seat at the bedside. Zael thought about the woman she'd come to know, upbeat and full of life. She was devastated at the thought of Raven being taken from them under these circumstances. She had watched this woman fade over the past several months. *I wish I knew how long we'd have together*, she thought as she neared the door.

"Three days, apparently," Raven said.

Zael stopped mid-step, turning with her eyes wide. She looked at Raven in shock.

Raven looked back at Zael. "I thought you asked how long they thought I was going to live. Okay, that's strange. I know you can't speak. I heard you ask as clear as a bell. It was even in your voice—the same one I remembered from the other side. I must be losing my mind."

Zael nodded, faking a smile, and tapped her fingers on her throat to confirm that she couldn't speak. She turned again to the door and left. Out of sight down the hallway, Zael felt her face and hands turn cold. *What just happened there? I need to tell Jairin!*

Jairin heard a knock on his door—about eight knocks, in quick succession. He sat up in his bed as Zael let herself in. Light from the lanterns in the hallway spilled into his chamber. He rubbed his eyes and checked the window to confirm that the suns had not yet come over the horizon. "Zael, you're awake! But it's still dark out. What's happened?"

Her face was nearly white. Jairin's eyes were adjusting to the lantern light. "You're in shock!" He jumped out of bed and put his arm around his adopted daughter, ushering her to his bed where he sat her down. "Take deep breaths. Is it Raven? Is she okay?"

Zael appeared to have trouble signing. Jairin looked at her chalkboard, which didn't provide any answers. "Is anyone in trouble? Has anyone died? Is anyone gravely injured?" he asked hurriedly. Zael shook her head. She took a few deep breaths, grabbing her knees with her hands.

"Okay," Jairin said, "Sign it out when you can." Zael, a bit too quickly, signed: *Raven came to otherworld, then left. Now she reads thoughts.*

Jairin nodded. "Okay. I need more help with that." Zael started again. In more detail, she explained that Raven was able to read her thoughts. She had come to the Other Place, met with her and Marax, and then was pulled back into this world.

Jairin's jaw dropped. "No, no. This isn't good!" Azil had told him that something was changing in his sister. He wondered if it was the magic that kept her alive, the artifact, having crossed to the other side, or just influence from the demon that allowed her to read Zael's mind.

"I'm devastated to see her like this, but I admit that a part of me is jealous." Jairin said. "She carries a burden that I always expected I'd keep for myself. I never realized that part of that burden would be staring down the face of death moment by moment. But because of that, she's had a chance to meet our father. I've always wondered what he'd say about my life—about the choices I made."

Zael signed back: *He loves you. He's proud of you and what you've done. Don't be in a hurry to pass to the other world. You've seen the vast empty spaces. There's not much more than that.*

"You're right. I'm being silly. This morning, when the suns

rise, I'm going to Retreol. We're going to confront Madigan."

Zael smiled. *I'm in*, she signed.

"I'd be grateful to have you. That will help make up for leaving you behind at Thadia. I'll take you, Barlemicus, Arik, and Jacob with me."

She nodded, the color having returned to her face. Zael hugged her father goodnight and left the room.

Jairin sat for a while on his bed, unable to fall back asleep, running through the variables of his plan. He muttered, "Demons are full of rage and pride, they feed on fear. Wizards use Vis to control Katrivis. The thrull warps magic fields and is immune. The wizards want Smeech for something. Oh crap, Raven may be able to read my thoughts.

"Pancakes, pancakes, pancakes, pancakes, pancakes…"

34 Exodus

As the suns rose, Jairin dressed and entered the hall, finding Arik, Barlemicus, and Jacob already at the table eating breakfast. The company rose from their seats as he entered. "No need," Jairin said. "And for the rest of this excursion, there is no bowing, no titles, and no formalities. I have a plan that we need to follow, but we're a company of equals. Is that understood?" His friends sat down and continued with their breakfast, not waiting for him to sit. Fresh eggs, bacon, wheat bread with cheese, tea, and tavali juice.

Zael entered a few minutes later. *Sorry I'm late,* she signed to her father. She filled a plate and sat down next to him.

Jairin smiled back at her, patting her hand with his own. He turned to the company and addressed them. "Today we're taking the coach north to Retreol." He turned to look specifically at Jacob. "The coach and the horses are all ready, I hope?"

"Yes, Sire."

Jairin shook his head. "Remember, we're a company—a group of equals."

"Yes…, Jairin," Jacob said.

"Good. We'll ride up in the coach, changing horses at Thadia. The road is still a bit bumpy, having been out of use for a few years. But we can rest as we need along the way."

"The road to Thadia is a quick trip," Arik said. "I know the coach doesn't travel nearly the speed of one man on a horse, but the time is very quick."

Jairin continued, "In Retreol, we need to stop at the City Hall, to take measure of how officials view this wizard. I don't expect help from the mayor, but I'll accept it if it's offered. From there, we find Madigan. There is another wrinkle, however. We need to keep Madigan and his apprentice apart. Finish your breakfast and I'll meet you at the carriage shortly. I need to say goodbye before we leave." He took a final bite and stood up.

Jairin knocked on Carmen's door. "Are you up, my queen?"

After a quiet pause, she answered. "Yes, please come in."

He entered to find her sitting at a small desk, reading a book. "I'm sorry I didn't join you for breakfast," she said. She set the book down and rubbed her abdomen gently as she smiled back at Jairin. "I was reading to our child. I also wanted to give you a chance to motivate your group before you left. I heard that we lost Raven for a several minutes. I'm afraid she doesn't have much time. Is this going to work?"

"I hope so," Jairin said. "We don't have any options left. Are you having second thoughts?"

"This is dangerous, but I don't see any other choices, either. I haven't said anything to Raven, or anyone else, for that matter. If this fails, though, we're in a great deal of trouble. While it pains me, I have to ask what your plan is for succession if you don't come back. Zael? Your child to come?"

Jairin sat on the bed next to Carmen. "Rule will fall to you, of course, Queen Carmen. Beyond that, I would request that you look to Zael and our child—whomever you deem worthy."

She nodded. "And so we're clear, you include Zael in this

line."

"Yes. She is to be as my own flesh and blood."

Carmen walked to the bed and sat beside her fiancé, wrapping her arms around his neck and moving close enough that their noses almost touched. "You're brave and honorable. I love that about you. I also have every confidence in you, despite this newly found reliance on magical mumbo-jumbo. I trust it only because it's kept Raven alive for these past months. Go and save her. When this is done, we'll have many things to celebrate."

"Goodbye, love." Jairin reached out and placed his hand on her belly. "Little Titan isn't kicking yet?"

"Pfft. If you intend to call him 'Titan', you'll have nothing but resistance from me. Besides, it's a girl. I want to name her Victoria after my mother."

"We already gave your parents a castle!" Jairin chuckled. "I'm coming back. We have time to decide these things." He gave Carmen a long kiss and rose, leaving her room.

"Be careful, my king. Return safely and swiftly!" she said as he disappeared into the hall.

Jairin walked down the hallway toward Raven's room. When he reached the place on the wall where he'd mounted the shield and the destroyed sword handle, he stopped and grabbed the shield from its mount. He turned it over to make sure the mounting clips were still in place and continued on to his sister's room. He remembered what Zael had told him of his sister earlier. He tried to clear his mind of thoughts before knocking.

"Come in," Raven replied in a much stronger voice.

Jairin entered her room, trying to keep his mind like a blank canvas. He had no intention of worrying her with the details of the upcoming confrontation with Madigan. She sat up in bed, with a small smile on her lips. It was the first time he'd seen her smile in months.

"Azil had to run out early this morning on some errand,"

Katherine told her brother. "He's given me at least a three-day expiration date at this point, unless he can find some more of that gross potion that he gave me yesterday." Her smile faded a bit as her expression grew more serious. "I don't want to die, Jairin. I would have no problem dying to save people from this demon, but Azil said that if I die, the demon is freed anyway. Tell me there is something we can do while we have this thing contained."

"I'm going to strike a bargain with Madigan. You aren't going to die, Raven."

"Be very careful with him, Jairin. So much more than my life hangs on this. And don't call me Raven. Raven was gone quite some time ago." A tear fell down one of her cheeks.

"You're not defined by the color of your hair."

"I know. There's a lot more to it. I'm always weak and tired. Fix that if you can, and you can call me Raven all you want." She struggled to smile again. "I'm sorry. I never meant for any of this to happen."

"The wizards have all admired your strength. They tell me I wouldn't have lived half as long putting up the fight you've had. Don't worry. We'll take care of you." Jairin had a mission to carry out. He filled his mind with one thought: *pancakes, pancakes, pancakes, pancakes, pancakes.*

Raven had closed her eyes, drifting to sleep. She shook her head. "No thanks, I'll eat later."

"What?" Jairin asked. It was clear that Raven's new ability wasn't limited just to reading Zael. She didn't respond to the question.

Jairin reached out and kissed his sister on the forehead. *Pancakes, pancakes, pancakes, pancakes, pancakes…*

A moment later, Jairin slipped from Raven's room, bolting to the front exit. When he passed through the door, he looked for the coach. "We're leaving!" he yelled to the coachman, who was helping the last of the company into the back. Jairin ran a few more steps and tripped forward, catching himself with his free hand on the ground just before his face would have been firmly planted in the driveway. He stayed on the ground for a moment, but with a grunt and a wince, he stood back up and ran the last several meters to the carriage. "Go, go, go!" he yelled to the driver. The coach driver gave a *yah* as Jairin jumped in, closing the door behind him. The horses pulled the carriage away from the lake home.

"No!" a voice yelled out from the home behind them. "Jairin! No!"

Arik strained to look out the window of the coach. "Was that Raven?"

"It's nothing," Jairin said. "She doesn't want us to risk our lives on her behalf." He tapped the top of his shield on the roof of the coach as they drove off. "Make haste, driver! We have a long road ahead of us."

Zael sat next to her father with Barlemicus and Arik on the bench facing them, backs to the horses. Jacob was seated on the front bench outside with the coach driver.

Along the road, they passed several new farmsteads that had been settled during the summer. It was an encouraging sign for Jairin to see that people were starting to return to the land now that the demons were gone. This reinforced Jairin's desire to banish the demon once and for all. Until he was gone and not simply contained, there would be the constant risk that he might escape and again destroy whatever got in his way.

The company stopped several times to give the horses a chance to drink and eat from feedbags. In the early evening, they arrived at Thadia and handed the horses over to one of the stable masters. Within an hour, the carriage was hooked up to four new horses. During the break, the party ate as well in the lower hall of the tower, then boarded the carriage again to head north to Retreol.

As night came on, Zael leaned her head to rest on his

shoulder. He put his arm around her, and the girl fell asleep with a smile on her face. He'd missed his family this past week when he was away in Barrington. He was glad to have her volunteer on this trip. *I can keep most of them out of trouble,* he thought. He'd send Zael, Arik, and Jacob after the apprentice.

As the suns set, the road ahead was illuminated by two lanterns lit by the new driver they'd picked up in Thadia. They rode on, making a single stop in the middle of the night to let everyone take a break and to feed and water the horses. Jacob joined the group in the carriage and Arik sat up front with the driver. After the carriage got underway for the last leg of their journey, Jacob looked over and seemed to take an interest in Jairin's weaponry. "If I may ask, your highness, why have you brought that beaten hand shield with you? I've never known you to use a shield before."

Jairin looked at Jacob. "Would you have chosen another one?"

Jacob tipped his head, shrugging. "No, I suppose it's as good as any. It just looks old, very well used, if you know what I mean. In a fight, or as a show of power, there are several good pieces I could have helped choose from the armory."

"That's probably true," Jairin said with a laugh. "I chose this one partially for its small size, and partially for its special nature. Diplomacy is our goal, but if all else fails we may end up in a fight, I'm afraid."

"You'll get no complaint from me, your highness. Are we going to be fighting men or wizards? I don't fancy our odds in the latter."

"I don't know how this will play out. It wouldn't be smart to take on a wizard alone, and I certainly don't plan to die on this trip. If we can't strike a deal, we also have Barlemicus." The old judge stirred at the mention of his name but didn't appear to awaken.

The carriage hit a small rut in the road and jerked gently as it continued on its path. Jacob looked back at his king. "I'm not afraid to die in the line of duty."

They hit another small rut and Jairin sat quietly, watching the two men opposite him in the back-facing bench. He was silent for a while, but finally spoke, "Death is overrated." The king reached for his shirt, feeling around for the token hanging on its chain beneath. Satisfied, he sat back again. Soon, Jacob had fallen asleep and then Jairin drifted off as well.

"Firestorm!" Barlemicus yelled. "Driver! Firestorm!" The company was awakened by the cry and maneuvered to look out the windows.

The driver brought the carriage to a halt. "Whoa!" He looked out at the light in the distance. "It's not a firestorm," he said. "That's far enough away to be Retreol, but it would have to be an intense fire to see it from this distance. Perhaps it's an ironworks or something?"

"No," Jairin said. "The ironworks forge is intense, but not that big. Something's amiss."

"Everyone hold on," the driver said. "We have more ground to cover before we get to the city. We're going to start moving again. Yah!" The horses sprang back to life and the carriage moved forward with a jerk.

The road from Barrington had joined them on their journey north, and about a half-hour later, they neared the south entrance to Retreol, and the city wall arose on the horizon. Smoke rose in the distance from inside the city, but there were no visible flames as they approached. The rising suns bathed them in a sea of morning light. Arriving at South Town gate, the carriage slowed and then stopped. A sentry came to speak with the driver. After a few moments, the sentry turned and waved to guards up in the tower.

The driver turned back to the carriage as the gate ahead

slowly opened. "There was a fire in the warehouse district. They lost a storehouse of distilled spirits and two apprentice brewers during the night. It's under control this morning."

He urged the horses into the city and to the stables. There, the party collected their packs, and the driver checked the horses and carriage with the hostler. The driver paid the stable keepers and he and Jairin were given matching tokens.

Jairin pulled the driver aside. "Check at the stables for a note from me—once each morning and once after noon, starting the day after tomorrow. I'll leave word here for our return trip." Jairin gave the driver a handful of silver coins. "For your expenses in town."

Jairin led Zael, Arik, Jacob, and Barlemicus to the main cross street. As they left behind the wafting scents of the stables, something new hit them. Arik sniffed the air several times and turned to Jairin. "What's that smell?"

35 The Grand Return

"I know time is short, but I for one am starving, and that bakery smells amazing!" Arik said.

Jairin inhaled deeply. "We made good time to the city. I'm famished as well, and I don't think anyone would take issue to a bit of breakfast. We won't get far if we don't eat." The two-story stone building ahead was painted a light green, chipped in a few places to reveal the natural gray stone beneath. The sign hanging overhead had a picture of a rotund man holding a rolling pin, reinforcing for the olfactory challenged that it was a bakery. He knew Dinthroe's Baked Goods was legendary in the region and a cornerstone of Retreol's Gant Street.

The fresh smell of toasted wheat and hot blueberry muffins filled the air. From the window outside, he could make out a sea of fresh pastries, breads, and baked goods. A young man exited the bakery with a sack and more of the sweet smell billowed through the doorway.

Jacob looked over at Jairin. "I grew up in North Town. Even there, we knew that it's hard to beat Dinthroe's for a filling breakfast. We can be in and out in just a few minutes."

"We have time to eat, but then we must make haste to the Town Council chambers." They entered the bakery. The sights and smells inside dwarfed the sensations from Gant Street. Jairin urged them to pick out a few items and head back out to the street. They each drank a large mug of breakfast tea and Barlemicus filled a sack with croissants, apple turnovers, and iced strawberry tarts, and another with half a dozen long sausages for the journey.

Once they were back on Gant street, Jairin turned to Jacob. "Which road do we follow to get to city hall?"

"We need to follow Gant to the Central Corridor, then take Central into the heart of North Town over the bridge to the city offices."

Zael signed to Jairin before they started walking down Gant Street. She and Arik had been sharing their concerns about Raven, especially with the cry they'd heard from the lake house as the carriage drove away. The company started a brisk walk down the street as the conversation continued. "I won't understate her condition," Jairin said. "But the best we can do for her right now is to forge ahead and meet with Madigan. In the meantime, Azil has given her an elixir—something that will keep her alive for the coming days. Hopefully she can recover some strength. Azil has worked wonders. I've seen it with my own eyes."

"I'd remind you that your injuries were a very different case," Arik said.

"How so?" Jairin asked.

"You carried the sword with an enchantment against shadows. Even then, you said you returned by tricking the keeper of the dead."

"That's true, I suppose. But it was Azil's magic that healed me. Who is to say the sword even had anything to do with it? I think the sword's power was always overvalued. Don't forget that Gestron turned it to dust with just a touch."

Arik looked over at Jairin. "I thought you weren't using his name any longer."

"I can't deny his existence. He has a name. I shouldn't be

afraid to use it."

Zael and Arik exchanged quizzical glances.

Jairin continued, "Time is short. Let's not get sidetracked. Council first and then other business."

Jacob shook his head. "I know how the council and the mayor work. Even if they grant us a hearing, it won't be for several days."

Jairin slowed to a stop and they halted. "We don't have a few days. Our mission is urgent, even though Azil said he can keep her stable for now. I'm starving. Can I have a sausage?"

Barlemicus opened the smaller wrapped package with the meats and held it out for Jairin to grab one. He asked Jairin, "What exactly are we going to ask of them if we are granted an audience?"

"I need to make a plea regarding their wizard," Jairin said, grabbing one of the sausages. The rest of the company helped themselves to food from Barlemicus' bakery bags.

"Madigan?" Barlemicus asked.

"The same."

"Why?"

"We need to get Madigan to banish the demon for good. He more than anyone knows how dangerous the demon is when set free," Jairin said. "He had the power to summit it. He will know how to release it."

"What if he refuses?" Barlemicus asked.

Jairin tapped the shield that hung from his belt several times. "If he refuses to do it, we'll have to take care of the situation in another way."

Jacob turned to Arik, whispering, "He's lost it." He looked back at Jairin. "If we're a company of equals, Jairin, am I free to voice a concern?"

"Yes, of course."

"That doesn't make any sense. You have a sword and an old heirloom shield. With that, you are going to fight a wizard?"

"Diplomacy first," Jairin replied. "If that doesn't work, then we need to remember that he is a wizard—not a fighter. And I will have a Thrull with me." He looked at Barlemicus, who nodded.

Jacob shook his head. "I don't see all the moving pieces, but if you are certain of what you're doing, I won't second-guess you."

"We both know there's no certainty in this. Madigan relies on his magic as I rely on my steel. If I can't convince him to do what he must do, then we'll defeat him by turning his magic against him." Jairin took a bite of the sausage and resumed his pace, continuing his conversation with Jacob, loud enough for the others to hear. "Raven's life is in danger. As you know, I get focused too narrowly at times. The first thing we need to do is approach the city council. They swore fealty to my father in ages past. I don't know if they wish to resume that status, but we have to coax them to our side. At the very least, we need them not working for Madigan. That's leverage we need to negotiate with the wizard."

Jacob said, "My family has been sending me news from here. There is growing discontent—people disappearing, increasing violence, and distrust. Like the fire we saw on our approach. I'm not sure that was an accident at a distillery."

"That's how it started at the castle when I was young. I always thought it was the demon that was wreaking havoc, but now I think it's Madigan. Whenever he's around, people disappear. Our time is too limited to deal with him the way we should. For now, we need to bargain to save Raven's life."

Arik said, "I agree. We can leverage that fear to bring the council to our side. They want peace. We want peace. They must at least suspect that Madigan is feeding these incidents. Accidents don't happen this frequently."

"I'll take Barlemicus," Jairin said. "The two of us can

confront Madigan and work on a bargain. If things go wrong, the wizard won't be throwing spells at a thrull. We aren't helpless here."

Jairin removed his backpack as he walked, fishing out a black cord that he handed to Zael.. "I'm putting you in charge of our friend, Mr. Smeech. The wizards believe he's ready to leave Madigan, and when he does, they want him to choose to join the order. I don't know what that means, but separating him from Madigan will help us all a great deal. When we find the wizards, I need you, Arik, and Jacob to give this to Smeech. We can't afford to fail in either of these tasks."

Jairin noted several major streets as they passed them: Optura Street, Gargoyle Way, Henschel Street, Cloudview. After half an hour they came upon Central Corridor. Jacob led the way up the corridor until they came to the Montamar River. A steel bridge crossed the river with several guards on each side watching over the waters below as a small skiff floated past. "There is the Council Chamber," he told them. It was a single-story stone building, less assuming than several of the fine houses surrounding it. Outside, it appeared the building was in the midst of a fortification process. Steel rods and bricks were set in piles around the two sides of the building they could see from the street. As the company approached, they saw two uniformed guards flanking the door with long pointed spears.

"That's strange," Jacob said. "The entry has always been guarded, but I don't know what all these new fortifications are for."

Jairin reached into his pack and pulled out his father's signet ring, the symbol of his office as King of Tarquin. He approached the door, holding out his signet for the guards, but not knowing what to expect. "Good morning to you both. I am King Jairin of Tarquin. I am here to meet with the City Council." He reached out to pull the handle on the door to enter the chamber, only to find the two bewildered guards outside had crossed their spears to block his arm and his advance.

"Where's Tarquin?" the first guard asked.

"You're in it," Jairin said. "The land around Retreol and even the city itself in times past."

The first guard looked at the second. "Well, there's news for you, Robert. Did you know we were in a kingdom and this fellow here is our liege?"

"Well, I certainly didn't," the second guard replied. "But he's got a fancy ring and everything. Why would anyone ever lie about such a thing? He must be. We should bring him right on in."

"With a pipe," the first guard added. "While we escort the king and his court into the offices of our elected city leaders, it's only fitting that he be given a pipe and some toast with fine jellies!"

Jairin stepped back. "Okay, you made your point. Would you please announce me to the council? They'll meet with me."

Robert turned and entered the chamber, pulling the door shut behind him. The other guard kept his spear at an angle to continue blocking Jairin's path.

Jairin signaled to Arik and Jacob to ready their weapons. In a few moments, the second guard re-emerged from the chamber. "The council will meet with you," he said.

Jairin stepped forward again. "Thank you." But Robert kept his spear crossed across the front entry.

"The council will meet with you… tomorrow afternoon."

Annoyed and frustrated, Jairin slipped the signet ring onto his finger and pointed ahead to his company. Arik moved in on one guard, Jacob on the other. With a few flicks of their swords, the guards were up against the building, spears on the ground in front of them. The two companions held them there at the edge of their blades.

Jairin stepped forward and threw open both doors into the small building before striding into the chamber, with Barlemicus and Zael behind him. Arik and Jacob followed, their swords to the necks of the outside guards.

It took a moment for Jairin's eyes to adjust. Despite the morning light outside, the room was shrouded in darkness except for a few strange lights fixed to the walls. If there were any windows in the room, they were shrouded. The lights didn't appear to be lanterns or torches of any kind he'd seen before. Jairin noted that they dimmed and flickered as Barlemicus passed near them. He walked to another set of doors at the far end of the entry room and threw those open as well before storming into the next room.

The council chambers were illuminated by similar lights. A massive table nearly filled the room, in the shape of a letter "V." Four men sat along one outside edge of the long table and three women sat along the other. At the point of the "V," in a taller chair, sat a red-faced, chubby man that Jairin assumed was the mayor. As Jairin entered the room, the man stood from the tall chair, clutching a small pile of papers. He was older, perhaps 130 years, with pure white hair. The man wasn't much taller standing than he had been while seated. His clothing reeked of poor style and self-importance. "What is the meaning of this intrusion?" he demanded. He looked at Jairin, and after a moment seemed to have spotted the signet ring. He threw the papers on the table with a *swoosh* and scrunched up his brow. "I said— tomorrow afternoon."

The mayor looked around the room and then back at Jairin. "I see. So this is the man who would be King and ask Retreol to be pledged to his kingdom? He comes breaking into our chambers at the point of a sword. If I refuse your demands, will you kill the elected leaders of this council, mighty King of Tarquin?"

"You're wrong, Mister Mayor, is it? Your Honor," Jairin

said.

"Hmph. Yes, I am Cartwright Anton, the mayor of this amazing city. We answered your letters. We even granted you an audience before the council. *Tomorrow*."

Jairin composed himself and addressed the council. "Your city council swore an oath to my father, the King of Tarquin, some eighty years ago. While that oath was never rescinded, my father, as you know, was ruthlessly and unexpectedly killed. The throne of Tarquin has been empty for many years, but I return to you now asking your great city what it will do in the coming days. As King of Tarquin, I refuse to arrive in Retreol in the morning to be told that I won't be seen until the following day. You have not requested release from, nor have I relieved you of, your oath of fealty. I carry the signet you swore to as your king and protector, and that is why I have come here today."

The mayor smiled. "Well then, King of Tarquin, let us talk of oaths and kingdoms." He paced back and forth, trying to recall old memories from his days as a young councilman. "I would argue it is the job of said King to provide a rule of law for any city for which he is bound to protect. I would argue that said King should provide patrols and oversee titles of nobility and at least contribute to the local justice for any city or which he is bound to protect. Yes, I see your father's features in you, and I have no doubt that you are the son of King Marax. But Retreol has been a free and independent city now for nearly twenty years. Remind me again why it is that we need said King?"

Several more guards entered the chamber. The mayor motioned for them to stay where they were. Jairin signaled for Arik and Jacob to put away their swords as well.

He turned back to the mayor, nodding. "Fair enough. As I said, I come to you not as one who is demanding that you uphold an oath, given the circumstances. There are, however, many benefits I can offer you which will not be available to a free city operating within the established border of Tarquin."

The mayor coughed and chortled. "An established border, you say? I have seen no signs of such. If any established city beyond our walls to the north or to the west would declare themselves to be within some kingdom, Tarquin or otherwise, you would make a much more compelling case with that argument."

Jairin continued, "I bring an alliance with the Wizard Kalari of the Eastern Domain and trade agreements with Rasheen, Gresenbaad, and Deltari."

The mayor stopped pacing. "These alliances are yours to offer? We already trade with Rasheen. Should I expect some armed resistance from you and your mercenaries if I were to still turn down your 'offer'?"

Jairin shook his head. "I'm not making any threats, Mister Mayor, but to say that I have unyielding respect for this council would be a lie. My sister holds title to property and land in this city, which this esteemed council has illegally seized. If you want to speak of legality, I would ask by what right this was done?" Several city councillors looked at each other, speaking quietly amongst themselves.

"Ah. Now we come to the issues at hand. An angry family member. A need for revenge, perhaps?"

"No. I'm not demanding that you yield out of revenge for my sister's house. But I do indeed demand satisfaction in that particular matter."

The mayor picked up several sheets of paper from the table, rearranging them in his hands. He looked back up at Jairin. "The nobility of your kingdom has caused unimaginable damage to my city—"

"That is an utter lie! My family has done nothing but add to the prosperity of Retreol," Jairin interrupted. "Raven has done nothing. Even if there was redress against her father, you have no right by law to confiscate her property."

Mayor Anton said, "We have no need of a king in Retreol. We have been under the protection of the wizard Madigan since the—"

The mayor was interrupted by one of the council members. "Your Highness… there are some on this council that would take your argument with more weight than our mayor."

Mayor Anton huffed and waved an arm at the councilman. "You are out of order, sir."

Jairin looked at the councilman, surprised. The man continued his statement to Jairin. "Councillor Gilvary of North Town, your Majesty. Since word of the shadow's disappearance in the south, Madigan has exerted an unnatural hold over the policies our mayor will entertain or fight for. I don't know what kind of…"

His words became overshadowed by a myriad of other councillors speaking over each other. Some stood and talked with others, angrily shaking their hands and engaging in side conversations. During this chaos, Councillor Gilvary approached Jairin and shouted. "This has been how our discussions go when it comes to the wizard at the north wall. It's as if a cloud of confusion and noise arises whenever Madigan's name comes up."

Mayor Anton banged his gavel on the table, silencing most of the other voices. "Councilman Gilvary, return to your seat. Everyone respect the rule of law or you will be censured. We *have* order in Retreol. As you can see, the council has its share of spirited discussions, but in the end Retreol chooses to live and die an independent city-state."

Councillor Gilvary, ignoring the mayor's call to return to the table, leaned in closer to speak directly in Jairin's ear. "The council will support you, King Jairin. If you can rid this city of the Madigan's toxic influence, the crazy chaos in this chamber will finally end. The mayor speaks only for himself, and perhaps the wizard." The mayor gaveled the table with a new volley of banging. The councillor continued, "Madigan brings upon our city almost nightly destruction. People disappear, screaming and crying in front of their neighbors, never to be seen again. Anton and his like look on in silent approval as others die in the night fires, so long as he himself remains safe and keeps his seat."

Mayor Anton banged his gavel a third time. "Out!" He motioned to the guards in the room and they picked up their weapons. Jairin and his company backed out of the room with their own weapons drawn.

Gilvary spoke again, loud enough for them to hear. "Free this city, King Jairin, and this council will stand behind you. This madness needs to end for Retreol to survive!"

One of the councilwomen called out to the guards. "Let them go. They are guests of this council and free to stay in the city." The guards stepped back and allowed the company to leave the chamber.

As they left, Jairin saw Mayor Anton glaring at Councilman Gilvary. The tension in the room had grown quickly to great intensity. Whatever was really going on, Jairin knew where it was coming from. He was surprised that Madigan was able to cause such chaos and violence while still appearing to be an upstanding member of the city.

The walked north, away from the council building. Once a good distance away, Jacob brought them to a small shop where they could purchase a map of the city districts. He looked at the map for a minute. "Madigan built his tower where Fisch used to be."

"He drained a lake?" Arik asked.

"No. F-I-S-C-H, Fisch Floods. It's an area where many poor and lame lived. They didn't have much money, living hand-to-mouth. There were dozens of people there."

Jairin nodded. "That sounds like Madigan. Set up camp amongst those who are missed the least and get rid of them first."

Zael signed to her adopted father: *What is the wizard doing? Why?*

"It's called wasting. Madigan did something that knocked his magic out of balance. Now he has to take the life from others to sustain himself. He has probably been behind these deaths for decades, blaming it on Gestron." Instinctively, Jairin reached for the chain at his neck and felt for the token hanging from it. Still there.

Arik shook his head. "That's one person who definitely wouldn't be missed if he were to disappear."

They looked over the map some more, finding cross streets and nearby businesses. Arik pointed out a place Jairin was familiar with, and they decided to pay it a visit. They made their way back to the river along the north bank. Arik and Jairin led the company to the Root Cellar Tavern. As they had moved farther from the Council building, the sneers from passing guards had stopped. Word may not have reached this far west about their earlier encounter with the Mayor and the guards. They entered the tavern and found a table near the back wall. Jairin ordered a round of drinks for the group and they worked on their plan. After running through several contingencies, Jairin excused himself and approached a table of brawny-looking men. One of them seemed to recognize Jairin and stood to grasp his wrist. "Well met, my friend!"

Jairin smiled and introduced himself to the man who stood. "I'm King Jairin of Tarquin. I believe I met you here months ago on my first trip through the city. You said you were from a long line of King's knights."

The man noticed Jairin's signet ring and dropped to one knee. "I am Brandt, my liege. It would be my honor to serve the crown."

Jairin urged the man to his feet and searched around in a small pouch hidden in the band of his trousers. He pulled out five small gold coins and handed them to Brandt. "This is for your transport to the castle and a banner tunic. If you haven't changed your mind, I will bestow you with a title, Sir Brandt."

Brandt bowed and took the coins. "You won't regret this, Your Majesty!" And left the pub and his companions behind.

The company finished a second round of beverages, then left and made their way wearily back to the inn Jacob had recommended in North Town. Upon arrival, Jairin paid out another gold piece to the desk clerk. Zael and Jairin shared one room with two small beds. Barlemicus, Arik, and Jacob took a second room, each with their own beds.

From their second-story window, Jairin and Zael could hear a commotion in the distance. Smoke rose over South Town in the distance. Another fire tonight in the city. *This needs to stop.* He pulled the heavy curtains to keep most of the outside world out of the room. As he was drifting off to sleep, Jairin was startled first by a muffled scream outside in the distance and then a gasp from Zael as she sat suddenly upright in her bed.

36 Terrors and Trials

Raven awoke and looked around her room. It was dark with the door shut, though a few stray beams of light peeked through the drawn curtains to hit the ground below the window. She rose from her bed and walked to the window, throwing the curtains open to bathe her room with sunlight. *Why was my room kept so fitching dark?* She took a step toward her door, but stopped. Her memory was a little fuzzy. She'd been unable to get much restful sleep for weeks, maybe months. This time was different. She wasn't tired—or sore. *What's going on? I feel like myself again.* As her head cleared up, the rest of her memories flooded in. She rushed the last few steps to her door and opened it. "Jairin!" she yelled, lungs full of air. No reply. "Jairin!"

Carmen hurried along the hall toward her, short of breath. "Raven! You're up and around!"

Raven felt her face grow warm. "Is Jairin here? Do you know what he's planning to do?"

"I did." Carmen walked over to Raven, reaching out to embrace her.

"No, I don't want comforting," Raven said, backing away with her arms raised. "Is he here?"

"Jairin took Arik, Zael, and several others to Retreol.

They're going to meet with Madigan."

Raven took a few deep breaths. There was nothing to be done about the situation now. "My brother is reckless and foolish." Another voice talked over Raven's in her head. It was Carmen. *He's doing what he needs to do to save your life.* "I know he means well," Raven said, "but he…"

Carmen raised an eyebrow. "So it's true. You can hear people's thoughts?"

Raven nodded. "It seems as much. And I'm sorry for raising my voice. My complaint is with my brother. You've been nothing but kind to me these past months."

Carmen stepped up and embraced Raven. "We'll get through this."

Raven smiled. It was her first real smile since she'd imprisoned Gestron. For now, the demon's voice in her head was silent.

Jairin was looking out the window when Zael finally got up and joined him. The suns were coming up, illuminating the city. Several men scurried from post to post with small stepladders, snuffing out the streetlights for the day. Jairin turned to his daughter. "Did you get any sleep?"

Not much, she signed. *You?*

"Hardly a moment. Every time I closed my eyes I saw fire. I thought I smelled smoke and burning flesh, but it was a figment of my imagination. The screaming, as we first laid down to sleep—that was real. As if we needed any more terrors to stop us from getting any rest."

Zael frowned, setting her hand on her father's shoulder with a sigh.

"This will end today," Jairin said.

She took a step back, looking Jairin in the eyes. She signed: *What if he refuses to make a deal?*

"I said before that we'd try to negotiate. I won't do anything to put Raven in jeopardy. We can't afford that. But the people of Retreol deserve better than this. We can't leave Madigan to continue slaughtering the people of this city."

They took turns freshening up, changing behind the wooden dressing screen, and walked next door to where the others had slept. Jairin knocked on the door. "Yes?" one of their companions replied, sounding like he'd been roused from sleep.

"Breakfast," Jairin said. "We'll meet you downstairs." They headed down to the dining hall.

Zael grabbed her father's arm as they arrived at the bottom of the stairs. She pointed to his waist, where the shield hung from his belt. *Why are you bringing that to breakfast?* She signed.

"It's my good luck charm." This reminded Jairin to check the chain on his neck for the token. It was still there.

The two entered the dining area and filled up on fresh juice, a bacon and cheese omelet, hash browns, and fruit. As they finished their breakfast, the rest of their company made their entrance and joined them at the table. At the moment, there were only a dozen other people in the dining area. Aside from a few quiet conversations and an occasional laugh, the hall was calm.

Jairin had some last-minute instructions to share with his companions. "This morning, we'll head north and east to Madigan's tower. But first, let's find the site of last night's fire. We should look around there for clues to who is setting them. I need to know what Madigan is responsible for before we run into him, then we'll find someone from North Town who can tell us what to expect once we arrive at the tower. I don't forgive any of what Gestron has done to my family or the people of my kingdom, but I've come to understand that he was just an agent of a far more insidious force." Jairin snapped his eyes shut with a cringe. A shock ran through his spine, a burning sensation running from his feet to his head. He dropped the apple he'd been holding—tightening for a moment by reflex.

Arik's eyes widened. "Jairin! Are you okay?"

Jairin took a breath as the sensation passed. "I'm okay. Madigan must have realized I was here," he lied. "I was saying… Gestron was blamed for a lot more deaths than he caused. The deaths didn't stop with Gestron's containment —only the way they were killed has changed. These fires? It's a cover for the wizard. The City Council know he's up to something. The mayor is covering it up, too. Madigan has grown either careless, or overconfident."

Zael signed to her father: *I love you. Be careful!* She put an arm around his neck with a concerned smile.

"And I you."

Arik contested, "We're losing focus here, Jairin. Are we diplomacy first or violence first? I'm not willing to sacrifice Raven for a prolonged vengeance war."

Jairin nodded. "I agree, and I know that. I just want to make it clear that placating the wizard could save Raven, but it won't do anything for the next hundred victims."

Jacob spoke up. "It sounds like you've ruled out any diplomacy at this point?"

"No," Jairin said. "Raven is our first concern. But beyond that, no peace is worth making a deal with this man. Would anyone be okay with letting him walk free among those you love after what he has already done?"

Barlemicus looked at Jairin with concern. "I hope you haven't overestimated how much I will be able to help you."

After so many years of waiting to get his revenge on Gestron, Jairin found himself in a fragile position. He knew Madigan had no interest in simply helping him. There was no reason he would. When it came down to it, however, Madigan was just a man. He was a wizard, but any man could be killed, and Barlemicus could help keep the wizard's magic under control. Jairin had developed a deeper understanding of how Gestron thought, but it was a dark place he dared not linger in.

His thoughts turned back to Madigan. Here was a man who killed, apparently randomly, just to keep himself alive. Jairin's sense of justice couldn't let that continue. He needed Barlemicus, but he knew that wasn't enough. None of his companions would have approved of his real plan. He'd convinced Carmen that it could work. Raven had probably figured out what he intended if she really could read his thoughts.

He pulled himself together. "We'll save my sister first, but Madigan needs to be brought under control." When the time came, he hoped it would work. Luckily, the rest of the company didn't seem to realize all the ways this could go wrong. He was sending them on the other quest to keep them alive. He'd brought the only magic he had. Tannis had given him the pieces to the puzzle. He hoped he had put them together properly.

Leaving the inn, they followed the smoke to the site of last night's fire, about a kilometer away. When they arrived, they found the smoldering ruins of what looked like a two-story apartment. A crew of workers were walking around the second level, attached to safety ropes thrown over a pair of unburnt rafters. They were knocking out charred walls and pulling out anything that had survived the inferno. A few guards in front of the building blocked the company's way as they approached.

"Nobody's allowed to enter," the guard said.

"What happened here?" Jairin asked.

"Like the others, the fire was set during the night and engulfed these apartments. They were lost before the fire brigade had even been alerted."

Arik looked around the scene. "What about the buildings around it? They look untouched."

The guard nodded. "That's how these fires have burned. Someone is setting them, and they're doing it in a way to take out single buildings without engulfing the others."

"Did the residents make it out alive?" Jairin asked.

The guard shook his head. "Ten people, burned to the bone. I need you to clear out." He shooed the company back from the building.

Several crew members exited the building holding a covered stretcher. An arm protruded from under the cloth covering. It was really just a pair of burned bones with a mangled hand dangling from the end. Something didn't look right, though. The workers quickly tucked the bony arm back under the covering and took it away.

Arik turned to Jairin. "The bones are charred, but with a fire hot enough to burn through the whole body like that, you'd expect more damage to the surrounding buildings."

"That is odd," Jairin said.

Barlemicus joined the discussion. "There's more, Jairin."

Zael tapped Jairin lightly on the shoulder. He didn't acknowledge her interruption as he continued talking with Barlemicus and Arik. She tugged on his sleeve, also without response.

Barlemicus said, "This is the work of—"

Zael cleared her throat and grabbed Jairin's shoulder, turning him in another direction. Smeech. About ten meters away, he was watching the crews picking through the ashes of the fire as the smoke continued to rise in small puffs from the cooling cinders.

Smeech glanced in their direction and seemed to recognize them. He turned and briskly started walking away. After a few steps, his pace turned into a run.

"After him!" Jairin yelled, motioning to the second team.

Arik, Jacob, and Zael ran after Smeech, leaving Jairin and Barlemicus at the fireside.

"…magic," Barlemicus said. "This is the work of magic."

Jairin had heard that these fires had been breaking out across Retreol for months, taking dozens if not hundreds of lives. He was furious for what had been allowed to smolder under the cover of darkness, but it was beyond that. A malice began to grow, fast and hot through his body—something he couldn't control.. He had to save Raven, and that was his first objective, but he felt a growing fervor to destroy and rip apart the bodies of the wizards that had wrought this chaos. It was reckless malice he fought now to control within himself. "I'm scared, Barlemicus. I'm scared of the way I'm going to react when we find Madigan."

"Keep it together, Jairin. You'll have your chance soon. Don't fall apart on me now that we're so close."

Jairin shook his head. "I'll try not to. I feel my blood boiling, but I think I can hold it together."

They hurried back to Central Corridor and made their way toward Madigan's tower. Several men on the street assured them they couldn't miss the tower. It stood against the north wall of the city, rising above the city wall. After a brisk half hour walk, the tower rose before them about ten meters in height, a full story higher than the wall and any other buildings nearby. The air here, away from the center of the city and the fires, was much clearer.

Arik ran as fast as his injured leg would allow. Luckily, the people and carts along the city streets were slowing Smeech down. The wizard was still ahead of them, but they were gaining ground. Occasionally, Smeech would glance back over his shoulder at them, which slowed him down a bit.

The three companions were closing in on him. Buildings passed them in a blur as Arik gritted his teeth against his old injury. It no longer hurt to walk, albeit with a limp, but running still caused pain. Smeech seemed to be slowing down, but Arik, too, was running out of energy for the pursuit. As they closed in, Jacob passed him and moved ahead.

Smeech was only about twenty meters ahead of them

now. He threw over a cart full of potted plants. They hit the ground, sending shards of broken clay and a spray of dirt into the air. Smeech reached the next cross street and turned left. They followed him and realized they'd entered a dead end.

Smeech reached the end of the alley and stopped. He turned, faced his chasers, and raised his arms. He made a motion with both hands and his palms filled with balls of fire.

"Wait!" Arik yelled.

Smeech rotated his thumbs across his palms and the small balls of fire grew larger. "I remember you folks, from the tavern." He nodded his head to Zael. "Your girl there has the Scourge."

Jacob moved to the side, clearing a path for Smeech and Arik to talk with a clear line of sight. Arik said, "She doesn't possess any power that you should be afraid of. She faints. Is that what offends Madigan so much?"

"What do you want?"

Zael stepped forward with her hands raised, palms out. Arik called out, "It's okay. Zael was told to seek you out. She is here on behalf of the Kalari. She's not armed, and she has no way to harm you."

Smeech lowered his hands, the tiny balls of fire sparking and then flashing and disappearing. "You know nothing about magic or wizards. I suggest you turn around and go back the way you've come."

Zael took a few more steps until she was just a few meters from Smeech. He looked at her with caution. She slowly put one hand into the pouch at her waist and fished around for something. Smeech watching every movement.

She pulled her hand out, clutching a shimmering black band. She held her hand out for Smeech to take it. Without breaking eye contact, he reached out and took it from her. Only then, he looked down. The expression on his face softened and he moved his other hand carefully across the surface of the band, causing it to emit a dim glow. Smeech looked back up at Zael. "This is the day, then? I've wondered when the Kalari would force me to choose. I imagined some kind of elaborate ceremony or maybe even a kidnapping in the middle of the night. Instead, they send a child and two mercenaries to tell me I'm at a crossroads." He smiled back at Arik. "I want you to know I didn't cause the fires or the deaths. The Kalari must know that. Make sure the king knows that, too. I am—or was—a bound apprentice. I ran Madigan's errands, but all of this chaos was of his making. If the Kalari believes I'm done with my apprenticeship, I won't fight their decision. Let me pass and I give you my word I won't return to my former master."

Jacob pulled out his sword. Zael heard the *ring* of the blade and turned to him, waving off his action. She looked back at Smeech and nodded, indicating he could go. Smeech walked around the three company members and continued back to the street.

Arik approached Zael. "That's it?" he asked.

She nodded. Zael pulled out her chalkboard and wiped it clean. The men watched as she wrote a new message on it: *Jairin explained this to me. Smeech will decide his path. He is no longer Madigan's.*

Zael made a motion with her hand that looked to Arik like a bird in flight. Smeech was gone.

Barlemicus and Jairin grew closer to the tower ahead. At the main entrance, two guards of about three meters tall paced before the front door. Barlemicus was the first to name them. "Stone golems!"

"They're small for golems. But I suppose you don't need full-size golems to protect a man-sized door." Jairin felt himself zone out for a moment. "It's odd to see them here at all. Madigan can't create golems."

"How in oraj would you know that?"

Jairin said, "The fundamental component structure is different. Madigan can't manifest this kind of particle matrix. It's a redoubled semi-flexed granite. It can't be animated in that form. These are just an illusion."

Barlemicus looked even more confused. He looked at the golems, marching back and forth, and then back to Jairin. "Are you sure?"

"They're an illusion. I'm positive," Jairin said. He shook his head, trying to dispatch the fog that had set in.

Barlemicus approached the doors, triggering the golems. The two guardians raised massive stone clubs above their heads and turned, facing the approaching thrull.

"Are you crazy? What are you doing?" Jairin yelled, "They're going to smash you flat! Run!"

Barlemicus stood motionless. The first golem swung the massive club and it came crashing down at the thrull. Jairin looked away, waiting for a thump or a spat or some other horrendous sound. Nothing. He looked back and was surprised to see both of the stone golems smashing away at Barlemicus—their massive clubs passing right through him and silently pounding the ground over and over.

Jairin approached his friend in disbelief. Barlemicus smiled. "I'm immune to magical spells, but illusions appear real to me until I disbelieve them. But once I know, I see them for what they are. Just an image."

"But how did you know they were just illusions?" Jairin asked, now nearly upon Barlemicus.

"What do you mean? *You* told me they were illusions. You said you were positive." Barlemicus looked back at Jairin and raised a brow. He put his hand on Jairin's forehead. "Should I be worried about you?"

Jairin shook his head. "No, I'm fine. I mean—of course I knew. Sorry." He reached out and turned the handle of the door to the tower. With a soft *click,* the door was free and

Jairin swung it open.

37 Madigan's Tower

Barlemicus looked at Jairin. "I can stop direct magic, but if he uses magic to throw an ordinary object at us, there's nothing I can do about that."

"Noted. And diplomacy first, but if it comes to a fight, I can fight." In the distance, the illusionary golems continued smashing the spot where Barlemicus stood a few moments ago. "I think those guardians are broken." Jairin stepped through the threshold into the tower.

"This whole place is broken," Barlemicus said. "There's strange magic emanating from the tower. It's making my skin crawl."

Inside, Jairin found himself in a grand entryway, easily three times what it appeared to be from the street and two stories high. "Ugh. Wizards. If this doesn't smell like magic, I don't know what does."

Entering behind Jairin, Barlemicus looked around. "Living in an imaginary palace while killing for sport."

The floor appeared to be polished quarry stone, angled downward toward the center of the room where a column of water fell freely from a source above into a drain in the floor. The walls were covered in intricate, gold threaded, colorful tapestries, depicting scenes of the hunt, holidays, and social gatherings. Large urns and pedestals were dotted around the room, many of the latter supporting stone statues of dryads, minotaurs, golems, and other creatures.

When he saw the last pedestal, Jairin drew his sword and fell backward, feeling drops of cold sweat fall down his face. "No, no, no!" His breathing quickened.

Barlemicus rushed to help him up. "No, that's not a demon." That alabaster statue looked human, except for a pair of outstretched wings, resembling those of a bird. "They're like elves, Jairin. They aren't hostile to humans."

The last time Jairin had encountered a humanoid statue, it had tried to kill him with a club the size of a horse. The time before that, they nearly took his life in the statue garden near Glensong. He had developed a special distrust of stone likenesses. Trembling, he stood, calming his breath. "These alatar really exist?"

"Oh yes. Wonderful people."

As they approached the waterfall, Jairin could feel the water vapor in the air. At the far end of the room, two spiral staircases crisscrossed as they extended up to the next level. The entire entry was brightly illuminated, but there was no sign of any torches, lanterns, or other devices. As they climbed the stairs, Jairin heard a heavy *slam* from the entryway they'd just left. He looked back to see a solid wall where the front door had been. "Damn! It looks like we'll need to find another exit."

Barlemicus looked back. "Hmm. I'm guessing he knows who just broke into his tower as well."

The next level was equally well-lit. The lone hallway here was crescent-shaped, with the falling water in the open center. This level had no statues or decorations, only stone pillars rising from floor to ceiling. Barlemicus stopped and ran his fingers across an inscription on one of the pillars. "Something about the light of the path. Maybe, 'Living light reveals the path?' My Telmarian is very rusty."

Jairin found a small doorway set into the stonework of the wall with a hand-sized notch cut into it. He reached into the stone to pull the door open, but it was shut fast.

Barlemicus ran his hand along the door. "I can feel the magic holding this shut. Let me try." He motioned for Jairin to move aside and put his own hand into the crevice. With a *click*, a hidden mechanism released, and they were able to pull the stone door open. The judge smiled at Jairin. "I may need some help spotting illusions, but bypassing magical barriers is my specialty."

"You've proven yourself invaluable yet again, Barlemicus." Jairin patted his friend on the back and they passed through the doorway. Inside, they found another set of winding stairs leading farther up into the geometrically challenged tower. Barlemicus led the way as they cautiously climbed the stairs. Every few steps, he waved a hand through the space ahead of him. After a tense minute, they arrived at the top to find themselves in another chamber.

Unlike the lower levels, this third-level room seemed to match the building dimensions they saw from the street, ten meters wide and deep, filled with a dim light. It appeared to be a storage area. The walls were lined with shelves and hooks, holding a wide assortment of both mundane and impressive-looking items: boxes, large jars, weapons, a broken statue, food stores, something that looked like a massive, mummified foot, piles of clothes, and some books.

Barlemicus looked around. "I don't like this. I feel the pull of magic, but it's not coming from this room. It's as if something were creeping up on us."

Jairin heard several footfalls and he tugged Barlemicus's sleeve. "Be ready."

A man stepped forward from the shadows.

Madigan smiled. "Prince Jairin, my friend! Oh, I'm sorry. You are calling yourself King Jairin now, I hear." His tone was soft and melodic. "I haven't the slightest idea why you've come to visit my home. Had I known you wanted to visit, I'd have sent an invitation. But this break-in is *most* unwelcome. How did you get in?"

"The door was open," Jairin said, following that up with, "mostly."

Madigan looked from one to the other. "I am dismayed that you have very recently dispatched my apprentice."

Jairin looked to his companion, who seemed equally confused. "That wasn't my doing, directly. The Kalari sent the message to Smeech. We were just the deliverers."

"Yes, quite," Madigan said. He took a few steps toward Jairin. "He's a smart boy. No doubt he'll make his own way now without standing in my shadow. You have relieved me of something else recently, I noticed. That demon was quite draining, and I'm relieved to be free of him. But you've caused me a great deal of trouble these last few months."

Madigan took a few more steps. "And Barley!"

Barlemicus nodded in acknowledgement to the wizard. "Madigan."

The wizard continued. "Our young king has decided to bring a thrull with him into my home. Now, I have to ask myself why you would do such a thing if we are having a civil conversation."

Barlemicus took a step forward, standing between Jairin and Madigan. "Watch out, Jairin. He's casting."

Madigan chuckled. He turned his hand over and moved several fingers, producing a soft glow in his palm. "You've brought me an artifact! Your shield has some kind of enchantment I can't make out. I don't suppose it's some kind of peace offering?"

Jairin reached down, checking that his sword and shield were both with him, without looking away from the wizard's hands. "We came to talk, Madigan."

"Yes," Madigan said. "I'm sure you would like that. The man with the losing hand always wants to sue for peace. The problem is, just as your father before you, you've gotten in my way." He threw his arms into the air, releasing a thunderous explosion. A block of stone burst forward from Madigan, striking Barlemicus in the chest. The old thrull was thrown back several meters into the far corner of the room.

Jairin pulled his sword from its scabbard with one hand and thrust his shield forward with the other.

Madigan dropped his hands back to waist-level, making a fist with each of them. Again, a thunderous explosion echoed through the room as the wizard thrust his fists into the air. A wall of stone rose between Jairin and Barlemicus as the wizard let out a hearty cackle. "Ha ha. Fools!"

Jairin now stood alone. "Barlemicus!" he yelled. He needed the thrull. Whatever spell Madigan cast at him next, he had no way to stop it. He tried to charge the wizard but felt a force holding him back. He strained to move forward, but there was a barrier in front of him, an unseen wall.

"I'm okay," Barlemicus said. The voice was quiet, distant, beyond the wall of rock. "I'm sorry, my King."

Fear crept over Jairin. *No,* he thought. *Fear won't help me. I need anger.* "Stay strong, Barlemicus!" Jairin yelled back.

Madigan took a few more steps toward Jairin, just a few meters away now. "I do hope you can excuse my rudeness with your friend. I am not a fighter, so I rely on my magic to defend myself. I can't let someone walk into my home with a sidekick who bends magic and then confronts me with some devious plan to harm me. No offense, you see."

"Tell me, Madigan, why have you taken it upon yourself to kill so many people in cold blood? All of these people had families of their own—people who had done you no harm."

"And now we come to that," Madigan said. "I guess I owe you that much. I have a small problem, my young friend. Like that demon you somehow destroyed, I find myself needing to feed on the Essence of others. Somewhere in the distant past, I must have overlooked something—performed some selfless act that disturbed the Balance. Though I don't expect you to understand these matters."

"You're wrong, you bastard," Jairin replied.

"Really? You know about such things?" Madigan stared questioningly at Jairin, but then his face softened. "Ah. One of your Kalari friends. Maybe the wizard that told you to come steal my apprentice away?"

Barlemicus yelled from the other side of the wall. Jairin couldn't make out what he was saying, but at least it was a reassurance that the old judge was still alive.

"The Balance is disturbed when you try to use more power than you can control. You killed hundreds of people. Innocent people."

Madigan smiled evilly. "Hundreds? I've killed thousands. None of them were important." Saliva frothed from his mouth now as he spoke. "I'm a fitching wizard and when an ant gets in my way, I *squash* it. The tapestry around us drained my Essence until I could no longer feed it. Am I supposed to lie down and die? No! No cost is too great to keep me strong! You couldn't possibly understand my value!"

The wizard whipped his arm down in a slashing motion, throwing Jairin to his knees. Madigan's wild smile grew as his eyes widened. He stared down at Jairin, within arm's reach. "Now… This is the way things should be. On your knees, before me, where you belong. We've talked enough about me. Let's talk about you."

Jairin fought to stand, but something was holding him down. He tried to push forward, then up, only to be repelled by a barrier he couldn't see.

Madigan continued, "I fancy myself a bit of a diviner. While you call yourself a king, I know there are no cities of any importance backing your claim. As you've seen, Retreol is clearly siding with me. There will be no lasting peace with the kingdom of Rasheen. You will go to war and the kingdom will fall. Your sister will soon be gone. The tart of a woman you left at home carries your child—your *real* child, a daughter who won't be long for this world. The rundown monastery where you hid for so many years will soon be torn apart. All of this will come to pass and there is nothing you can do to stop it."

Jairin's heart sank in his chest. *No, these have to be lies.* He had no reason to believe that Madigan knew the future or that he'd tell the truth even if he did. *There's no peace I could strike with this wizard that I could live with. An animal that targets innocent townsfolk and children?* Madigan threatened everything he loved and everything he'd promised to keep safe. Jairin took a long breath, but it didn't slow the oncoming storm. His sword hand trembled. "I came here to talk to you about Gestron."

Madigan looked surprised. "Very well," he said. "But first you need to tell me how you were able to banish him. Since his summoning required a great effort, I know how much it would take to send him back. I dare say it's more than I could muster, even if I'd wanted to. You reek of the Kalari. They say they won't interfere, but I see no other explanation. They will have to answer for this."

"It's wasn't the Kalari. I did this on my own. Raw strength of will." Jairin felt himself starting to slip. "He curses your name, you know. He said you were sickly and weak."

The wizard looked perplexed. "Weak, you say? You want to talk about weak?" Madigan's eyes filled with rage. "I summoned the most powerful demon I could find. He was angry and resistant, yet he bent to my might. I bound him to the mountains and fed him with only the smallest bit of Vis I felt like sparing for him. There he sat for decades, in filth and darkness while I combed the countryside killing farmers and merchants in his name, keeping their Essence for myself."

The world grew blurry as Jairin felt himself continue to slip. He thought back to the horrors of his childhood, seeing his family's kingdom crushed into the ground. Countless townsfolk disappearing from their households as villages fell into disease. The smell of burned bodies in the villages rushed back—the living burying husbands, wives, and neighbors. He thought of the fire crews in Retreol, carrying bodies away that were barely recognizable as human after being burned alive. He'd been forced to watch Raven shrink from a carefree young woman to a tormented shell before his eyes. This wasn't anger. This was pure hatred.

The wizard didn't have remorse for any of the atrocities he performed. He was gloating over it.

As the rage built, Jairin didn't try to hold it back any longer. Some of this terror was the work of Gestron, and some he knew now was Madigan himself. It didn't matter. The rage all swirled together. He was angry that he couldn't swing a sword at the wizard right in front of his face. He was angry about the city of Retreol being under siege. He was angry about Glensong having been left a ruin. Finally, he saw the image of his father being crushed in Gestron's hand and dropped on the floor like a bag of rags. "No!" Jairin yelled, shaking the walls with its reverberation.

Madigan smiled again. "The beauty is that this worthless demon takes the blame. While I feast on the insignificant here in Retreol, the blame falls on the demon—and now on you as well, Jairin." Madigan took a step back and waved a hand, forming a fireball. "Goodbye, Jairin." He pulled his arm back and pitched a ball of fire.

Jairin instinctually raised the shield to cover his face. Fire poured past the edges of the shield in all directions. The handle grew scorching hot, as the edges of the shield took on the yellow, red, and orange glow of molten steel. Jairin didn't let go. Something in the building rage stopped the flames from burning him. He raised his sword hand to find the invisible wall was gone. He stood up and took a step toward the wizard.

Madigan started another fireball. "This will be your end, Jairin, King of nothing."

Jairin burst into flame. It wasn't Madigan's fireball. It poured forth from inside him. His vision was gone. The air around him screamed back even as he dropped the sword. Fumbling around, he found the clips on the back of his shield and disengaged them. Pain swelled in him now. "Ahhhhhhhhhhh!" Something fell to the floor with a *clank* and Jairin focused enough energy to utter three more words: "I release you." He collapsed to the floor in agony and darkness.

Madigan stopped his second fireball spell. Jairin's body lay near his feet, next to whatever the king had discarded. It was glass—dark, but reflective with a silver frame. He recognized that it was some kind of mirror, but in that same instant, a swirling black mass escaped its smooth surface. Madigan readied a shield spell—too late.

Gestron's immense form poured from the Mirror of Wills. Screams and flame filled the room as Gestron rose up over Madigan's head, looking down on him with a gaze of pure vengeance. Madigan screamed as a plume of flame burned up his casting arm. Gestron lunged at the wizard, who was now engulfed in a ball of fire. Through the swirling torrent, the last thing Madigan saw was Gestron coming straight for his head, mouth gaping. The wizard felt a surge of intense pain, like he was being turned inside out. Then nothing.

Jairin lifted his head with a gasp. The hatred that had overwhelmed him was gone. He was in agony, but looked around to get his bearings. A few meters away, he saw Gestron holding something in his giant clawed hand. Blood dripped from the demon's jaw as he spat a head across the room. He clenched his fist. *Crunch, crunch.* It was a horrifying sound—one Jairin had heard before, a great many years ago. Jairin averted his eyes to avoid getting sick.

Gestron opened his fist and dropped the mangled corpse of the headless wizard on the floor. The demon then unfurled his wings, breaking open the ceiling as Jairin scurried to dodge a broken rafter.

Jairin looked around the room. Burned cloth, mangled steel, and broken containers lay all around, some items smoldering, others still burning. Madigan was no more.

The wall separating Barlemicus from Jairin and Gestron melted like water. Jairin finally managed to get to his feet and backed away from the demon. Gestron turned to Jairin. He stared into Jairin's eyes, and for just a moment, he didn't look like death incarnate. At the end, Jairin and Gestron had been joined in one body and the demon had protected him from the flames. Gestron exhaled a great breath and took another. "Go."

Barlemicus ran to Jairin. "Leave it all! We need to get out of here! Now!"

Jairin grabbed the empty mirror from the floor. Barlemicus hurried out, urging Jairin on to a faster pace than he could have found on his own.

Once in the hallway, Jairin turned to see Gestron stretching again to full height, wings causing still more damage to the ceiling above. The demon flapped his wings a few times and gave a final yell, "Arrgghh!" Jairin knew what was coming next. He slipped through the door and they ran back to the stairs. A moment later, the wall to the room collapsed with the force of a thunderous *boom*.

"What was that?" Barlemicus asked, breathlessly.

"No more wizard, no more demon."

They staggered back down the stairs to the first floor, dodging loose pieces of wall and ceiling stone as they cracked and broke. In the entryway, the fine tapestries and statues had turned to dust. The waterfall was also gone, but the entry door that had vanished was now back. They raced the last several meters to the front door and emerged in the street outside.

From a safe distance, Jairin looked back at the collapsing building. The outside hadn't been illusionary. It was the same size they had seen before. It had major structural damage, but the magic seemed to have been all on the inside.

Barlemicus looked at Jairin. "I don't even know what to ask. We were talking with Madigan and then everything blew up. What in oraj happened back there?"

Jairin held up the mirror. "I snatched this back from Raven just as we were leaving for the city. When we trapped the demon in the Mirror of Souls, instead of feeding off his summoner, Madigan, he started feeding off whoever possessed it."

"That should have given Madigan more power."

"It did," Jairin said, nodding. "But Madigan was too greedy. I don't know if there was any way for him to be rid of his wasting, but he was too arrogant to try."

"So where did the demon just go?"

"Gestron needed the wizard's power to stay in our world. When he killed Madigan, he sealed his own trip back to—wherever it is he came from."

Jairin and Barlemicus circled back to where they had been separated by the rest of their company earlier that day.

Two days later

"Yes," Carmen said, continuing her lesson. "You're a quick learner, Raven. I know field tactics are tricky, but you have a knack for planning out your next moves. It will serve you well down the road."

Raven brushed the hair from her brow. "Thank you!"

"Hmm," Carmen said. She reached out and ran her hand through Raven's hair. "I can't believe how much more color has come back today."

"The past few months are starting to feel like a bad dream."

With some lasting effects, Carmen thought.

"Yes," Raven replied with a laugh. "I can't handle being in large groups of people. I need to figure out how to control this."

"I'll be there for you, dear," Carmen assured her. "We all will."

A commotion arose from outside. "Raven!" Jairin's voice called out. Both women stood, and Carmen spun to face the door in time to see it burst open.

Jairin ran into the room, followed by the rest of the company. He ran to his sister and grabbed her in a bear hug. He then moved on to Carmen, pulling her into his arms. "It's done. This long nightmare is finally over."

"Gestron?" Raven asked.

"Gone!" Arik said, taking a turn to hug Raven.

Jairin took a step back and tossed the mirror onto a table near his sister. "You can't keep this," he said. "I just wanted you to see that its occupant has been sent back."

Barlemicus and Jacob took a turn bowing to Raven and then to Carmen.

Raven wiped tears from her eyes, looking around. Zael approached with her arms out. "I'm so glad you've all come back," Raven said.

Jairin turned to the rest of the company. "Tonight, we feast!"

As she turned to talk with Jairin, Raven felt a tug on her sleeve. She turned back to Zael and heard the girl's soft voice speaking in her head. *We need to talk.*

Epilogue

Smeech dropped the small mesh bag of herbs and spices into his mug and grabbed the kettle from the stove. He poured boiling water over the bag in a circular motion. Someone knocked on his cottage door. He never had visitors. Nobody in his new village had stopped by to introduce themselves, and he didn't have much interest in getting to know them, either. He set the kettle back down on the stove. "One moment, please." He grabbed his staff and walked to the entry. A young woman stood at his door, with long, black hair with a few wisps of white. He knew her from somewhere. A street performer perhaps, from Retreol?

Uninvited, the woman stepped into the threshold. "Hi. My name is Raven. I think you know my niece." She motioned back outside and Zael walked up behind her, waving her hand at the wizard.

"No, no, no!" Smeech said. He took a step back and attempted to close the door. Raven's foot blocked it from closing. "Leave me alone!"

The two women pushed their way past Smeech into the cottage. Raven smiled at the young wizard. "As I was saying, my name is Raven and this is my niece—no—my sister, Zael. Unfortunately, Zael isn't able to speak. She can talk to me, but she needs to use a chalkboard or hand signs to talk to others."

Smeech looked on, nervously. "I don't want you here. You've all been nothing but trouble."

"Oh, Smeech, where's the love?" As the women cleared the door, Raven closed it behind them.

"My name is Joshua," he said. "That stupid 'Smeech' was Madigan's joke. I won't ever answer to that again."

Zael signed to Raven, who smiled as she relayed the message. "My sister is wondering what your new cool wizard club name is if you aren't 'Smeech' anymore."

"I don't know. And I haven't decided if I'm joining the Kalari. What do you want?"

Raven reached out and put her hand on Joshua's shoulder. "Well, the way I see it, you owe me."

"I certainly don't!"

"Your boss had my house seized and razed. Your demon —"

Joshua interrupted, "It was Madigan's demon. He was my teacher, but I had nothing to do with that."

"Your demon nearly killed me. I need to thank you for giving me a purpose, however. My brother had a spell book, and I only ever learned one spell from it before he had it taken back to the library at the monastery. I'm told that because I can't wield magic of my own, I can cast it once and then it will be erased from my memory."

"What do you want?" Joshua asked again.

Raven took another step, moving close to his face, gently placing her hand on his cheek. "I need you to awaken me, Joshua. I need to be able to see magic."

"There is no way," he said. "What would possibly make you think I'd put you through the awakening?"

Zael tapped her sister on the shoulder. Raven turned and watched her sister's hand signs. Raven nodded and turned back to Joshua. "Both of us. You need to awaken both of us."

Joshua laughed. "You must be kidding. Your sister has the Scourge. Awakening her is forbidden, even if I wanted to—which I don't."

"No, no," Raven said. "We checked on that. It is forbidden for a member of the *Kalari,* but you aren't a member—you said you hadn't decided yet."

Joshua shook his head. "Your request is preposterous. I'm not doing it."

"You'll do it—because I have your staff and you want it back."

Joshua lifted the hand with the staff. "You guys are crazy. I don't know what your game is, but I'm going to ask you to please leave." He took a step and reached out to open the door.

Raven smiled and started speaking an incantation,

"tenere utas motum anasa rey munda de amei..."

"Oh smeck!" Joshua said. He opened the door and tried to make a run for it. Too late. He felt his joints lock up as Raven continued her incantation. He was frozen in place right outside his door, fully aware of his surrounding as the black-haired young woman walked up and grabbed his magic staff from his hand.

Raven smiled at the immobile wizard. "Come back inside when you're ready—when this wears off. I'm first."

Joshua watched helplessly as she walked back into his home. Inside the cottage, he heard her say, "There you go, Zael. We're getting magic!"